Evvie Drake
Starts Over

Evvie Drake
Starts Over

Linda Holmes

HODDER

First published in Great Britain in 2019 by Hodder & Stoughton
An Hachette UK company

This paperback edition published in 2020

2

A CIP catalogue record for this title is available from the British Library

Paperback ISBN 9781473679276
eBook ISBN 9781473679269

Printed and bound in Great Britain by Clays Ltd, Elcograf S.p.A.

Hodder & Stoughton policy is to use papers that are natural, renewable
and recyclable products and made from wood grown in sustainable
forests. The logging and manufacturing processes are expected to
conform to the environmental regulations of the country of origin.

Hodder & Stoughton Ltd
Carmelite House
50 Victoria Embankment
London EC4Y 0DZ

www.hodder.co.uk

To Nona, who always saw me

Evvie Drake
Starts Over

First

GO NOW, OR *you'll never go*, Evvie warned herself.

She didn't want to be there when he got home from work. It was cowardly, yes, but she didn't relish the whole *thing* it would turn into, the whole *mess*. He'd say, not unreasonably, that leaving with no warning at all was a little dramatic. After all this time, he would wonder, why now? He wouldn't know that, today exactly, Evvie had been with him for half her life. She'd figured it out on the back of a grocery receipt a few months earlier, and then she had circled this date on their wall calendar in red. He'd walked by it over and over and never once asked her about it. If she let the day pass, she thought she might start to disappear, cell by cell, bone by bone, replaced by someone who looked like her but wasn't.

She popped the trunk of her Honda and stuffed a fat envelope of cash into the glove compartment. This part might be silly. She didn't think Tim would cancel the credit cards or close the accounts. But her life had a lot of "just in case" in it, and she needed money just in case she didn't know him as well as she thought. It wouldn't be the first time she'd stumbled while trying to predict him.

She went into the house and opened the hall closet. She pulled down the worn, hard-sided blue suitcase with the stickers all over it—PARIS, LONDON. It was light, and it rattled from inside as she made her way down the porch steps and pushed it into the backseat of the car. The sounds of her feet on the driveway pavement tempted her to smile.

There was more to retrieve from the house, but she slid into the front seat and closed the door, leaning back against the headrest with her eyes closed. *Holy shit, I'm really going.* In a few hours, she would be in some chain hotel with scratchy bedspreads and a ragtag cable lineup. She would buy a bottle of wine, or a box of it, and she'd lie dead center in the king-sized bed and drink and wiggle her toes and read for as long as she wanted. But then she began to wonder what she would do tomorrow, and there wasn't time for that, so she took a deep breath and got out of the car to get the rest of her things. She was walking up the driveway when her phone rang.

The ringtone always startled her a little bit—a metallic arpeggio that sounded like an electric harp. The call was from the hospital in Camden where Tim sometimes saw patients. She didn't want to talk to him, but she needed to know if he would be home early.

"Hello?"

"May I speak to Eveleth Drake?"

It was not Tim.

"This is Evvie."

"Mrs. Drake, my name is Colleen Marshall, I'm a nurse at Camden Hospital. I'm calling because Dr. Drake was brought into our ER about half an hour ago. He's been in a car accident."

A thump in Evvie's heart traveled out to her fingertips. For one tenth of one second, she wanted to tell the nurse to call Tim's parents, because she was just leaving him.

"Oh my God," she said instead. "Is he all right?"

The pause was so long she could hear a doctor being paged in the background. "He's badly hurt. You should come in just as soon as you can. Do you know where we're located?"

"Yes," she choked out. "I'll be there in, ah . . . probably twenty minutes."

Evvie's hands shook as she tapped out a text to Andy. *Tim was in a car accident. Bad. Camden Hospital. Can you tell my dad?*

She turned her key in the ignition and pulled out of her driveway, heading toward Camden. She later figured, from her phone and all the paperwork, that he probably died while she was waiting at the stoplight at Chisholm Street, a block from the church where they got married.

FALL

One

EVVIE LAY AWAKE on the floor in the dark. More specifically, on the floor of the empty little apartment that jutted awkwardly from the back of her house into the yard. She was there because, upstairs in her own bed, she'd had another dream where Tim was still alive.

Evvie's Scandinavian grandmother had claimed that young women dream about the husbands they want, old women dream about the husbands they wanted, and only the luckiest women, for a moment in the middle, dream about the husbands they've got. But even accounting for the narrow ambitions this formulation allowed, Evvie's dreams about Tim were not what her nana had in mind.

He was always angry at her for leaving. *Do you see what happened?* he would say, again and again. He'd felt so close this time that she'd dreamed his cinnamon-gum breath and the little vein on his forehead, and she was afraid if she turned over and went back to sleep, he'd still be there. So she'd thrown off the blankets and made her way down to the first floor of the house that had always been too big and was *much* too big now. Descending the wide curved staircase still felt like transgressing, like sneaking down to the front desk of a hotel late at night to ask for extra towels. She'd stopped in the kitchen to put on a pot of water for tea, come directly into the apartment, and stretched out on her back to wait.

When they'd first bought the house—when *he'd* first bought the house—they'd planned to rent out the apartment. But they never got around to it, so Evvie had painted it her favorite shade of peacock blue and used it like a treehouse: *KEEP OUT*. It was still her favorite place in the house and would remain so, unless Tim's ghost started haunting it just to say he'd noticed a few little bubbles in the paint, and it would really look better if she did it over.

Nice, she'd thought to herself when that thought first intruded. *Welcome to Maine's most ghoulish comedy club. Here is a little joke about how my husband's ghost is kind of an asshole. And about how I am a monster.*

It was a little after four in the morning. Flat on her back in her T-shirt and boxers, she took rhythmic breaths, trying to slow the pounding in her temples and belly and wrists. The house felt empty of air and was totally silent except for the clock that had ticked out *pick-a-pick-a* for thirty-five years, first in her parents' kitchen and now in hers. In the dark apartment, she felt so little of anything, except the prickle of the carpet on her skin, that it was like not being anywhere at all. It was like lying directly on top of the earth.

Evvie thought from time to time about moving in here. Someone else could have the house, that big kitchen and the bedrooms upstairs, the carved banister and the slick staircase where she'd once slipped and gotten a deep purple bruise on her hip. She could live here, stretched out on her back in the dark, thinking all her worst thoughts, eating peanut butter sandwiches and listening to the radio like the power was out forever.

The kettle whistled from the kitchen, so she stood and went to turn it off. She took down one of the two public-radio fundraising mugs from the cabinet, leaving behind the one with the thin coat of dust on its upturned bottom. The tag on her chamomile teabag said, *There is no trouble that a good cup of tea can't solve*. It sounded like what a gentleman on *Downton Abbey* would say right before his wife got an impacted tooth and elegantly perished in bed.

Blowing ripples in her tea, Evvie went into the living room where there was somewhere to sit and curled up on the deep-green love seat. There was a *Sports Illustrated* addressed to Tim sticking out of the pile of mail on the coffee table, and she paged through it by the wedge of light from the kitchen: the winding down of baseball season, the gearing up of football season, an update on a college gymnast who was quitting to be a doctor, and a profile of a Yankees pitcher who woke up one day and couldn't pitch anymore. That last one was under a fat all-caps headline: "HOW TO BECOME A HEAD CASE." "Way ahead of you," she muttered, and stuck the magazine at the bottom of the pile.

By the clock on the cable box, it was 4:23 A.M. She closed her eyes. It had been almost a year since Tim died, and she still couldn't do anything at all sometimes, because she was so consumed by not missing him. She could fill up whole rooms with how it felt to be the only person who knew that she barely loved him when she'd listened to him snoring lightly on the last night he was alive. *Monster, monster,* she thought. *Monster, monster.*

Two

"LILLY CHUCKED HER milk at the floor." Andy took a sip of coffee. "I'm in trouble with her teacher."

Andy and Evvie's Saturday breakfasts at the Compass Café had started four years ago when he got divorced, and they'd never stopped. Some husbands might have minded, but Tim hadn't. "I have plenty of work to do, so as long as you're not complaining to him about me, I don't care," he'd said.

Andy would have the ham and cheese omelet, and Evvie would have the blueberry pancakes, a side of bacon, and a large orange juice. They drank at least two pots of coffee and reviewed the weeks past and ahead. They stayed as the place filled and emptied and filled again. They eyeballed the tourists and tipped extravagantly, and locals they knew wandered by and said something about the weather or asked what Andy's little girls were up to. And, for this last year or so, people would stretch their necks to peek, or happen to stand at a politely investigatory distance, to check on Evvie and satisfy themselves, just *make sure*, that the death of her husband hadn't turned her into a shriveled little husk, sitting at home humming ballads to

Tim's favorite shirt as she rocked back and forth, clutching it to her chest.

"Why did Lilly chuck her milk at the floor?" Lilly was Andy's younger daughter, who had recently started kindergarten.

"Good question. The teacher says she just threw it. No warning. Yelled, 'Milk is melted yogurt!'"

Evvie smiled. She could picture it, including the face full of fury Lilly had worn on and off since infancy. "I see how she got there, I guess."

"So the teacher tells me she gave her a time out. I say, 'That seems fine.' And the teacher says, 'I think it would also be good to follow up at home about respect.' I say, 'Respect for you?' And she says, 'Well, yes, but also for property.' And I'm thinking, *Are we talking about teaching my daughter respect for milk?* Because I can't figure out what else she wants me to teach her. What she means by 'respect for property.'"

"Capitalism?"

"Maybe. Anyway, I'm working on it. I'm working on teaching Lilly to have more respect for her teacher. And respect for milk."

"Lacto . . . reverence? Lactoreverence? Is that something?"

"No." Andy paused to push his coffee cup out to get a refill from Marnie, a young mom with a grown-out stripe of purple in her hair who had been their regular server for a couple of years. "I'll tell you, she was a biter when she was little, but I don't know what this is. Even when she's loving all over me, she's *so mad*. I went to pick her up the other day, and she goes, 'Dad! Hug me!' But she shrieks it, like a howler monkey. Very take-charge, if you want to think about it that way, like she's . . ."

"Jerry Orbach."

He frowned. "In *Dirty Dancing*?"

"In *Law & Order*."

"Fine, Jerry Orbach." He paused. "My point is she's bullheaded, which I think is great, but I don't want to be bailing her out of jail when she's nine."

Evvie smiled again. "I can't wait for her teenage years."

"She can come live with you."

"Oh, no. I'll do periods and bras and birth control, but I live alone."

"Well, for now," he said. "I meant to ask you, are you still thinking about renting out the apartment?"

She chewed on a piece of bacon. "Maybe. Eventually."

"You're not using it, right?"

"Not except to lie on the floor in the middle of the night and contemplate my existence." He stopped chewing and his eyebrows popped up. "I'm kidding," she said. He wouldn't understand. He'd just worry. "I never go in there."

"I was thinking, you know, it's money you're leaving on the table if you let it sit empty. Finance-wise." The logic was impeccable. It was probably a trap.

"I suppose that's true," she said suspiciously.

"It is true." He pointed. "Your sleeve is in the syrup."

She dabbed at a sticky dot on the cuff of her shirt. "Do you want me to rent it to someone in particular? Are you evicting Rose now?"

"Ha." He didn't laugh. "No, I think the kids should be at least ten before they're fully independent." He took a slug of coffee. "By the way, before I forget, Rose has a dance recital a week from tomorrow, and she told me to tell you that she'd like you to come over and do 'the hair with the swirly braids.'" Rose was seven, and she did not trust her father with her recital hair or her Matchbox cars.

"She's a planner, that one."

"The other day she called me 'Father,'" he said. "Like we're on *Little House on the Prairie*."

Evvie frowned. "That's 'Pa,' though."

"Who am I thinking of? Who's called 'Father'?"

"Priests," she said. "And Captain von Trapp."

"So can I tell her you're coming?"

"Of course," Evvie said. "Now tell me who you want to stash in the apartment."

"Right, right. I actually have a friend who's going to be in town for a few months, and he's looking for a place to live."

She frowned. "What friend? Somebody I know?"

"My friend Dean."

Her eyes got a little wider. "Baseball Dean?" She knew one of Andy's friends was a pitcher, but she'd never met him.

"Not anymore," he said. "He retired recently. He's going to come up here and take it easy for a while. Enjoy a little of our fine salt air and all that."

"I always forget professional athletes retire in different decades from normal people. What is he, mid-thirties? And he retired? Must be nice."

"It's a little more complicated than that. Which you would know if I didn't steal all your issues of *Sports Illustrated*."

"I probably still wouldn't read them," she admitted. "There's a new one at the house, by the way."

"I know," he said. "Dean's in it."

She snapped her fingers. "Wait. Baseball Dean is the head case?"

Andy squinted at her. "He's not a head case. He lost his arm. I mean, not his *arm* arm; he lost his pitching arm. He has both arms. And he's not crazy."

"What's wrong with him?"

"Well, he was a very good pitcher, and then all of a sudden, he was a very bad pitcher. Other than that, no idea."

Just then, Diane Marsten stopped by the table. She ran the thrift store Esther's Attic, which had been her mother's before it was hers. Diane often ate at the Compass on Saturdays with her husband, sometimes in the unsanctioned company of her little dog, Ziggy, who didn't seem to be around to thumb his tiny nose at the health code today. "Morning, you two."

"Hey, Diane," Andy said. "How are things?"

"Can't complain." This, Evvie knew from experience, was not true. Diane turned and put a hand on her shoulder. "Good to see you out and about."

Evvie shot a look at Andy, then screwed on her smile. "Thank you, Diane. It's good to see you, too." Diane provided a few updates about neighbors with ailments (politely vague to the point of futility, like "troubles with his system") or personal issues (same, like "the business with the one daughter"), then went off to enjoy her French toast. "Honestly." Evvie sighed.

"She cares about you, Ev."

"I know. I know. But they all . . . hover. 'Out and about,' she says, like I had the flu. They act like all I'm doing is"—she switched to a hard whisper—"sitting at home grieving."

"She said it was good to see you."

Evvie shook her head. "It's the *sympathy*. It's all the pats on the arm, all the soft voices. That tree-planting thing at the clinic is in a couple of weeks, and it's going to be even worse then. Everybody's just going to sit there and watch me cry."

"You don't have to cry. Everybody knows how much you loved him."

In fact, everybody didn't know. Andy didn't know.

"I don't get it," Evvie said. "Nobody pities Tessa Vasco because her husband died and she's not out partying all the time."

"Tessa Vasco is ninety-two."

"So?"

"So you are *not* ninety-two. And unlike Tessa Vasco, you don't need a walker or an oxygen tank to go to the grocery store." He wiped his mouth. "And not to pile on, but I feel like I have to point out that Tessa does water aerobics."

"Why would you know that?"

"Because my mom also does water aerobics. She's only sixty-nine, though. Little less embarrassing for you."

Evvie put one hand up. "All right. It was a bad example."

"So can I get back to trying to sell you on a tenant?"

She looked around the restaurant, then back at Andy. "Why does a professional athlete want to rent an apartment in my house? I thought they lived . . . I don't know, on private islands or something."

"Dean lives in Manhattan. World's least private island. He says he can't get a cup of coffee without somebody taking his picture. He wants to get out of the city for a while, and I told him I thought up here, people would leave him alone. He's not staying long enough to buy a place, but he's staying too long for a hotel. I can't put him up because I have the kids. I thought maybe he could have the apartment. That way, I'd know he wasn't renting from somebody who was going to Snapchat him in the bathroom or sell his trash to TMZ. You'd get some money coming in, and maybe you'd be friends. Win-win. I told him maybe you'd take $800 a month."

It would take a big bite out of the bills. "$800 would be okay."

"So, yes?"

She looked into her coffee cup, with its lazy hairline curl of cream still on top. "So, bring him by the house." Evvie sensed a tiny puff of exasperation, and she tensed. "I've never met him, Andy. What do you expect me to say?"

"You'll like him," Andy said. "I like him."

Evvie straightened her back. "You like a lot of people. Who knows what smelly college drinking buddies you would drag through my kitchen if I let you."

"I didn't meet him drinking. I met him in Cub Scouts. He was in my wedding, Ev, you've seen the pictures. And if you remember, he's the one who sent me and the girls to Disneyland after the divorce. He's not going to steal your jewelry."

Evvie smiled. "I don't own much jewelry."

"Well, he's not going to steal your . . . cozy sweaters with holes in them, whatever."

She frowned. "Low blow. Look, like I said, bring him by and let me meet him. If it seems like a good fit, I'll be glad to have the money." She thought briefly about the overdue bills that were rubber-banded together in the kitchen drawer. That was what a year without a doctor's income would do. She could put somebody in the apartment, leave the door closed, collect the rent, and she might not even notice he was there.

Andy sighed. "Thank you. He needs . . . I don't know, quiet. Plus, like I said, it wouldn't be the worst thing in the world if you had company."

"I have company," she said. "I'm sitting here with company."

"Company other than me. And my kids. And your dad. You know"—he gestured at her with a fork full of eggs—"it's not good to be alone too much. It'll make you weird." Andy's sandy, wavy hair and narrow frame made him look like he was in an indie band, perpetually about to put on something plaid and pose for the cover of an album where he played a lot of washboard. But the dad in him ran deep, seven years in.

"I'm fine. I'm not weird. If I get bored, I'll get Tessa Vasco to take me to a Zumba class." He looked dubious. "Andy, I'm fine. I'll meet your friend." Suddenly, Evvie narrowed her eyes at him. "This isn't a setup, is it?"

Andy laughed through a bite of his breakfast, swallowed, and washed everything down with coffee. "That's what he said, too: 'Is this a setup?'" She didn't laugh. "It's not a setup. After all, I think my mom still hopes I'm going to marry you, which definitely won't happen if I set you up with former professional athletes."

"Oh, no," Evvie said. "Would you tell her already?"

"Tell her what?"

"'Tell her what.' Tell her we earnestly tried to look meaningfully at each other. And that it was the least sexy thing that has happened between two humans, maybe ever."

"She wouldn't believe me," he said.

"She would if she'd been there," Evvie said.

"Oh, when you cracked up laughing? That's the truth."

"We both cracked up laughing."

"You laughed harder," he said, accusing her with the points of his fork.

"Okay, I'll give you that."

Three

DEAN SAT IN his truck in Andy's driveway. He'd left New York City more than eight hours earlier and had stopped only once. He took a deep breath. "Okay," he muttered, as he made his way toward the house and rang the bell.

The door opened and Andy grinned. "Hey, man." They did the backslap-hug they'd been doing since they were about thirteen, and Andy extended a bottle of beer. "Come on in."

Andy's house was a modest green rambler with a lot of wear on the siding. But inside on the living room floor, the girls' plastic dollhouse was decidedly ornate, with three floors and an elevator on a pulley. Today, it looked like it had been knocked over and set right again, leaving an array of little plastic lamps and furniture on the carpet. A hula hoop leaned against the arm of the sofa, and the sounds of the TV and two girls giggling floated down the hall from behind a closed door. "Welcome to my party house," Andy said as he gestured to an armchair for Dean to sit. "I'm raging, as you can see."

Dean grinned. "How old are they now?"

"Rose is seven and Lilly is five." Andy pushed the hula hoop out of the way and sat on the sofa. "They're in the playroom watching *Ghost-*

busters for the fiftieth time, so I'm thinking they'll be lady scientists for Halloween. I'm honestly pretty psyched." He took a swallow from his own beer. "How was your trip?"

Dean involuntarily twitched against the memory of his stiffening back. "Long, but it was good. It's good to see a different place. And good to see you, too. I was trying to think—it's been, what, three or four years?"

"Yeah." Andy thought for a minute. "It was right before Lori left, I think. When we came down for your party, your ESPN thing? That would be four years."

Dean cringed. "Yeah, that. It's way too long."

"Well," Andy said, "since then, Lori left. I still teach math. I'm still single. I recently became the faculty advisor to the yearbook, which I'm counting as coaching a sport. And now you're pretty much up to date." His eyes went to a picture of himself and his girls that was sitting on the end table. "It doesn't seem to have been as much of a surprise to anybody else as it was to me that my marriage didn't work out."

Dean picked up a stuffed panda off the floor, then put it back down. "I know I should've come up after she left. I meant to, and I didn't get around to it. I was pretty busy being a big shot."

"Yeah." Andy tipped his head to one side. "Pretty brutal, all that."

Dean laughed into the bottle in his mouth. He swallowed and wiped the corner of his lip with his thumb. "For me, too. Apparently, I'm a fucking disaster."

"That's what they say."

"Oh, I know they do."

"How have you been doing?"

Dean dropped his head back against the chair. "Not my best year."

"Yeah."

"And I have gotten probably a hundred thousand letters and emails and goddamn *tweets* about it. Mostly from people who know for sure what it would take to fix me."

"Hard to believe they haven't solved it yet."

Dean smiled. "I mean, did you know this might all be in my head? Did you know that when I went from being able to strike out guys who are going to wind up in the Hall of Fame to barely being able to hit a car with a fucking beanbag it made some people think I had a psychological problem?"

"Psychological, huh?"

"Yeah, the consensus is that it's all right up here," Dean said, tapping his temple. "Just need to concentrate. Focus. Get in touch with my inner Zulu warrior."

"You have to be kidding me. Nobody said Zulu warrior."

"Oh, hell yes, they did. They said inner Zulu warrior, they said inner Peyton Manning, somebody said inner fucking Hannibal Lecter, like I'd want to find *that* if I had it. They kept writing to me: 'Did you try hypnotism?' 'Did you read Sun Tzu?' 'Did you try a therapist?' Like I'm trying to fix my arm with a socket wrench and they're going to save baseball in New York by telling me I need a therapist. Like I'm in the city where baristas write their shamans' names on your fucking coffee cup, and it's Margo from Greenpoint who's going to come up with 'Try a therapist.' 'Thanks, Margo, I never thought about trying a therapist. How would I have known to try a therapist?'"

Andy nodded. "So you tried a therapist?"

Dean reached over to rub his right shoulder. "Yeah, make your jokes. I went to eight sports psychologists and two psychiatrists." He started counting off on his fingers. "I did acupuncture, acupressure, suction cups on my shoulder, and candles in my fucking ears— which, ask me about *that* sometime. I quit gluten, I quit sugar, I quit sex, I had *extra* sex, I ate no meat, *just* meat. I took creative movement classes, I was hypnotized a lot, and I learned how to meditate. That's the one I still do, by the way." He looked at Andy, who had his mouth twisted into a perplexed curve. "Where did I lose you? Extra sex?"

"No, 'creative movement classes.' I think Rose did that."

"Oh, it's some elegant shit. It was supposed to help me align my spine, move more naturally. I looked like one of those inflatable tube guys that blows around outside a car dealership. They kept saying I needed to have loose bones. Nobody on Twitter had diagnosed me with tight bones, so fuck the Internet, I guess, right?"

Andy shook his head. "I'm sorry, Dean. I wanted to call you, find out how you were. But it's a lot easier to call Greenpoint and check with Margo."

"You're not funny."

Andy grinned. "So now that you're up here, what do you want to do?"

"Stay off the Internet," Dean said. "Figure out what I'm going to do now that I've got a free, what, fifty years?"

"Any ideas yet?"

"Fuck if I know, man." Dean stretched out his shoulder again. "I could coach, once I'm a little less famous for not knowing what I'm doing. There's announcing, but I didn't exactly make many friends in sports media. I've got money left, so I've got time to think about it. But I've been thinking about it for about a year, and I've gotten about as good at *Overwatch* as I'm going to get."

Andy tried not to smile when he said, "Can I ask you something?"

"Yeah."

"Is it true about *Dancing with the Stars*?"

"It's true that they asked. Hey, don't laugh. I was up for the dancing part. Did you see it when Emmitt Smith did it? Smooth as hell. But my sister-in-law watches every season, and she told me that if I did it, they were going to keep making me talk about how this was my only chance to redeem myself, and how they'd make me do a waltz while they played 'Take Me Out to the Ball Game' on a cello or some shit, so I told 'em no. They went and got that skater who fell in the Olympics and bled all over the ice instead. One washout's as good as another, apparently."

"You're not a washout," Andy said, putting his hand on Dean's shoulder. "You're a head case. It's completely different." They laughed, and Rose poked her head out of the playroom down the hall and hollered.

"Dad, I can't hear, you guys are so loud!"

"Do you need an ear cleaning? Should I bring in the garden hose? Or I think the Dirt Devil is around here somewhere," Andy called back to her. There was more giggling, and the door slammed shut. "Awful children," Andy said, shaking his head. "So. I put sheets on the foldout bed in the basement. I figured you can stay here for now. Tomorrow, I'll take you over to Evvie's. She wants to say hi, make sure you're not violent and you don't have a musical instrument."

"Anything I should know?"

"About Evvie? She's the greatest. You'll like her. She's a lot of fun. She's cute; she kind of looks like . . . your sister."

Dean frowned. "I don't have a sister."

"I'm saying she looks like *everyone's* sister. Like someone's sister."

"Whose sister?"

"Nobody's. She's an only child."

Dean shook his head. "You are not good at this."

Andy shrugged. "Brown hair. A lot of sweaters. Brown eyes . . . I think."

"Any other intel?"

"Just get her name right. As she always says, 'Evvie like Chevy, not Evie like Max Greevey.'"

"Who the hell is Max Greevey?"

"A cop on *Law & Order*. Evvie didn't watch much TV when she was a kid, so she's been catching up. She's up to about 1998. She just started *Dawson's Creek*."

"Wow, old school."

"But she's great. She saved my life when I was first on my own with the girls. Do me a favor and don't let her take care of you, because she'll get completely carried away and you'll wind up a much better person than you should be."

"Got it. And you said she'd take $800?"

Andy nodded. "Between you and me, I think she could use the money. The husband didn't have life insurance."

"Ouch."

"Yeah. I mean, whatever. You know what they say about 'don't speak ill of the dead or the guy your best friend married.'"

"You two aren't a thing? You're not mooning about it?"

"Nope."

"You're both single now."

Andy used his foot to nudge a little plastic lamp back toward the dollhouse. "Yeah, but when we met, we weren't. And she was married until last fall. We tried to have some kind of a . . . moment in her doorway like six months ago. It seemed logical. I don't know how to explain it, but it didn't take. It was like trying to put a sex scene in the middle of one of those videos they play before your flight takes off, where they show you how to buckle a seatbelt. I think we know each other too well. Not that I've convinced my mom."

"Oh, Mama Kell. Did she lose it when you got divorced?"

"She was worried that the girls might end up leaving with their mom. But when she found out they were mostly going to stay up here while Lori kinda did Lori for a while, I think she got that it was for the best."

Dean took a drink, then tipped his head back until it rested against the chair again. "How are things with Lori anyway?" he asked in a low voice.

"They're okay. We're friends. Or at least friendly. She gets bored all the way up here, so she comes as far as Portland, I bring the girls down, she sees them. And she calls. She loves them."

"She just started over, huh?"

Andy nodded. "I couldn't have left without them, if it were me, but it's her life. And as Evvie pointed out to me once, guys have done it forever. Nobody even blinks. And the kids like Charleston all right. They visit Lori's family for a couple of days, they drink sweet tea until their teeth fall out, they come back saying 'Y'all gonna eat that lawb-stah?'"

"Always good to speak a second language."

"Right. Big picture, it could be much worse."

"I guess I'd say the same thing."

Dean had spent a lot of nights in Andy's living room when they were kids in exactly this way, biding his time. He waited for elementary school and then high school to be over so he could move on to what was next. But that was when he had known what was next. Now his only plans were dinner and bringing his duffel in from the truck. The part of the future that was in focus had shortened; the part that was just a wall of fog went on forever. He still woke up some days and believed for fifteen seconds or so that he had something to do, until he remembered he didn't.

The sixteenth second was a killer.

Four

 CALCASSET WAS IN the part of Maine well-suited to the name MidCoast because it resolutely doesn't mean anything, and a description that resolutely doesn't mean anything is a powerful indicator of communally owned modesty. Even the weather changed politely: every year, as fall began to take over from summer, there would be crisp mornings that would warn that one day soon, it would truly be cold.

As soon as Evvie woke up and put her feet on the cool wood floor, she knew this was one of the days when fall would poke its head out. She made tea, ate a bowl of oatmeal with raisins and maple syrup, and threw her favorite gray cardigan over her Calcasset High School Band T-shirt—still hanging in after fifteen years—and jeans. The sweater left a trail of fuzzy puffs everywhere, but she'd had it since college. When she wore it and drank something hot, she liked to imagine it gave her autumnal superpowers and a certain cozy appeal.

She could work. She should work. There was a little voice getting louder and louder, saying, *Do something, do something.* She had emails to answer, including one from Nona Powell Brown, a professor at Howard, with the subject line, "Your attentive ear."

Evvie sometimes called herself a professional eavesdropper, but she was a transcriber. She worked mostly with interview tapes from researchers and journalists, though she also had what she called "cha-ching clients" who wanted documentation of board meetings or presentations. She knew it sounded boring to people who figured she could be cheaply replaced by decent software. Tim had once cracked that she should get business cards that said, "For when technology barely won't do." And she did have automation breathing—or buzzing, or whatever—down her neck, not that everyone she worked with didn't, too.

But she'd always thought it was sort of fabulous. It meant slipping on headphones and listening for hours to people's stories, imitating their accents, being surprised by their voices cracking or tumbling into laughs. Often, she'd develop elaborate ideas of what they looked like or what they wore, and she'd image-search them at midnight, sitting in bed with her face lit up by her laptop screen to see if she was right. She was good; she could type almost as fast as she could listen, and a reporter for *The Boston Globe* called her "the only woman who can reliably translate mumble into English." He was the one who'd connected her with Nona, her favorite client, a labor economist who wrote what she called "occupational biographies." The last one had been about logging, and Evvie had transcribed almost two hundred hours of tape for it. She could tell you what a whistle punk was. She knew logging had the highest per capita death rate of any U.S. occupation. This did not come in handy at parties—or, it would not, if she went to parties.

Nona's email said that she was planning a book on Maine lobstermen, and she wouldn't be starting the work for at least a year, but she wondered if Evvie was interested in helping with the research. Not just transcription, but the interviewing, too, and helping Nona navigate. This would be a promotion of sorts. "I always try to team up with a local," she'd written, "and I naturally thought of you right away. I don't know what your schedule is like these days, and it's still a long way off, but let me know when you have time to talk."

Right now, though, Evvie's attentive ear was mostly on hiatus—and she hadn't yet answered Nona. She did little jobs here and there so she wouldn't be broke, but the very thought of going out into the towns up and down the coast, having her work interrupted by condolences that would make her circle back into her marriage was too much to even think about. Most things were too much to think about.

So instead of returning emails to clients, she devoured books that moved with her from table to table, chair to chair, as she read and stopped and read more, sticking a scrap of paper between the pages to mark her place. On this occasion, she was a third of the way through a fat Southern novel she'd been wanting to read ever since she heard the author on *Fresh Air*, talking about how he grew up living above a beauty parlor with his family and their illegal pet monkey.

She was stretched out on the sofa, trying to ignore the *Do something, do something* voice, when she heard a knock that had to be Andy and the potential tenant. She hopped up and started for the front door, but along the way, she stopped. Her eyes settled on the fireplace mantel, which held two marbled scented candles and a driftwood sculpture she didn't like from somewhere salty where she and Tim had once had a lobster roll. She yanked open the drawer of the writing desk in the corner and pulled out her silver-framed wedding portrait. She'd loved the gazebo; she'd hated her dress. But propped up between the candles, the photo would perhaps testify on her behalf that she was properly grieving and was not a *monster, monster*. She walked to the door.

When she opened it, Andy wasn't there. There was only a man, strikingly tall, with green eyes and dark hair flecked with gray. He had a sunburn on his left arm, likely from hanging it out a car window. "Oh," she said. "Hi there." Andy hadn't mentioned that the guy was particularly good-looking, but he probably didn't even know. Andy was such a decent guy, and he was such a dummy about this stuff.

"Evvie," he said.

"I bet you're Dean," she said, extending her hand.

He clasped it and said, "Good to meet you. I hope you don't mind. I was afraid if I brought Andy, you'd feel like you should say yes to shut him up, so I left him at home."

She looked at his eyes, his wrists, his high cheekbones, all the years of sun on his skin, and the way he didn't look as young as she'd thought he would. "Sure, come on in, it's fine." Remembering to let go of his hand, she stepped to the side, and he squeezed past her into the house. As she closed the door, she encountered his shoulder and got a whiff of detergent and maybe bacon, which she figured Andy had been putting in front of him all morning, next to the same frozen waffles the girls favored on the weekends. "When did you get to town?" she asked.

He looked around the living room a little. "I got here yesterday afternoon. I caught up with Andy and his kids. We haven't seen each other in a few years."

"That sounds like fun. Did the girls ask you about where you live? They're very into geography right now. Maps and globes, the shape of the coast."

"They did. I had to promise to take them on the subway someday. I think they're going to be disappointed that it doesn't feel as much like a roller coaster as it looks like on a map."

"Did Lilly ask you to play Doc McStuffins?"

"Yeah. She was very thorough. I'm supposed to go back in six months for a follow-up."

Evvie nodded. "Abundance of caution, sure."

"I've been in worse hands." He smiled, about a third of the way. It was a pretty good third of a smile.

"So you drove up from Manhattan? How long does that take?"

"Eight hours, give or take."

"Yikes."

"Yeah. The good news is that there's a lot of radio to listen to."

"What do you like? Sports talk and stuff?"

"Oh, no. Jerks who don't play sports fighting about sports is not my idea of a good time," he said. "I'm more of a public radio guy."

"Hey, me, too," she said. "Or podcasts."

"My brother's trying to get me into those. I'm always afraid it's going to be, like, three guys on Skype getting high and talking about jam bands. What kind do you listen to?"

"One about music, one about design, a couple about politics when I can stand it. A bunch that are just, you know, 'Today on our show, a man who learned everything and nothing at all.' That stuff. And one where a guy summarizes horror novels. I'm not sure how I got listening to that one; I'm not a horror person."

"It's not bad to know a little something about the things you don't care about," he said.

She laughed. "That's how I am about *Sports Illustrated*, no offense."

"Oh, none taken."

"So," she said, "anyway. This is the house. The apartment is in back. It doesn't have a separate entrance, so you'd come in this way, or there's a side door into the kitchen from the yard. But it's a straight shot"—she walked him through the house—"back to the kitchen, and then it's this door, right through here." She kept the apartment door closed, and she hadn't had the heat on in there, so it was a little chilly when she opened it up. "It stays nice and warm normally, promise."

He stepped in behind her and closed the door, and then they were standing in the middle of all that beige carpeting with the cloudy gray light coming in the big windows. She reached up and pulled the chain on the overhead light, but after he'd walked around a bit, he reached up and shut it off again. He went to the bathroom door and swung it open, then shut it again and came back to her. He seemed to be stretching out a sore shoulder as he opened and closed the refrigerator in the kitchenette. He walked back and stood with his hands on his hips. "I feel like I should ask you questions."

"Do you have questions?"

"I'm not sure."

"Well," she said, "let me think of answers. You can have whoever over that you want, of course, it won't bother me. I'm usually working upstairs, or in the living room where you came in. You've got the kitchenette in here, but if you need anything in the big kitchen, there's plenty of room."

"I'm only good at grilled cheese," he said. "And Pringles. I'm also good with Pringles."

"Just cans of Pringles, or, like, you cook with Pringles?"

"Just Pringles. I buy them, I open the package, and then I stuff them straight into my face."

"Ah. Got it. That's how I make Oreos," she said. He grinned, and she told him about the washer and dryer, the gas grill outside, and the spot beside the house where he could park.

He looked around the empty space. "It looks great, just right. I know you weren't sure about renting it out. Not knowing me and everything."

"I thought about it more after I talked to Andy. It makes a lot of sense. It can be open-ended, you don't have to get into a big"—she waved her hand—"a big thing that's not convenient for your situation. It's more space than I need."

He nodded slowly. "House rules? Other stuff?"

"No smoking. Do you have pets?"

"I don't have pets, and I also don't smoke. True story, by the way: a friend of mine had a Great Dane who used to try to eat his Marlboro Lights. Wound up in the dog hospital once."

"Well, at least they were lights."

"Yeah, he pulled through. You're not a dog person?"

"No, I am. Always meant to get one. I guess I didn't get around to it."

"Ah, that happens," Dean said. "Andy said you were asking $800?"

"To be honest, Andy was asking $800," she said. "He does all my negotiating."

"Seems reasonable." Dean smiled and looked out the window, where the biggest tree in the yard shook. "Getting windy out there."

It got quiet. She heard a car go by outside, and more wind. A swarm of leaves blew across the yard. "It seems like a cup-of-tea day," she said, finally. "I assume you like Gatorade or something. Do you drink tea?"

"I do drink tea, when it's cold," he said. "Hot Gatorade is not good."

Back in the kitchen, they sat across from each other at her wooden table. She wished she'd thrown out the wilting bunch of parsley she was storing in a jar of water. "So you grew up with Andy in Denver." He nodded. "What was after that?"

"I went to Cornell to play baseball. Graduated from there, then I got drafted, played in the minors in a couple different places, and then I went to the Marlins in 2008."

"Mi . . . ami Marlins?" she ventured.

"Exactly. But back then, the Florida Marlins, before they got the new stadium. So I lived down in Miami for a couple years, then I got traded to the Yankees, and I went to New York. And now I'm unemployed. You?"

"Nowhere near that interesting. I grew up right here, in Calcasset. My husband, Tim, and I went to USC, and then he went to medical school out there. Then Tim did his residency in Portland. I lived up here, so we were semi-long-distance. Then he moved to Calcasset, and we got married and got this house. That was four years ago."

When he immediately looked at the floor, it seemed likely that Andy had told him how the story ended, at least as much as Andy knew himself. His version did not include her in her car with her birth certificate and a wad of cash.

Dean looked back at her. "I'm sorry about all that, by the way," he said.

"Yeah, thank you." She nodded. Her mind was digging through options, seeking for anything else to ask. "How long were you thinking of staying?"

"I don't know. Six months? A year at the most. I'll have to get back to New York, that's where my real life is. But right now, I'm kind of clearing my head." He smiled. "That's about as far as I've gotten for now."

She nodded. "I can relate."

The amount of time people who have just met are supposed to look directly at each other, particularly without talking, is a unit that's both very short and very precise. When you exceed it, you get suspicious, or you get threatened, or you get this flicker of accidental intimacy, like you've peeked at the person naked through a shower door. They both smiled, and it ended. "Right," she said. "So, I think you should take it. The apartment. You should take it." She could see that he was carefully considering whether to say something. "What?" she asked.

"I'm wondering if I should promise you no funny stuff or something."

She raised an eyebrow. "Do you need me to promise *you* no funny stuff?"

Now he seemed a little more serious. "I do think we should have a deal." She looked at him expectantly. "You don't ask me about baseball," he said, "and I don't ask you about your husband."

She blinked. "I didn't ask you about baseball."

"I know. I didn't ask you about your husband."

"But you want to have an official arrangement."

He rubbed his eyes. "I don't know how much you know about it, Evvie, but I have had a shitty year. A shitty couple of years. And I have talked about it a lot. And I think maybe you're in the same position. If you're okay with this, you'd be doing me a favor, and you'd be doing me an even bigger favor if it can just be normal. I'll say hi, and you can say hi, and we won't do, you know, the whole thing with the mysterious sad lady and the exiled . . . fuckup."

She squinted at him a little. "So, like, as an example, I won't mention that 'exile' and 'fuckup' both strike me as a little unfair."

"Right. And I won't ask you why 'mysterious sad lady' doesn't."

Her hand stretched out across the table. Instead of taking it in his handshake hand, his business hand, he took it in the hand on the same side. "Do we have a deal?" he asked.

She nodded, noticing the freckles on the back of his wrist.

Oh, stop it.

Five

A FEW DAYS LATER, Evvie was stuffing the second notice on her electric bill into her kitchen drawer when she heard a bang from the apartment. She went and knocked, and Dean opened the door wide. "Hey."

"Hey," Evvie said. "Everything okay?"

"Yeah, yeah," he said, "sorry about the noise. Knocked a box off the counter. It's never the box with the sheets in it, you know? It's always whatever will make it sound the most like you tried to murder a robot by throwing it down a couple of flights of stairs."

Evvie laughed. "Are you settling in okay? I wasn't sure I'd told you how to open the windows."

"Oh, no, you did, they're open, I've got a breeze going. You want to come in? I'm unpacking. I got lucky at your thrift store. I got furniture, I got dishes, I got my grilled cheese pan."

Evvie peeked inside. "You didn't get a bed."

"It's on the way. Diane told me a used mattress might give me bedbugs."

"Smart lady. I'd be happy to put you in the guest room until it gets here."

"Nah," he said. "I've slept in airplane seats with guys who were spitting tobacco the whole time, I can make it a couple more days bunking with Andy. I'm pretty sure Lilly wants me back tonight anyway to look at some sketches of a superhero she invented. Her dad told her I like Batman."

She stepped into the apartment, which was so different with *anything* in it. Even boxes made it breathe differently, and he had set up a pair of big, comfortable-looking club chairs sort of facing each other. "Batman, huh? You're one of *those* guys."

"Yeah. I sneaked around at Comic-Con in San Diego in costume a few years ago. Full thing, big cowl over my face. Missed a couple of days of practice and got fined, but it was worth it."

"Because?"

He stopped unpacking. "I'd never been. I'd always wanted to go. I saw a guy in a picture who was decked out like Boba Fett—you know, from *Star Wars*?"

"I know who Boba Fett is."

"Anyway, I figured Comic-Con was the one place I could wear a mask and still blend in. Probably the most normal I got to be that year, walking around in a superhero costume."

She smiled. "Maybe that's why Bruce Wayne did it."

He laughed. "Yeah, maybe."

"Well, it looks like Esther's Attic treated you right," she said. "I haven't bought anything over there in forever, but she's amazing. Diane, not Esther. Esther's been dead since I was in high school. But Diane can tell you who gave her everything she has in that store. I was about to buy a sweater from her once when she told me that my dentist brought it over with a pile of his mother's stuff from when they moved her into a home. I couldn't do it. I figured it was bad enough I was drawn to an old-lady sweater without literally buying an old lady's sweater."

"She says nice things about you." He looked up from his unpacking. "She promised you would be a very nice landlady. She put her hand over her heart when she said your name and everything."

Evvie sighed. "Uch. I bet. A lot of people will tell you how nice I am, which mostly means they feel very, very sorry for me and they're very worried about where they're going to find a new doctor."

"She said you were a trouper."

"Yes, that sounds like something she would say."

"I met her dog."

"Ah, Ziggy."

"Yeah. She said he's a . . . fluffernutter or something? Scared the hell out of me. I thought he was stuffed, and then he started walking toward me. I think I almost screamed."

"He's a miniature goldendoodle. At Christmas, he wears antlers. On St. Patrick's Day, he wears a hat with a buckle on it."

"Can't wait."

"Town treat you well otherwise?"

"Yeah. I like it. It's nice and quiet. It's, uh . . ."

"Quaint? Fishy?"

"White. It's very, very white."

"Oh," Evvie said. "You noticed that, huh? You know, Maine is the whitest state in the country. Oldest, too. Freezing cold in the winter, full of tourists in the summer. On the plus side: lobster."

"What do people do for fun?"

"Sometimes the kids from the high school throw bricks through the windows of our deserted shoe factory." She paused. "Is that not what you meant by 'fun'?"

He smiled and set a blender on the counter. "It seems like nobody gives a shit about baseball, which is helpful."

Evvie laughed as she dropped into one of the chairs and inspected the upholstery on the arm. "That is not true. They don't care about major league baseball. But they care intensely about baseball, I promise."

He frowned. "Really?"

"You are in the home territory of the Calcasset Claws," she said. He looked at her, puzzled, and she held up her fingers in a sideways V. He just stared. "You didn't see 'Go Claws'? Esther's has one in the window, I think."

"Oh," he said. "Right, that's what that was. Hey, you want a water?"

She nodded, and he tossed her a small plastic water bottle. "We had an Atlanta Braves farm team back in the '80s, and then we lost it, and a few years later we got the Claws, who play in the same park. They're part of the Northern Atlantic League. Unaffiliated minors."

He hopped up to sit on the kitchen counter. "Is this okay?" he asked, gesturing generally to his perch. She waved dismissively. "So," he said, "Claws are big."

"They're huge. Couple summers ago, there was a scandal, though." She raised then lowered her eyebrows.

"You don't say."

"Intrigue at the cereal-box races." She swiveled in the chair so she was sitting in it sideways with her legs slung over one of its wide, soft arms. "At every home game, between the third and fourth innings, three kids from town get into these foam cereal-box costumes. There's a Cheerios box, a Wheaties box, and a Chex box. And they run around the bases, and whoever comes in first gets an autographed ball and a gift certificate to the DQ."

"Wow, the DQ!" he said. "Giving away the good stuff."

"Exactly. As you can imagine, it's very serious. And everybody in the stands jumps up and knocks over their beers, you know, 'CHEEEERIOOOOS!' or 'WHEEEEEEATIEEEES!' So. Anyway. There's this kid Mike Parco, who at the time is eight years old and is a serious, total asshole. I know you're not supposed to say that about children, but I swear, it takes most men at least two divorces to be as mean as this twerp. His mom, Talley, ran the lobster-roll stand at the ballpark, and everybody knew that, at the time, she was sleeping with Doug Lexington, who was in charge of fan relations, like, ha ha."

Dean grinned at her. "Oh, Talley."

"So, probably because of favoritism, Mike got to race in the Cheerios costume for about ten games in a row. But, because fan relations can get you into the outfit but not around the bases, he never won. And Talley started to complain that it was the costume. She believed that the cereal-box races were *rigged*. So she writes a letter to the *Calcasset Neighbor,* and she's demanding that somebody do something about this injustice and restore public confidence."

"Boy, that's a lady going a long way for a free Dilly Bar."

Evvie laughed. "Right? So she raises this *huge* stink, and finally, the word goes out—Mike Parco is going to wear the *Wheaties box* at the game against Concord. By the time the night arrives, this story has everything—sex, sports, official corruption—so everybody is there. *Everybody.* You could have walked into any house in the entire town and cleaned it out. Taken absolutely everything they owned. And they're not there for the game; they're there for the *cereal-box race.* Not for love of the community, not for the spirit of the town—they're there because they *care who wins the cereal-box race.* It is the least uplifting thing that has ever brought a town together. It is the opposite of the end of a Hallmark Channel movie."

He nodded. "I'm not going to lie; this would not happen in New York."

"Yes. Here's to MidCoast Maine, home of a surprising number of people whose Fridays are available." She smiled, raising her water bottle. "So Mike's in the Wheaties. Dutch Halloran's kid—we call him Double Dutch because his real name is Addison and it does not fit him—is wearing the Chex. And in the supposedly cursed Cheerios box is Bree Blythe Netherington, who is the shortest girl in the third grade. In fact, Bree is so short that we're all pretty sure she can't see out of the eyeholes."

Dean smacked his hand to his forehead. "Oh, no."

"Oh, yes. So they're all standing there, and finally Denny Paraday—who plays shortstop and is emceeing the thing—says, 'GO!' and they go. And they're sort of run-waddling toward first, and Bree is so short that the costume comes down to her ankles, but for reasons that defy the laws of physics, she's *motoring.* And she's the first one to get to first base, but the actual bases have been removed so the kids won't trip. And she can't see, so she keeps going, and she's clearly going to run straight into the Righteous Heating and Plumbing sign on the right-field fence. Somebody yells, 'Turn, Cheerios!' And she pivots, and with some kind of internal GPS or magnets in her head or whatever, she heads straight for second. She's like a *bloodhound*. And when she gets there, they have to do it again—'Turn, Cheerios!' She turns.

"After they get her around the turn at third, it looks like she's going to win. Mike is ahead of Double Dutch, but he's about a step behind Bree. And then somebody thinks they see him trying to trip her. And you hear these voices going, 'Wheaties is cheating! Wheaties is cheating!' Bree is still on her feet. She's still going to beat him. But then—absolutely everybody sees it this time—out from Mike's Wheaties box comes this foot, he sticks it right out in front of her, and she trips and falls flat on what is, under about half a foot of foam, her face. So Mike crosses the plate while Bree is lying on the ground with her hands and feet sticking out, waggling. She's like a foam turtle. In the shape of a Cheerios box."

"I assume somebody helped her up. I mean, she's not still there."

Evvie cackled. "No, no. She's not. They got her up, and her mom put the video on YouTube and called it, 'The Video the Claws Lobster-Roll Stand Doesn't Want You to See.' Eventually they revoked Mike's gift certificate, and Bree got free DQ for a year. Fan Relations Doug dumped Talley out of shame, and she had to quit the lobster-roll stand, so now she's a manager at the CVS in Camden. Mike was banned from the cereal-box races for life, in part because he was told to give a public apology, got up to the microphone at a game, and made fart noises with his elbow." Evvie took a deep swallow from her water bottle. "That is all true. My hand to God."

"It's not surprising they don't give a damn about me."

She grinned. "Believe me, they know all about you. It's a different gossip economy. They're worrying about the Claws and the sorry state of the soccer field at the high school, and the fate of the Maine lobster, and whether the tourists are going to come. I'm sure that's why Andy thought it would be a good place to take a break. They're just . . ."

"Not petty?"

"Oh, no," she said as she peeled back the corner of the label on the bottle. "They are very petty. But they're petty about insiders more than outsiders. They only violate your privacy if they've known you since you were a child."

"They've known you since you were a child." He looked over at her.

"They have," she said slowly. She hadn't been listening to the refrigerator, but it clicked off, and suddenly she was very much listening to it not running. "Anyway. What are you going to do while you're here? I assume you're not looking to get into the lobster business."

"Your local signs certainly make it seem like an option, especially since apparently I'm not going to get in at the shoe factory like I was hoping."

"Oh, the lobster thing is real. It's what my dad did. He bought his own boat when I was little, and he had it until a couple years ago, when he retired."

"Is he still with your mom?"

"No. She's been in Florida since I was eight. She's remarried to a real estate guy, and she makes jewelry and sells it to tourists. Last I checked, she was doing something with sea glass and old dimes. Don't ask me what aesthetic that is."

"Maybe she's inspired by those guys at the beach with metal detectors. I saw a lot of that in Miami."

"I'll bet. Anyway, tell me your plans."

"Read Vonnegut," he said. "Write poetry. I play the ukulele a little. I make driftwood sculptures."

She suddenly realized her brows were knitted together and she popped them apart. "Oh. Oh."

"That's a joke."

Evvie rolled her eyes. "Mm-hmm, hilarious."

He laughed. "I'm not sure. Not baseball. Just ... Maine, I guess. Probably hang out with Andy. I'm sort of on vacation from everything."

"Honestly, I would have thought New York would be a good place for that, for blending into the background."

"For most people," he said, then briefly tilted his head to indicate how much there was that they weren't talking about.

She stood up. "Right, fair enough. Okay, I should go and do work for a little bit."

"Oh, right. Andy said you work with journalists."

"I do," she said. "I'm transcribing an interview one of my clients did with an extremely famous musician whose name rhymes with . . . Baylor Biffed. And Baylor has got some tales to tell."

"Baylor's got nothing on you," he said as he went back to unpacking a couple of boxes. "You tell a good story."

She smiled. "If that's true, it's all the years of hearing other people do it."

"I appreciate all this," he said as she paused at the door.

"Appreciate what?"

"Just, you know, place to stay. Cereal-box story."

"Ah. Well. You're very welcome. If you ever want to see the Claws play, let me know; they'll be starting up again in the spring if you're still here." She paused. "Is that weird? To take you to the game?"

"Because I'm a head case?"

She put her hand up. "Never mind. I'm asking about baseball." She paused, then nodded. "Okay. I'll see you around."

Six

IT WAS A pretty day for a tree-planting ceremony, Evvie had to admit.

Assertively crisp, she'd call it, though that only made her want a glass of wine more than she already did. Andy met her in the parking lot, and they made their way across the lawn to the stone bench. There was Dr. Schramm. There was Tim's friend Nate, and there was Tim's favorite nurse, with whom Evvie knew he had flirted incessantly. There were a few other people she didn't recognize, maybe from Camden or Portland, wearing fall jackets and sad expressions. And there was a hole with the wrapped ball of a tree in it. All that was left now was to put back the dirt they'd disturbed, like they'd done a year ago on a similar day, in similar company, when they'd buried him.

Evvie found Tim's mom and dad among the subdued faces. Lila was wrapped in a navy blue car coat, with her mostly gray hair twisted into a bun. Pete had his arm around her, and the two of them were looking at what seemed to be the same spot on the ground in front of them. Evvie went over to them, forcing every step like she was sinking into the grass, even though she knew she couldn't be. When she came near, Lila stood up and embraced her. "Hello, sweetheart," she said, hanging on tight. She smelled like roses, as always, even now. Lila had spritzed Evvie with this scent on the night of the senior prom, and on the day of her wedding.

"It's good to see you. I'm so glad we're doing this," Evvie said. Lila deserved for this to be true, and in the moment when Evvie felt Lila rub her back, it was.

"I still can't believe it."

"I know. I know." Evvie pressed her hand to the back of Lila's head.

Paul Schramm stepped up to them and said quietly, mostly to Pete, "We're going to get started."

Evvie and Lila stepped back from each other and Lila sat down beside her husband, who reached up and, with an even smile, squeezed Evvie's hand.

Dr. Schramm began to speak to the little circle about how they were all gathered for this purpose, in this place, to remember one of the kindest doctors and one of the best men any of them had ever known. Andy had an arm around her, and she leaned against him a little. She was sure there were people standing around this lumpy little dirt ball, staring at a tree that wasn't even a tree yet, who had drawn the wrong conclusions. About their breakfasts together, and about the fact that his girls would jump into her arms with such familiarity. She was sure there was talk about this, some of it excited and some of it about whether she was moving on too soon, like there was talk about everything else. Why wouldn't there be? This had to be much hotter gossip than cereal-box racing.

She wondered sometimes if they'd ever thought she was good enough for the doctor. For them, she had gone directly from lobster-man's daughter to doctor's wife, and because they didn't know any-thing, they figured it was a promotion. This was how she knew without a doubt that reputation, in many forms, was bullshit.

Tim had been effortlessly charming to nearly everyone who hadn't married him. He was especially good with patients and people he outranked, because they most obligingly did what he told them to, and if they didn't, he had reason to maintain that they should have. Evvie herself had thought of him as a very good boyfriend through high school and college.

Later, when he had brought her to Christmas parties and she wouldn't dance, she knew that all it did was make them love him more. They'd all say, "Oh, Eveleth, don't be silly." She'd say no, she wasn't feeling well, and then they'd look at Tim with sympathy, like *What a good man you are to love this.* They wouldn't have believed that the reasons she rarely felt like dancing with him had to do with the way he was at home. She knew the way he sort of glowed for most people. She probably knew it better than anybody, because she'd traded away more than anybody in return for it.

Evvie had been almost sixteen on the day in March of her sophomore year when Tim found her alone, dripping wet, and out of options. She was back from a band trip to Augusta, and she had a fleece jacket on and her clarinet case under one arm. The bus had come back at 4:20 and her dad had been scheduled to pick her up at 4:30. But it was 5:30 now, and it was raining. If her father was still working, she didn't want to bother him, even if she could find a phone. She watched for anyone she knew, even though most of her friends were in band, too, and they'd already been picked up by parents or they'd driven off in twos and threes, laughing and waving. Evvie was just starting to wonder how, exactly, to get herself home when a blue Lexus pulled up to the curb in front of her. The license plate said DR8KE, which didn't quite scan.

She and Tim Drake had been in the same class since third grade, but she didn't know him very well. Still, the class was small, so she knew enough. She knew his dad was a lawyer, his mom owned a real fur, his sister was three years older than he was, and their dog was named Kenny—supposedly for Kennebunkport, where his mom grew up. Evvie and Tim had two classes together, and he'd held a door for her not long ago, throwing her a sideways smile. Other than that, they were effectively strangers.

He rolled down the window of his car. "Hey, Evvie. Did you call a taxi?"

She frowned. "What? A taxi? No."

He looked away, smiled, and looked back. "Do you need a ride? I'm asking if you need a ride."

She laughed. "Oh my God, I'm sorry, yes. That makes sense, sorry." It was raining a little harder. "And, I mean, yes, a ride. A ride would be great."

"Okay, it's open."

She hustled around to the other side of the car. "Thanks," she said as she realized she was getting the seat of his car wet. "I think my dad forgot to pick me up."

"That's okay. I remembered." He smelled like cinnamon gum.

"Thanks."

"Oh, no problem." They sat in the car, and they didn't move. "You live out by the water, right?"

"Oh! Right! I'm sorry, I live on Wexler. Do you know where that is?"

"You live near the bookstore."

"Yeah, that's where you turn, and then I'm down the hill."

"Do you mind if we stop off?"

"At the bookstore?"

"Yeah. I like it in there."

Evvie had been cold and wet with no ride home. A guy who smelled like cinnamon had picked her up in a Lexus, and now he wanted to stop at the used bookstore. "Sure," she said. "That'd be fine. I'm not in a hurry."

She couldn't believe how smooth his windshield wipers were. They made the faintest, most soothing electric hum, nothing like the *whappety-konk, whappety-konk* of the blades on her dad's truck. As they glided through town in the deepening dark, she felt . . . something. She looked over at him. "Um," she said. "I think—it feels like the—"

"Oh, they're heated seats," he told her. "Great, right?"

Cute boy, dry car, bookstore trip, and now a warm ass. It was like the universe had forgotten her first fifteen birthdays and was rolling them into one big gift. "Yeah. Is this *your* car? It's great."

"It's my car," he said. "It's new. Sometime when it's not raining out, I'll open the sunroof for you." *Sometime*. He'd blinked a future into existence. It was sorcery.

"I just got my permit," she said. "I live with my dad, and we only have his truck. I want to get a job so I can get a car, but I don't know if it'll happen."

"My parents got it for me for my birthday," he said, like he hadn't heard her. "It's like what they drive."

They talked a little about classes and the new house his family had recently moved into, a big Victorian that had been owned by a local land developer named Van McCrea. Evvie told him a story she'd heard from her dad about the time Van's wife set the kitchen on fire deep-frying a turkey indoors on Thanksgiving, and he assured her that you couldn't see a trace of the ashes now. And then he pulled up to Breezeway Books, a little house that had been converted into a bookstore, if by "converted" you meant "filled up with shelves that hold so many used books that there's barely room to walk, so step carefully and keep your elbows tucked in."

You could get up to a grocery bag full of paperbacks for ten cents each, so Evvie wandered around plucking romances and mysteries until her bag was half-full. She turned a corner where a sign hand-made with cardboard and markers said SCIENCE, and she ran into Tim, who was holding a hardback copy of a book called *Man and His Diseases*. She opened her eyes wide.

"I'm going to be a doctor," he said. "That's . . . that's why I'm holding this book."

She laughed. The boy with the dry car and the heated seats who wanted to go to the bookstore was going to be a doctor. And he was funny. "Ah. For a minute there, I was a little bit worried. You know, for you."

He grinned at her. "You have a cute smile."

She never stood a chance.

A breeze brought Evvie back to the memorial. One of the nurses was reading a poem. Something with angels. Something that rhymed "heaven" with "ten or eleven," and "sky" with "cry," something familiar. Evvie tried to place where she knew it from, thinking maybe she'd heard it from her mother, who had a soft spot for simplistic sentimentality, or had seen it on a wall hanging. It took a minute, but she finally remembered: it had been read at a very important funeral on a very highly rated television drama series. *Somebody asked you to say a few words,* she thought at the nurse, *and you googled "poem from season finale of* Cole Point." *You did. What's wrong with you?*

Dr. Schramm's assistant brought a bouquet to Evvie and pushed it into her hands, then took an identical one to Tim's mom. Evvie looked down at the flowers, orange and red for autumn, tasteful for grieving, and to her great relief, she felt tears start to tense her throat. Andy's hand, soft on her back, drew them the rest of the way out. *Thank God,* she thought.

The good thing about a ceremony packed with busy people is that they don't linger. The tree was planted and the dirt was shoveled, people said things about how much they'd loved and admired Tim, and Evvie felt eyes on her the entire time. She tried to breathe right, sigh right, smile right, hold the flowers right.

It was at the very end, when a former patient of Tim's asked to say a few words, that Evvie was most sharply reminded of how devoted to him they were and what they believed he had been. The man talked about how Tim had sat by his bed and helped him figure out how to break it to his daughters that he had cancer.

When Evvie was in college, she'd come down with a flu that filled her lungs with cement for two weeks. Between classes, Tim would come sit on the bed and read to her from his biology textbook in the voices of various cartoon characters. Tweety Bird and Yosemite Sam and Pepé Le Pew told her about microbial diseases and molecular genetics. She had loved it; it hadn't occurred to her to mind that even his close attention was a performance. In fact, it was too bad that "solid cartoon mimic" wasn't something she'd thought to say at his funeral, because it would have sounded affectionate and been the truth, a combination she'd found hard to get right on that day.

Reminding herself that things like that had happened—that he could be sweet, and he could be fun, and he could be focused on her in a way that made her feel almost *high*—had kept her in the house, married to him. They were the tethers. And the rarer those moments got and the unhappier she got, the more often she picked through every bit of evidence of every day when she had ever been happy. She kept ticket stubs, dried flowers, receipts; she kept the flash cards he'd made in medical school. She kept whatever made her good memories occupy space. She threw away everything from her bad days, especially after they were married. The day after Tim lost his temper and dented the drywall throwing his phone, she donated the clothes she'd been wearing when he did it.

It wasn't as if she'd had no early warnings, no chances to extricate herself. In the spring of Evvie and Tim's senior year of high school, the Calcasset Small Business Association gave its Young Scholar's Medal, and the associated $3,000 scholarship, to Zoe Crispin. She was a straight-A student who worked in the school's tutoring program and edited the yearbook. But Tim had expected to get it himself—so much so that he'd drawn an X over the banquet date on the calendar he kept in his backpack. They were at school when he found out Zoe had won. He didn't talk, he just bang-bang-banged his books into the locker, then he slammed the door so hard that everyone in the hall turned to look. Evvie tried to get him to meet her eyes. "Hey," she said. "I'm sorry it didn't turn out how you wanted."

Tim adjusted his pack on his shoulder, shrugged, and said, "They probably had to give it to a girl."

From time to time, late in her marriage, Evvie had fantasized about an alternate past in which she punched him in the gut and ran. But she didn't. She nodded, she smiled, and she grabbed his hand. She said, "Probably." And it quieted him. It ended the scene he was making, all the *noise* he was making. She felt older, and special, like she'd slipped through a door into the future. She knew how to settle him down; everyone noticed. She heard the next day that one of his friends had nicknamed her "TD," and when they were having lunch outside, she asked Tim what it meant. She was afraid it would be something gross, and he hesitated to tell her, but after a while he grumbled that it stood for "Tranquilizer Dart." Evvie blushed and took another bite of her apple.

She didn't know then, as she would later, that he wouldn't settle for reassurances that he'd been wronged. There would have to be justice. Tim's father, Pete, went fishing four days later with Bill Zeist, the president of the Calcasset Small Business Association. And two days after that, the CSBA announced a new distinction: the Leadership Medal, to be given to the high school student who best demonstrated the potential for future contributions to the community. It also carried a $3,000 scholarship, and it would be given at the same banquet where they honored Zoe. The first recipient: Timothy Christopher Drake.

They'd given both medals every year since, meaning that every year, Tim's bruised ego helped another student attend college. Every year, a room full of people gathered, without knowing it, to eat roasted chicken, honor Tim's ego, and applaud the way his parents loved him so much that over and over, they had made him worse.

She had made him worse, too. She was the one, after all, who had graduated second in her class, right behind him, after tanking her math final because she knew how much it meant to him to be valedictorian. He first told her he loved her on the day he learned he'd edged her out.

Andy patted Evvie's back, and she snapped back into her body. It was done. As people left, they gave Evvie a familiar and encouraging squeeze—some had graduated these moves from her elbow to her shoulder around the six-month mark, as a sign that it was time to buck up and stop bumming everyone out. She told everyone thank you, hugged Lila again, let Pete pat her hand again, told them all goodbye. She and Andy walked in silence to his car. "You okay?" he asked.

"Yeah," she said, trying to keep her tone light. "Pretty painless, actually."

"You sure?" he asked. "You'll tell me, right? You'll tell me if it's too much for you? That's our deal."

"That's our deal," she said. It was their deal, and it was too much, but she couldn't tell him why, and it was just one more thing she knew she was doing wrong.

Seven

S HE TOLD ANDY when he dropped her off that she had errands
to run, then she spent the rest of the day in bed, with the quilt up
to her chin, lying on her side, reading a romance novel on her Kindle.
When the sun went down, she went to the kitchen for a bagel and a
Diet Coke and brought them back up to her room. She ate in the dark
by the light of her reader, listening to the winds that weren't uncommon so near the water. After a while, she put the book down and lay
on her back on the bed, listening. When it started to roar, she got out
of bed and stretched out on the thick area rug. She waited for that
feeling of floating, like she was dropping into the earth. But she
couldn't stop seeing herself from above. Couldn't stop thinking about
how silly she must look stretched out on the rug by her bed like a
crazy person. *What adult lies down on the floor?* Tim had asked her
this once when he caught her snoozing on the carpet in the apartment.

She went to the window and pulled back the curtain to see how
windy it was. She was startled at the sight of someone moving in the
semi-dark in the side yard, almost out of the porch light's reach, until
she realized it was Dean, heading for the trash barrels with a garbage

bag. As she watched, he whipped the lid off—she could never get it off smoothly like that, how did he do it?—and dropped the bag in. He took a couple of steps back toward the house, into the light, and paused when he inadvertently kicked what she soon realized was a big pinecone.

He picked it up off the ground and seemed to weigh it in his hand. She saw him look around the yard, over at the driveway, and even— she thought—up at her window. She instinctively stepped back. He tossed the pinecone into the air and caught it. He turned his body, those big shoulders, to face the house, then pivoted his head until he was staring across the wide backyard. It took her a minute to realize what he was doing, and then she saw his leg kick up, his shoulders rotate, his arm whip around, the pinecone fly across the yard and smack into the fence. He stared for a minute after it, at the spot where it had landed, and then he rubbed his right shoulder. He walked slowly over to examine the spot where it had hit, touching the wooden fence like he could read the splinters with his fingers.

He leaned down and picked up the pinecone, and he walked back to where he'd been standing. He repeated the motion: settled his body, stretched, rotated, let it fly, listened to it smack into the wood. Up by the window, Evvie moved the curtain aside a little more and leaned down.

He picked it up again. He walked in a couple of small circles, resting his hands on his hips. He tossed the pinecone in his hand, just a few inches, and caught it. Finally, he set himself again. This time, when his shoulders rotated, he uncoiled his body with such force that he almost knocked himself over. And this time, when it hit the fence, she saw the pinecone break apart and hit the ground in pieces. He stood for a minute with his hands on his hips, then bent down to rest his hands on his knees, like he was out of breath. Finally, he came toward the house.

It wouldn't be fair at all to spy on him and then run downstairs so she could pretend to coincidentally run into him as he came in. If she was curious about what he was doing out there, she would just ask.

She would at least tell him she had been watching. Spying was bad. Being nosy was bad. These were all the things Evvie was thinking as she took the stairs two at a time, down to the kitchen, where she snatched the kettle off the stove so that she was filling it just as the side door opened. "Oh, hey, I didn't know you were out there," she said as he came in, still wiping his hands on his jeans. "I was making some tea. Can I make you some?"

"Oh," he said to her. "Sure, thank you. How's everything?"

How's everything with you? What happened? Why can't you pitch? How did you get the trash-can lid to come off like that?

"Everything's good," she said, plunking down in the kitchen chair. "How have you been settling in?"

"Can't say I've done that much exploring. I should be getting out a little more."

"I say that to myself a lot, believe me." She fidgeted with the salt shaker. "And I'm sure the last few months in New York were hard, privacy-wise."

"You could say that," he said with a barely perceptible smile, or maybe a barely perceptible grimace—it really was . . . barely perceptible.

She listened to the clock. She wondered if he'd say something, but he didn't. They sat there together, and nothing happened. The kettle started to make a noise like a long exhalation, and they still sat there. Her chest felt tight.

She put down the salt. "There was a memorial thing for Tim today," she said. "They planted a tree." She figured he had to be startled that she'd come right out with this. She certainly was.

"Oh, boy." He leaned forward, but she didn't immediately go on. "How did it go?" She knew they were breaking their deal, punching a little hole in the rowboat in which they'd decided to float. Just this once. You can always patch a hole.

"Well, a lot of people said a lot of things about how wonderful he was. So that was great for his mom and dad. He has lots of friends. Well, he had. One lady ripped off a poem from a TV show, so I think she might be disqualified from the Grief Olympics, but there was a patient he helped who had lots of good things to say." She rubbed the back of her neck.

"How was it for you?"

She wrinkled her brow. "What do you mean?"

"You said it was great for his mom and dad, his friends. I'm asking how it was for you."

Evvie licked her lips. "Um." And she couldn't believe it. Couldn't. Now she was going to cry. Now, in her kitchen, while she was making tea, while she was talking to someone who was probably not ready to be promoted north of "acquaintance," she was going to cry. She'd had to pray for wet eyes at the tree-planting, had to coax a lump into her throat while everyone else was sniffling away, and now this. She took a couple of deep breaths, trying to look like she was thinking about what to say. Finally, she felt herself calm.

"I felt bad," she said, "because they all loved him so much, and I didn't. I mean, I loved him originally, a lot, but I didn't when he died. He wasn't nice to me. He didn't hit me or anything, but he was sometimes pretty nasty. And then he died, and now when I'm around people who miss him, I don't know what to do. Sometimes I can't sleep because I don't miss him so much, which sounds crazy. But . . . that. It's that, that's why I'm . . ." Her voice trailed off, and she waved a hand in front of her face. "Nobody knows all that, by the way. Not even Andy. So, if you don't mind." It had just tumbled right out. Not all of it, not the leaving, but more than she'd expected. It might have been sheer exhaustion, or the sight of him throwing at ghosts under her outside light.

Dean met her eyes. He nodded. "I've only done one thing seriously since I was ten, and I can't do it anymore, and nobody can tell me why," he said. "So I don't know what to do either." He ran his hand over his hair. "It's not the same at all. I don't mean to say it's the same."

"Honestly, I don't know if it is. I don't know . . . a lot." She sighed. The kettle *haaaaa*-d louder and they sat. Finally, the hiss became a whistle. She got up, and as she passed him on her way to the cabinet, he reached out and grabbed her hand with one of his. He squeezed, then let go.

She pushed her hair behind her ear and moved the kettle off the burner, listening to the whistle fade. The quiet came up behind her. "Did I tell you about the time Andy and I won $100 with a scratch-off ticket?" she asked. "We spent every penny of it on Reese's Peanut Butter Cups." She poured the tea and told the story, and they talked about the weather and the repairs his truck needed.

When the mugs were empty and he'd vanished into the apartment, she cleaned up the kitchen and went upstairs to her bedroom. She took her laptop down from the dresser, sat on her bed, and did something she had not done yet: she googled Dean. And she read everything. This was when she learned that what had happened to Dean was called "the yips"—although right now, they were also calling it Dean Tenney Disease.

On June 17, 2000, struggling Yankees second baseman Chuck Knoblauch tried to make a throw to first. Instead, he threw the ball into the stands and hit Keith Olbermann's mother. If it were possible to take everything currently known about the yips and reduce it until only its very essence remained, the result might be Knoblauch in this moment, unable to manage a throw he'd been executing for many years.

Twitchy golfers, tennis players who suddenly can't serve, aces who lose their touch at darts and cricket, basketball players who go up on their toes and freeze, unable to complete a free throw: they can all have the yips. Coinage of the term is most commonly credited to golfer Tommy Armour, who came down with the condition in the 1920s.

For a long time, in baseball, they called it Steve Blass Disease, after a pitcher for the Pirates who lost all ability to throw accurately after the 1972 season. He later wrote a book called *A Pirate for Life*. "It got to the point where I didn't want to go to the grocery store, didn't want to go out, because I was so humiliated," he wrote. There was a time when they called it Steve Sax Syndrome, after the 1982 Rookie of the Year—a second baseman, like Knoblauch—who also lost his throw to first. At least in baseball, whoever had it last gets to carry the yips as his personal codenamed whammy. Mets catcher Mackey Sasser lost the ability to throw back to the pitcher, so for a while, they called it Sasseritis. And now, they called it Dean Tenney Disease.

A 2014 *New Yorker* article by David Owen rounded up the latest research in the field of head-case-ology, which holds that the yips are a complex soup of psychological and neurological ingredients. Maybe anxiety, maybe something physical, maybe more like an injury than a curse. But you'd be hard-pressed to watch somebody with the yips and not think the most likely explanation is that he once annoyed a vengeful demon, who then pointed a long, bony finger and said, "*You.*"

Evvie watched Mackey Sasser on YouTube as he triple-pumped trying to throw back to the pitcher. She watched throws from Sax and Knoblauch pull first basemen off the bag, force them to leap, or sail right past them, a foot or ten feet out of reach. She watched Knoblauch hit Olbermann's mother.

And then, for the first time, she watched Dean Tenney pitch in a professional baseball game, in a low-quality bootleg video, where he threw two wild pitches and walked three batters in an inning against the White Sox. Caught in close-up, he clenched and unclenched his jaw. She noted in passing that he'd had a bit of a scruffy beard at the time and that she was against it. The announcers pitied him openly, and one speculated that maybe it was this rumored romance with this Hollywood actress—he wasn't saying she was a jinx, he was only saying this was the kind of situation where fans often *said* she might be a jinx.

"Sexist asshole," Evvie muttered.

She stopped the video. She found another that was called "Tenney Strikes Out the Side." Pitching against the Orioles before his troubles started, Dean mystified, puzzled, and confused three batters in a row.

The first swung wickedly at two pitches and let two go by, and then it was like he was in slow motion as he watched the next pitch thunk into the catcher's mitt, and he knew instantly that he had made a terrible mistake, even before the umpire threw his arm and bellowed. The next batter struck out after gamely trying to put his bat on a pitch that dropped like it had been suspended over a dunk tank. The last guy hung in for a while, but then Dean stretched, wound himself up like a spring, and hurled the ball. There was a swing like the guy wanted to hit it all the way to Philadelphia—a swing so hard he almost knocked himself over. And then there was just Dean, walking to the dugout, wearing exactly one-third of a smile.

Eight

THE NEXT AFTERNOON, Evvie heard someone pull into the driveway and cut the engine. She went to the window and saw a low-slung black Miata, from which a woman in khaki pants and a green sweater-coat was coming into view. Evvie waited, and sure enough, there were five quick knocks on the door, which Evvie's ear heard as *I-don't-have-all-day*.

But when she opened the door, the woman was smiling rather warmly, clutching a leather notebook in one hand. "Can I help you?" Evvie asked her, suddenly feeling stumpy and lumpy and like she wished she'd thought to pull her hair back.

"I'm Ellen Boyd. I'm with *Beat Sports*."

It didn't mean a lot to Evvie, but she'd seen the name. She knew enough. "Can I help you?" she repeated.

"I'm looking for Dean Tenney. I understand he lives with you."

It wasn't a secret that Dean was renting here; he'd been in town long enough to be greeted at the gas station and the grocery store, and he had a flock of admirers among the girls who sat around the coffee shop all day, drinking sugar bombs with whipped cream and never seeming to gain an ounce. A few people had even gotten up the nerve to tell him how much they'd liked watching him pitch. When she'd seen it happen, he'd smiled and said thank you and followed with, "What do you do?" or "What are you shopping for?" or "Do you think it's going to rain?" Or, if he got desperate, there was always, "What's your favorite way to cook a lobster?"

But it wasn't a secret. He lived there. So she said it: "Yes, he does." But almost immediately, she rewound the question and her answer in her head. "Well, I mean, yes, he lives in the house. He doesn't live with me. Like, he doesn't *live with* me, we don't live together. There's an apartment in back."

"Is he at home?" Ellen Boyd with the leather notebook wanted to know, even though Evvie suspected she'd waited until his truck wasn't here to show up.

"He's not, no. I can take your business card if you like, and I can ask him to call you." This was what Andy had done for Evvie when a couple of reporters came around knocking, asking about Tim's accident. She still had the cards in an envelope; she'd never looked at any of them.

"Could I ask you a few questions?"

"Oh. No, I can't be helpful. You should talk to Dean."

"Would you happen to know if he's been drinking since he's been here?"

Evvie's hand tightened on the doorknob. "I'm sorry, what?"

"I'm curious about how he's doing. Has he been drinking since he's been here?"

"I don't know what you're asking, but I'd like you to go, I don't have anything else to say." She started to close the door, but Ellen put her hand on it to keep it open.

"Totally understand, but you'll be helping him if you answer a question or two, because then I really can go. If it's no, say no, but if it's yes, you can get it over with and I won't be back, okay? Do you know whether he's having issues with his mental health?"

Evvie paused. She pulled the door back open and stepped into the doorway. "You should get off my porch."

"Did you and Dean know each other while your husband was alive, or did you get together more recently, or . . . ?"

Evvie's head felt light. "Listen," she said, making every syllable the precise equivalent of every other, "you're standing on a porch my father rebuilt when it was ninety-five degrees outside. I grew up here and I know everyone, and nothing will happen to me if I kick you down those steps with your notebook and your shit shovel."

"So you don't want to get into how the two of you got involved."

Evvie grabbed the notebook out of Ellen's hand and threw it. It landed with a thump in the grass. "You dropped something." Evvie nodded toward it and pushed the door shut.

Once it was latched, she leaned back against the door. "Oh shit, oh shit," she whispered to herself, letting out a hoarse, nervous chuckle. She spun around and peeked out the window. She wondered whether Ellen Boyd would be out there, calling the police, reporting that Evvie Drake had destroyed her property and needed to be arrested. She half expected to see cop cars wailing up her driveway with their lights and sirens going. What she saw was Ellen brushing dirt off the book, talking on her phone, and laughing as she walked to her car.

Forty-five minutes. That's how long it took for Ellen Boyd to file her story, get a photo of Dean added, and throw it on the *Beat Sports* blog that went by the name "Off the Field." And an hour after that, Evvie got the link from her cousin Steve, and thirty seconds after that, there it was on her own screen.

When Dean Tenney vanished from New York in September after choking as spectacularly as any pitcher in memory, rumors swirled that he was on drugs, was depressed, or might have a gambling problem. More adventurous folks suspected it might be personal. Maybe a woman whose situation was complicated. Maybe a relationship in trouble. Maybe with a man, even.

Evvie was willing to bet Ellen had started these rumors herself, assuming they existed at all.

> But a month or so ago, he turned up in Calcasset, Maine, which most assumed he'd chosen because it was the hometown of longtime pal Andrew Buck, and a place where the locals probably don't even have cellphones or high-speed Internet, let alone spend time on Twitter.

Uch. #condescendingNewYorkdouchebags.

> Shortly after he got there, though, Tenney moved in with a young widow named Eveleth Drake. Drake's husband, a beloved local doctor his patients called Doc, had died in a single-car accident less than a year before.

Evvie realized it was awfully petty that out of this scurrilous pile of crap, the word that was sticking in her craw was "beloved." And didn't patients call every doctor Doc?

> Drake answered the door at her house (a great big but still cozy property that looks like something out of a movie) earlier today, but when I asked, she claimed Tenney wasn't around. After admitting they were living together, she refused to answer questions about whether he'd been drinking and insisted she didn't know anything about any mental problems he might be having.
>
> But how did a widow from Maine wind up living with a guy who was a New York Yankee two years ago? Could this all have really come about just in the time since Doc died?
>
> Whatever the answers to these questions, when she was asked whether she was involved with Tenney prior to her husband's death, the former Mrs. Drake ended the interview and threw in a threat of violence.

"I didn't threaten violence," Evvie muttered. "Or I threatened very little violence, anyway." She had to give it to Boyd: the reporter had made all she could out of nothing. And even though it was innocent, it didn't look innocent. And everybody she knew would read it. Her father would read it, Tim's parents would read it, everybody who already thought she was a bad wife would read it. And, of course, Dean would read it. Why hadn't she closed the door?

Evvie was watching TV on the couch when she heard his key in the door. Dean came to the living room doorway and stood there for a minute. Finally, he raised his phone in one hand. "Saw it," he said.

She put her hands over her face. "I'm so sorry," she said into her fingers. "I'm *so* sorry."

He came over and sat next to her on the couch. "What? You're sorry for what?"

Evvie took her hands away and looked at him. "Oh, for making it sound like we were sleeping together. I'm sure that's not exactly what your public image needs right now."

"I don't know," he said. "I think it reflects pretty well on me. I don't know about you. Besides, my favorite sports site recently voted me First Athlete We'd Throw into an Active Volcano, so I don't think my public image can really be hurt."

"I also might have threatened the reporter, which I'm sure isn't exactly what I'm supposed to do. I'm guessing your people will not like that."

He narrowed his eyes a little. "What people are those?"

"Don't you have ... I don't know. People? Lawyers or agents or, like, PR people?" She waved a hand by her ear. "People with little headsets who run around barking about whether the limo is going to be on time and whether everyone is in position?"

"That sounds ... like a maître d'. Or a wedding planner," he said. "I don't have a wedding planner."

"You know what I'm talking about."

"I used to have a lot of people." He nodded. "But now I have a lot fewer people, and I don't talk to them as much. And when I do, I don't pay attention to anything they say. What I was going to tell you when I sat down was that I'm sorry a reporter came to your door and started badgering you about your life and your husband, since I doubt that's a lot of fun for you."

"It's not fun," she agreed. "I still shouldn't have threatened her."

"What did you say?" he asked with a grin.

She put her hands back over her face. "I said if she didn't get off the porch, I was going to push her off."

Dean offered a broad display of shock. "You *did* threaten her!"

"Well, I told her that I was going to kick her down the stairs with her notebook and her . . . shit shovel."

At this, he bark-laughed. "Did you really?" She nodded miserably, and he pulled her hands down from her face. "Stop pretending that's not awesome. That is awesome. You know it is. That's a fucking enforcer is what that is. I'm going to call you Bruiser."

She made a drawn-out, miserable moaning sound.

"Look, fifteen months ago, they burned me in effigy at a bar I co-owned. They shot out the windows of my next-door neighbor's apartment with a BB gun because either they can't count windows or they can't tell the difference between 816 and 818."

"Plus, active volcano," Evvie said quietly.

"Plus active volcano, yes," he said. "So trust me, the people I have left are not going to get all upset because you yelled at a reporter. And I appreciate what you did."

She smiled, just a little bit, just until her shoulders relaxed. He raised his hand and said, "Up top." She didn't respond. "Come on, Eveleth. Up top." She reached up and slapped his hand with her own. As he walked back toward the apartment, she heard him say, "Shit shovel. I'm stealing that. That's mine now."

Nine

DEAN WAS ANSWERING an email from one of his brothers the next morning when he heard Evvie's distinctive double-knock. When he opened the apartment door, she was standing with a gray-haired guy in a Calcasset High School warm-up jacket. "Hey," Evvie said. "Dean, you have a visitor. This is Ted Finch. He coaches football over at the high school. And he won't tell you this, but his son Jake is also our star . . . running back, right?"

"Running back," Finch said. "Yes."

"Hey, Coach." They shook hands a little awkwardly.

"I have to tell you," Coach Finch said, "I watched you pitch on television quite a lot. It's a pleasure."

"Oh, thank you."

Evvie nodded at them. "Maybe you guys can come in here and talk at the table? I have to go upstairs and get some work done. Good to see you, Ted."

"You, too, Eveleth," he said.

Dean watched Evvie disappear up the stairs, patting him on the elbow as she passed. "So," he said to the coach.

"So. How's the town treating you so far?"

"Great, great. Everyone's been great. Good to be out of the city, you know."

"I can imagine." Finch smiled at him. "I was sorry to hear how things turned out in New York."

Dean nodded. "Yeah, thank you." He gave the silence a few seconds to settle. "So, what can I do for you?"

"Uh, well," Finch said, "I came to ask you a favor. I've got a football team that's most of the way through a pretty strong season. I've got young men who are working very hard, they're a little beat up by now, and I'm always tryin' to think of ways to get them motivated. Keep them from gettin' lazy. Sometimes I bring in different men to talk to them, give some advice about football. Or generally. Just general advice."

Dean began to see the cloudy outlines of this visit sharpen. "Okay," he said, affecting the noncommittal eyebrow wrinkle of a man who didn't get it. Maybe Ted wouldn't be able to bring himself to explain it. Maybe Dean wouldn't have to say no.

"Well, you're a pro. You've worked with the best, you've handled pressure. It's not baseball, but I'm pretty sure it would kinda translate. I was hoping you'd maybe be willing—"

"Oh." Dean looked at him even more quizzically. "Coach, you know that I washed out of professional sports, right? That's pretty much what I'm known for."

Finch shrugged his big shoulders. "Yuh. I know about all that." He rattled what sounded like a big set of keys, school keys, coach keys, in his pocket. "I don't much go in for all this 'head case' stuff. Every guy wakes up one day, finds out he's done. Coaches, too."

Dean paused, waiting to find the argument ridiculous, something a small-town coach would say because he didn't understand big-time sports. But he found himself giving a nod of grudging acknowledgment instead. "I guess you're right about that."

"Nobody's ready. Doesn't always happen when they're in the middle of a game, I give you that. Doesn't always happen on television. Doesn't always make the news. More often it's the foot speed or they're hurt all the time. Sometimes they wear out. But they all wake up done. You might have woke up done, but you're still the best these boys are ever going to meet, chances are. I think it'd be good for them, knowing that life's not all one thing, as far as win and lose."

Dean had to admit there was some sense in it. He could at least explain what it took to get him where he'd been, even if he didn't know a damn thing about how to stay there. Maybe he could even do them some good. He could at least tell them not to give their money to quacks in the event they *did* become professional athletes and *did* make a lot of money and then *did* spectacularly implode.

Still, there had already been one reporter at Evvie's door. He felt bad enough about drawing one to her house; he didn't want to draw them to the school or to football practice, and who knew whether the football team would even want to hear from somebody who not only didn't play football but was pretty much set on fire and sent out of town because he couldn't outpitch the guys on a high school staff?

"We'd keep it quiet," Coach Finch told him, mind-reading as a man might learn to do after spending twenty years reading the complex behavioral signals of the seventeen-year-old male New Englander. "Not a show. Just talk to some kids. And if it works out, who knows? You help run drills, you do a little assistant coaching maybe, instead of sitting inside playing video games like I bet you're doing."

Dean chuckled. "I haven't played football since high school, and I wasn't that good."

"Doesn't matter."

"I don't know if it's a good idea, Coach. Kids are online, all that, people talk."

Finch shrugged again, waved that hand again. "Eh. My boys are solid. I tell 'em it's not for Twitter, they'll keep it quiet much as they can." This was Dean's favorite part—it came out *nawt fuh Twittah*.

"I hate to tell you, Coach, but I think they all gave up Twitter. That's for old guys like you and me. I think now you have to tell them it's not for . . . something else. Instagram, maybe."

"Oh, for the love of Gawd," Coach muttered. "I get a hold of whatever they're doing with their phones and they're on to something else. It's like grabbin' at eels." He continued: "Anyway, they're good boys. Worst thing that happens, everybody finds out you're working with a bunch of kids. Right now, they're sayin' you've gone dog-bone loony, so you've got nothing to lose, right?"

Dean had played for an awful lot of coaches. And Coach Finch of the Calcasset High School Hawks was the first one who'd ever come to him for a favor and called it a favor. Hard to say no.

Ten

IN THE THIRD week of October, Dean opened the apartment door and called to the living room, where Evvie was reading a dancer's diary from the 1920s, to tell her that it was ten minutes to *Halls of Power*, a dopey political soap they made a point of watching at the time when it aired, but mutually vowed to deny they knew anything about if they were ever asked.

When the door wasn't closed, they could hear well between his apartment and her kitchen, and sometimes they'd leave it open so they could chat while she made dinner or he opened a bunch of his forwarded mail. Now and then, if she made something she was particularly proud of, he'd come in and eat with her, or she'd flop into one of his club chairs with a beer and he'd tell her on-the-road athlete stories, which they'd agreed didn't count as talking about baseball. He told her about a guy he'd hid from an angry ex-girlfriend, two guys he'd smuggled into a hotel when they missed curfew, and a time he'd had to sneak into his hotel room naked, trying to block the view of himself with a towel and an electric guitar.

"I still can't believe you got this ridiculous, enormous TV," she said, settling in for *Halls of Power*, "that I really love." He'd mounted it on the wall opposite the club chairs, so she flopped into her seat and threw her feet over the arm. "Remind me where we were," she said.

"The lobbyist you hate was paying off Special Agent Flathead of the FBI."

"Ah, right." She rubbed her arms through her sweater. "And the president was . . ."

"Giving the VP the old pocket veto."

Evvie turned toward him. "If we watch this show long enough, I'm going to find out how many governmental sex euphemisms you have."

"I don't even know myself. Try me again."

"Okay. What was the president doing?"

"Giving the VP the old advise and consent."

"Stop."

"Well, stop laughing."

Evvie stretched in her seat. "It seems cold in here, are you cold?"

"Little bit." He went to pour her a drink.

She got up and went to her kitchen, where she fetched a foil-wrapped brick she'd sometimes used to flatten roasted chickens. She propped open the apartment door. "Better air circulation," she said. She sat back down. "So, how was today?"

"Actually, I was going to tell you something. I don't know if you heard, but the Drakes are setting up a scholarship at the school."

Evvie nodded. "I had heard they might do that. I'm not surprised."

Dean shook his head. "Guy casts a shadow, huh? I mean, if I can ask."

She nodded. "Yeah. I mean, went off to California and came back. Worked in town, lived in town . . . it was a big deal."

"Just that he came back and lived here?"

"Yeah." She took the glass of whiskey from him and shook her head when he held out an open can of Pringles. "A couple of years ago, somebody told us that Tim—who was class of 1999—was one of only two valedictorians from our high school who graduated after 1994 who still lived here."

"Why's that?"

"It's demographics and economics and stuff."

"Go ahead. Tee it up, nerd. I went to college."

She laughed. "Well, basically a lot of eighteen-year-olds with good options don't stay in a place like this. And when they leave, they don't usually come back. So the town gets older, tax base gets smaller, things get harder. Long story short? Too much leaving and dying; not enough arriving and being born."

"Oldest and whitest state in the country." He nodded.

"Exactly." She took another drink. "So with Tim, I think a lot of people knew that if he were their kid, they might have encouraged him to get out. But he didn't, and they loved him for it."

"I guess I can understand that."

"Besides, he was cute, he was friendly as long as you didn't live with him, and he married his high school sweetheart. He just had that thing. That *thing* that makes certain guys kind of glide across everything." She skimmed her flat hand through the air. "To some of the people who had watched him grow up, I think he was . . . a unicorn."

"He didn't want bigger things?"

"No, he did."

"Then why come back?"

Evvie shrugged. "Because anywhere else, he'd just be a nice-looking horse." She smiled and pointed to the TV. "Show's starting."

When she went to bed that night, she moved the brick and shut the door, but when Dean came into the kitchen to share a pot of coffee with her the next morning, she waved her hand. "Put the brick back," she said. After that, they closed it only at night.

Eleven

EVVIE HAD SAT out Thanksgiving the previous fall. She'd sent her father off to eat turkey with Andy and his kids and Kell, and she'd spent most of the day in bed with a book, putting on the nightstand a bottle of wine, which she opened at noon and finished at ten thirty at night.

This year, Andy had started working on her a month ahead of time, telling her he wanted her and her dad to come with him and the girls to Kell's in Thomaston. Kell had invited Dean's parents as well, and they were so eager to see him and so enticed by the pictures he'd sent that they'd decided to make the trip. Evvie promised to go, then planned to cancel, then got a supermarket flyer in the mail for frozen turkeys and cried in the bathroom, then called Andy and promised him she would bring the pumpkin bread.

There was a half-inch of snow on the ground when she woke up on Thursday and went downstairs with her thick robe wrapped around her to put the coffee on. She could hear that Dean was up, so she went over and stood at the closed door. "Morning," she said to it.

"Morning." He sounded barely awake. It made her smile.

As she scooped coffee into the filter basket, the door opened. "You want coffee?" she asked.

"I do," he said, coming into the kitchen and settling in one of her chairs. "I was at Kell's way too late last night. My parents' plane was delayed, so I didn't get them over there until midnight."

"They're settled in?"

"Yeah. They have about ten years of small talk to catch up on. Five boys between them, I'm sure they're keeping busy."

"It was nice of them to come all this way."

"I think my mom wanted to see for herself that I wasn't doing quite as badly as she kept reading that I was. How about you? Are you excited? Turkey? Family? Football?"

She gave a little "hmm" that wasn't quite a real laugh. "I don't know about excited, but it'll be good to see everybody. I didn't do last holiday season."

"Understandable," he said, rubbing his shoulder.

She poured in the water, pressed the button, and listened to the coffeemaker go *ffft-ffft-ffft* while she put away the clean dishes. The plates she'd gotten when she got married, which she still used every day, were white with a neat row of little yellow flowers around the edges. They'd always felt to her like dollhouse furnishings. "I can always tell I'm in a bad mood when I get annoyed about these dishes," she said.

"Oh, boy. Why?"

"They're not my style. There's something about registering for wedding presents that makes people think they're going to turn into other people. Like I was going to turn into a little-yellow-flowers person when I got married."

She put away the glasses, the flatware, the glass mixing bowl. They'd spent so much time sitting in her kitchen in the last two months that even with her back turned, she knew what Dean was doing. He was watching her work and listening to everything with a periodic narrowing of his eyes or tilt of his head. When she first met him, she'd thought he listened like a therapist, but now she thought he listened like a journalist. Everything she said, he treated like it ended in a semicolon. "I did not turn into a little-yellow-flowers person," she added. "I wound up with all this stuff I didn't pick, because there's this wedding-industrial complex, and you have to buy ugly dishes and not-soft towels and people *get angry* if you don't come up with pressure cookers and blenders and shrimp forks that you promise them you really, really want, and then you're stuck with them. I'm stuck with these flower dishes for the rest of my life."

"Why are you stuck with them?"

Evvie closed the dishwasher and turned back to him. "Oh . . . you know. I have them and everything. I mean, they're fine."

"But you're not stuck with them."

"Right, but I *have* them now."

"They're dishes."

"Right."

"So you could get other dishes."

"I have these, though."

"But you're the only person who lives here."

"You live here."

He tossed his head back toward the apartment door. "I live there. You live here." He tapped his index finger on the table. "You"—*tap*—"live"—*tap*—"here." *Tap*. "They're your fuckin' dishes. You're the person who eats off the dishes."

"I know that."

"So if you don't like them, get new ones. Diane could give you a whole box of them for a buck fifty. She'd probably throw in a set of salad tongs."

"Why are you mad about dishes?" she said, crossing her arms over her chest.

"Why are *you*?"

"I'm not!"

This silence was different. *Ffft-ffft-ffft* from the coffeemaker.

"There's a lot of things you don't get to decide," he finally said. "I think you can decide about this and you're talking like you can't."

She thought about the too-delicate wineglasses, the undersized table, the too-big house, the big shower she ended up with in place of the tub she wanted, and whether she'd ever chosen to live here at all. "I'll get different dishes. I promise."

The coffeemaker beeped, and she filled two mugs and brought them to the table. "My father will be happy to spend some time with you. He likes baseball, but I've made him promise not to mention it, and if you're curious about lobsters, he can tell you everything you want to know."

"How long was he in that business?"

"Well, he retired two years ago, and he started training when he was ten and doing it full-time when he was seventeen, I think? So . . . it's almost fifty years."

"But no lobster boat for you."

"It wasn't encouraged for girls so much when I was little. Plus, I think I knew from watching my dad that it was brutal. I never saw him before school, and then he'd get home right around when I had dinner ready."

"Good lord. I don't think I could heat up soup when I was that age."

She smiled. "Well, he was the one working hard. His back was—it is—a nightmare from hauling up the traps. He's had surgery on it a few different times, that's part of why he finally retired. He always wanted to make sure I felt like I could do whatever I wanted. 'There's more to life than eight hundred traps,' he used to tell me."

"Eight hundred traps?"

"That's how many one guy can have."

"That's a lot of lobster."

"It is. I think I . . . figured there were easier ways to live." She put her hands flat on the table. "Which I guess turned out to mean marrying a doctor."

"Did you want to do something else?" he asked.

She sighed. "I think every plan I ever had involved everything happening later. You're twenty-two, twenty-three, time is sort of infinite. It's like a pool where you can't touch the bottom. I knew there would be something else, but it was always *after*. After, after. It was like I was waiting for something to start, and I was actually in the middle of it the whole time. Does that make sense?"

"It does."

She picked at a thread on the sleeve of her robe. "You never wanted to do anything else besides baseball?"

He made a sound like *pffft*. "No. Never."

"Did your parents mind?"

He thought about it. "I don't think anybody wants their kid to have exactly one plan that could end in the time it takes for him to take a baseball to the eye socket. But they eventually gave up and went for it. Pushed me really hard to go to this All-Star Camp, and that's where I decided I wanted to go to Cornell . . . and you know the rest."

She remembered the smack of the pinecone against the fence when she was spying on him in the dark, and she wondered if he did this everywhere all the time, with oranges in supermarket alleys and snow globes behind souvenir shops and sea urchins from the tide pools into the sides of bleached-out boathouses, hurling everything over and over until it finally fell apart. She wanted to know if he thought he'd go back to pitching. She wanted to ask all the questions she'd promised she wouldn't—was he crazy, was he messed up, did something happen, what happened?

"I'm just saying," she told him, "that my dad is going to talk to you a lot about lobsters."

"I'm ready. My dad might ask about your homeowner's policy."

"Can't wait."

The door of Kell's house opened, and Lilly, Andy's five-year-old, looked up at them. "Hello and welcome to Thanksgiving!" she said.

She was the more adventurous dresser of the girls, hostessing today in brown-and-white checked pants and a white long-sleeved T-shirt featuring a frog made of sequins.

"Hello, lightning bug," Evvie said.

"Hey there, Lilly Buck," Dean added, giving her hair a muss with his right hand.

"Dean, doooooooon't-uuuuh," Lilly wailed with a grin, then she took off running into the house.

"Oh, boy, she is nuts about you, that one," Evvie said. A warm wave of turkey fumes drew them into the living room, where Frank Ashton was making short work of a dish of peanuts while voices chattered in the kitchen. Lilly had disappeared back into the finished basement, where her sister surely awaited with whatever inflatable fort or elaborate robot kit their grandmother had secured for them. Evvie called out a greeting. "Don't get up, Pop," she said as she bent to hug him and press her cheek to his. "How are you?"

He patted her encircling arm. "Oh, I'm doin' fine, sweetheart." She still loved the sound of her father's voice. She gave him an extra squeeze before she let go.

"Dad, this is my friend Dean," Evvie said.

Dean shook her father's hand. "Good to meet you."

"You, too. And I promised Eveleth I'm not going to say anything about baseball." Evvie froze.

"Right on," Dean said with a nod. "Excuse me a minute, I'm going to go kiss my mom." He took the pumpkin bread from Evvie and turned toward the kitchen. "You guys, I'm coming in there to see about the pie situation. Anything that's not covered up, I reserve the right to eat with my hands." She heard Kell laugh.

When Dean was out of earshot, Evvie leaned down toward her father's chair. "Pop, what was the one thing I asked you not to do?"

Frank threw his hands up. "I'm not askin' him anything. You didn't tell me I couldn't speak to the man."

Andy appeared at the top of the basement stairs. "Is Evvie hassling you, Frank?"

"You've got that right there, Andrew," said Frank as he popped four more peanuts into his mouth.

Evvie got up and walked over to her best friend. He hugged her so hard she grimaced. "I'm happy to see you," he said into her ear.

"Me, too."

"Your dad and Dean's dad have been bonding."

"Oh, that should be something. Dean's in the kitchen with the rest of the parents."

Andy released her from his grip. *"Dean, are you bothering my mother? Mom, is Dean bothering you?"* he bellowed as he walked away.

Evvie had barely taken her coat off when Dean came back into the living room. "Evvie, these are my parents, Angie and Stuart Tenney; this is Evvie."

Dean's mom was slim and pink-cheeked, with curly gray hair and glasses; his father was tall—though not as tall as he was—and broad through the shoulders. Evvie shook hands with them, but the impulse to hug his mother, in particular, was palpable. "We've heard a lot about you," Angie said.

Her husband stood with his hands on his hips. "Hopefully Dean's not throwing too many wild parties where you have to call the cops."

"Not at all," Evvie told them. "He's been a great tenant, I promise."

Kell came in from the kitchen, nibbling on an apple slice, with Andy following behind her. "Everything's doing what it's supposed to be doing in the kitchen," she said, "so why don't you all sit down?"

"So," Dean's dad said as they all settled, "we heard from Tom this morning. He's in Boulder with Nancy's family. Brian and David are at David's sister's place, and Mark and Alison are on a cruise."

"Those are all my brothers," Dean said to Evvie. "My dad is sharing all their news. Did he mention they're all married?"

"And Mark's on a cruise," Stuart repeated. "On Thanksgiving. Who eats pumpkin pie in a bathing suit on a boat in the middle of the ocean? With a little umbrella sticking out of your drink? Dumbest thing I ever heard."

Angie laughed and elbowed him. "Be nice. They like the water."

"I like the Runaway Mine Train at Six Flags Over Texas, but I'm not eating Thanksgiving dinner there."

"Say, Stuart," Evvie's dad said, "you mentioned you grew up in Jersey. Did you ever go to Coney Island?"

"Sure did," Stuart said. "Visited my mother's aunt out that way and rode the Cyclone. Have you been to Dollywood?" Frank shook his head. "They've got one there called Thunderhead. Rode it a few summers ago. I got off it and rewrote my will."

"I hope you left me something good," Dean said.

"We're leaving you the cat."

"Don't leave me that cat."

"Oh, yeah. We're going to leave you the cat," Stuart repeated, "and a note that says you have to dress it up every Halloween and walk it down Fifth Avenue or you lose your inheritance."

"We've got a lady in town walks her cat," Frank said. "Tourists think it's a local custom. It's on the Internet that people in Maine walk their cats on leashes. All because one idiot sees Lois yanking Pookie down Main Street like a poodle."

"Pumpkin, not Pookie," Evvie corrected.

"Whatever."

"All right, all right. Tell us about your work, Evvie," Angie said pointedly.

Evvie laughed. "I do transcription. I work with journalists and people doing research, mostly. I listen to their interviews and I type them up and sometimes do a little indexing so they can find whatever they're looking for. It's interesting to me, anyway."

"Dean knows lots of journalists," Stuart said with a twinkle. "He loves interviews."

Evvie turned to Dean. "Oh, really?"

"My dad is trying to start with me."

"Well, now I want to know," Evvie said.

"Tell her about Johnny Boo-Hoos!" Stuart grinned.

"Who's Johnny Boo-Hoos?" Evvie asked.

Dean rolled his eyes. "It's not a who. It's a what. It's a bar in Gowanus, in Brooklyn. My parents' favorite magazine article about me starts out with me stuffing chicken fingers into my face at Johnny Boo-Hoos. Those things always start with the food. How Jennifer Lawrence is eating poached salmon or whatever, or how they're at LeBron James's favorite place for burritos, like anybody cares."

"I'd love to try LeBron's favorite burrito place," Andy said, raising one hand.

"Not helpful," Dean told him, pointing one finger. Andy smiled and sat back in his chair. "Anyway. It starts out like, 'Dean Tenney is stuffing big fat pieces of industrial fried chicken into his maw while a sports reporter tries to get him to talk about how much he hates sports reporting.'"

"That's what they asked you about?" Evvie asked.

"They didn't have to," Angie said. "The TV in the bar was showing his favorite commentator."

"Pete Danziger," Stuart said darkly.

Evvie's father gave a dismissive snort. "Oh, *that* idiot."

"Thank you, Frank," Dean said. "See? Frank agrees with me. Danziger's a cable sports anchor. And an asshole."

"Dean!" his mother protested, but with a smile. "Kell, I apologize for my son." Kell waved her hand and took another sip of wine.

Dean went on. "It was maybe three years ago, and they were talking about this whole thing where Domenico Garza, who plays for the Mets, hit a home run, and he celebrated by doing this chest-bump with Florido Marquez. All these old guys got all bent out of shape, they said he was trying to show up the pitcher or whatever. And Danziger was talking about how players should be respectful, and I told the reporter nobody would have freaked out about it if Garza and Marquez were white."

"I'd believe that," Evvie said.

Dean sat up a little, like his body remembered the annoyance of it. "If Domenico Garza is named James Leo Francis Patrick Houlihan, you can bet your ass nobody decides he's being disrespectful. Then he just loves the game. That's what I told the guy, and they printed it."

"Danziger didn't love it," Dean's dad said.

"Yeah, well." Dean smiled thinly. "He got to report later that I threw four wild pitches in one game, so I think that made up for it."

Silence whooshed in under the doors and through the cracks around the windows. "I was proud of you," Angie finally said. "You were saying what you thought was right. That's why people love interviewing you. You tell the truth."

"Like about the environment," Stuart said.

"Oh, the environment!" Dean's mom put her hand over her heart.

Evvie leaned forward. "Really."

Dean leaned back, groaning like he was nursing a hernia, but Angie nodded. "He was on the red carpet for a movie that Melanie was in—she was his girlfriend at the time, very nice. And they asked what he wanted to say to his fans. And he said, 'Climate-change denial is flat-earth idiocy for people who want us all to drown.'"

"'Hardheaded dolts,'" Stuart corrected. "'For hardheaded dolts who want us all to drown.'"

"That's right," Dean's mom said fondly. "Hardheaded dolts."

"I didn't know you'd gotten so political," Kell said to Dean.

"Hell with politics. I just don't want to die in a war over the last gallon of water in Mad Max's kiddie pool."

Evvie caught the eye of Dean's mother, and they decided together not to laugh. "Dean is happy we're all here to celebrate our considerable blessings," Angie said, raising her glass in the general direction of her son.

"You're all a bunch of jerks," Dean said, smiling as they toasted him.

Frank eventually put the football game on TV, and conversations rose and fell in the living room and the kitchen. At one point, Frank got so riled up over a touchdown that he knocked a whole dish of guacamole onto the floor. Evvie swooped in from the kitchen with paper towels almost before he could ask.

In the kitchen, Evvie stood beside Kell and peeled potatoes. Kell was a feeder, a pourer, a hugger, and Evvie had watched during the last several years as her chic short hair got grayer and her chowder got better. She'd lost her husband very young, when Andy was only a baby, and once Andy and Lori had Rose and Lilly, she'd decided it was worth giving up her friends in Colorado—Stuart and Angie among them—to be in Maine with family. And so she'd moved to Thomaston and bought this great little house. It had a permanent bedroom for her granddaughters, for whom fruit was mandatory at Grandma's but vegetables were not.

Kell peppered Evvie with questions about Dean, no matter how many times she explained that it was purely a landlord-tenant relationship. This felt not *exactly* true now, but the last thing she needed was to pique the curiosity of a woman whom it had been so hard to convince that she and Andy were not getting married.

Evvie peeked through the oven door at the turkey now and then and watched as it crisped and browned, and then she helped with the potatoes and sliced her bread and put it into the basket. There were green beans and chestnut stuffing, and Kell made her own *real* cranberry sauce, thank you very much. "Taking something out of a can and putting it on your Thanksgiving table!" she would say at least once a year. "It's like you're eating in the lunchroom on an oil rig!" Sometimes she said "a college dormitory room," and Evvie's favorite had been "Well, you might as well eat it in your car over the gearshift."

When everything was ready, they sat around the big table, squeezed in and almost touching elbows, with Lilly and Rose at the desk pulled in from their room. Wine splashed into glasses, and Frank sat with the carving knife in his hand, prepared to operate. "This looks beautiful, Kell, thank you." And then he put the knife down. "I want to say something."

Evvie felt a flush in her face that wasn't the wine. She thought of her wedding, where her father had stood up and told a story she wished he'd kept to himself. It was about a time when she was twelve years old and they were going to the zoo, and he'd loaned her a pair of her mother's sunglasses that he somehow still had. Sometime during the day, she'd thought she lost them, and she had what she still considered her only real anxiety attack, huddled on a bench, unable to breathe, sure she was dying. To her father, this was a story of what a loving, sensitive girl she was, to be so distraught over a lost thing—especially when the glasses later turned out to have simply slipped into a side pocket of her bag. But to her, it was a story about the hole that her mother had left, and how anything, including panic, tended to rush in to fill it.

And then her father had given his toast. He hadn't said Tim was lucky to marry her, or even that she was lucky to marry him. Her father had said instead, very specifically, that she was lucky that Tim was marrying her. "My family is so lucky, and my Eveleth is so lucky, that Tim wants to be her husband." She knew he meant it to be general, generous gratitude. Frank was raised by a mother who worked to defeat the ERA and a father who spoke ill of "women's lib" at another memorable Thanksgiving dinner in 1997. He'd always wanted to make sure someone would take care of her, and as far as he was concerned, she'd gotten lucky.

She shook her head a little. "Pop, the girls are hungry. We should eat."

"Eveleth, it'll just be a minute," he said. "I want to say I'm glad we're all here. I'm glad we've got old friends and new friends together, and of course we have our Rose and Lilly. Seeing them grow up every year is a wonderful thing."

"Amen," Evvie said, gamely picking up her fork.

"Hey, not so fast there, don't rush the blessing," Frank said. "We're so glad Stuart and Angie could join us; we're grateful we're getting to know them and know Dean. And we're also happy to have my daughter here after the year she's had. She's got a lot of heart, as you all know."

"Pop," Evvie said.

Frank went on. "I think a lot of dads hope their girls marry doctors, even if not all of them would admit it. I didn't want Eveleth to spend her life taking care of some man bringin' a lobster boat back in every night, you can believe that. And she married a good man who saved my own life once. Eveleth could never do anything that would make me more proud of her than getting through this year on her own."

Evvie felt *seized* by something. That's how she would try to explain it later, and it was how it felt. She felt an ache melt through her body, felt it crawl down her arms and legs, felt pressure in her head like it might explode. And she put her fork down and looked at her father and said, *"Really?"*

He stopped. Everything stopped. Maybe even the earth.

It was Andy who spoke. "Ev" was all he said.

It wasn't enough, because nothing was enough. "I have been lying on my couch for thirteen, going on fourteen months. I have barely gone out. I have fed myself and made ends meet. I hope that's not the proudest of me you could be. I hope surviving not being married to a doctor anymore is not the greatest thing you can imagine for me. I went to school. I'm going to live another fifty years probably. I hope this isn't the highlight."

"That's not what your father meant, honey," offered Kell in her most soothing voice, sounding like the mother that Evvie would have given anything, *anything* to have right now. The way her body almost curled into itself wishing not for *her* mother in that moment, but for *some* mother, some *other* mother, like Andy and Dean had, was a thought so disloyal to her father that it might have been worse than anything she said out loud.

"Of course it's not what I meant, sweetheart, don't be silly," Frank said. "I understand—"

"Stop," she said. "You don't understand."

"We're talking about what we're thankful for," Frank offered. "And I'm thankful you're strong."

Evvie felt eyes on her, two nervous girls wondering why the temperature in the room had changed, near-strangers unsure what to say. She looked at Dean, who was sitting next to her looking down at his hands folded on the table. She looked at her father, who seemed baffled, unsure whether he was supposed to carve the turkey, unsure what was going to happen next. She didn't know either. It was like she'd smashed a glass in her own hand and had nowhere to put the pieces. She took a deep breath and the pressure in her head eased. "I'm sorry. I'm sorry. I don't know what's wrong with me."

"I understand," her relieved father told her as he picked up the carving knife. "I know you didn't mean it. Let's eat."

Twelve

THE TRIP FROM Thomaston to Calcasset took about half an hour. They'd taken Dean's truck, and on the way back, she closed her eyes and dropped her head back. "My dad talks about his feelings about once every five years," she said. "But when he does, you get your money's worth."

"That was something," Dean said.

"I can't believe I yelled at him," she said. Dean waited. There it was again, that semicolon. "I shouldn't have done that."

"You're going to have to tell him sometime."

"What do you mean?"

"Well, I mean. You're going to keep being pissed off as long as you're lying about everything. It's not fair to him. Or to you either."

She picked up her head and looked over at him in the dark. "What are you talking about? How am I lying?"

"Evvie, you can't expect your dad to know you didn't have a great marriage when you keep acting like you had a great marriage."

"Everybody's parents think they have a great marriage."

"Try again."

"'Try again'?"

"Everybody's parents do not think they have a great marriage, are you kidding? My dad took five years to get used to one of my brothers' wives. He bet me they'd get divorced. On their wedding day. Try again."

"I don't know what you're getting at." Eveleth rubbed her eyes. "I don't think anybody tells their parents everything about their relationships. My dad gets a version of my life that makes sense to him."

"So it's because he's your dad."

"Yeah."

"Then why doesn't Andy know anything? He's supposed to be your best friend."

"What does 'supposed to be' mean?"

"He doesn't know shit. He thinks you've been miserable for a year because you miss your husband. He's not your dad. He's not some townie your husband took a fishhook out of who won't hear that the doctor wasn't perfect. You say he's your best friend, he says he's your best friend, half the people you know think you're sleeping together, and he doesn't know shit. You have to start telling somebody the truth."

"This is against our deal," she finally said. "We're talking about my husband."

"Let's call it off," he said.

"Call what off?"

"The deal."

"The whole deal?" she asked.

"Whole deal. Let's call it off. We'll be friends instead."

Her first thought, she realized with some alarm, was to let all her bones go soft and collapse on his shoulder. But her second, better thought was not to. "We can't call off the deal. We shook."

"I just did."

"Okay, fine." She sat up. "Why can't you pitch?"

He flinched. She saw it, even in the dark. "Don't know. Tried a lot of things to figure it out, but I couldn't. That's that, and it's done. No point in crying about it. It sucked, but I'm over it."

You knock yourself over smashing pinecones in the dark, she thought. *Who are you kidding?*

Evvie said, "Mm," quietly but conspicuously, skeptically but compassionately. She always tried to do a lot of work with her noises.

"What did your dad mean about Tim saving his life?"

Evvie sighed. "Back when Tim was a medical student, we were all having dinner. My dad was complaining about this tight feeling in his back, and how he thought that he'd pulled something on the boat. Tim made him go to the emergency room, where it turned out he'd had a mild heart attack. He's fine now; this was probably ten years ago. But Tim got it right. If it had been up to me, I'd probably have walked on his back and told him to go to bed early."

"Wow."

"Yeah. Tim held it over me, if you can believe that. We were fighting one time, years later, and he said, 'You're so ungrateful, Eveleth. I might have kept you from losing the one parent you still have.' He said that to me. Right out loud, to my face."

"I believe you."

"I know." She paused, tapping the door with her fingers. She thought he might say something, but he didn't. "Another time, he was mad at me when I was a half-hour late to a dinner that was at seven, because he'd told me to meet him at seven thirty. I tell him, 'You said seven thirty.' He says, 'Evvie, I told you seven. You were reading.' It was like that with everything. He breaks his own phone throwing it down while he's watching hockey? Must be defective, because he put it down totally normally, even though I watched him *hurl* it at the floor. He even did it with stupid things. Just stupid, stupid things. If he left the door unlocked, it was because I told him I'd locked it. If I didn't get a phone message back when there were phone messages, it wasn't because he forgot to give it to me, it was because I didn't pay attention."

She figured Dean was sneaking a look over at her from the driver's seat, and she stared hard out the window. When they were near home, they drove by Dacey Park, where the Claws played, where the

Calcasset Braves had played before that, and she pointed it out to him. "What happens to it in the winter?" he asked.

"Nothing," she said. "It sits empty. The team hibernates, the park hibernates. We all do, I guess." She stared out at the white lawns and the mostly bare trees. "Have you ever played baseball in the snow?"

"Not a lot," he said. "You try not to. Pitching especially, when it's cold, your fingers don't work very well. But sometimes, in fall games, it happens."

He pulled into the driveway, and she reluctantly slid out of the passenger seat into what was now officially the cold of late November. They left their shoes by the door to let the last bits of snow melt onto the mat and she flopped down onto the couch. "You want to hang out? Should we see whether there's something on TV?" she asked.

"No, I'm going to sit here for a minute and see if I can digest the second piece of pie I definitely shouldn't have had." He sat next to her and they both leaned back, stuffed with dinner and reluctant to move. Finally, he turned his head. "Hey, can I ask you something?"

"Yeah." She turned her face toward his.

"You told your dad you're making ends meet."

"Yeah. You pay me, I pay my bills."

"Not to be morbid, but . . . you were married to a doctor. Why didn't he have life insurance?"

"He had life insurance."

"Andy said he didn't."

"Ah. Well, yeah. I told Andy he didn't." Dean looked at her. "Yes. I lied."

"Why would you lie about life insurance?"

"So he wouldn't ask me about it."

"Did you . . . get the money?" He raised one eyebrow.

She blinked twice and thought for a minute, then she took a breath. "If I tell you, you can't tell anyone. Not even Andy."

"Okay."

She looked back up at the ceiling. "I have it, but it's not mine."

"You gave it away?"

Evvie closed her eyes. "I'm going to. Everything got done, every-thing got cleared, they sent me a check. I went to a lawyer, I put it far away from my own money. It's . . . sitting."

"You don't want it?" he asked.

She turned back to him and chose this moment to notice how long his eyelashes were. Not the point. "Well, Dean, it's money. I have bills. Of course I want it."

"But you're not using it."

She turned away again so she was looking at the ceiling. "Nope."

"You want to tell me why?"

She breathed evenly, still gazing upward. "Not really. Not right now."

He looked up there, too. "Little weird," he finally said.

She laughed. "So are you."

They lit up the gas fireplace and sat there resting their hands on their full bellies and doubling back to the evening's better pieces of local gossip until he finally admitted he was beat and he was going to get some sleep. She sat up, and he hauled himself off the couch with considerable and noisy effort, then stood stretching out his back and shoulders and rubbing the back of his neck. "All right, I'll see you tomorrow."

"Night," she said, like always. But then, not like always, he sud-denly bent down toward her and she turned her face toward him with absolutely no time to react, and he kissed her on the forehead, just right of center.

"Happy Thanksgiving," he said and went off into his apartment and shut the door for the night.

"Happy . . . Thanksgiving," she weakly called after him. Her fingers went up to her forehead.

WINTER

Thirteen

THE ESSAY WAS called "Toward a Philosophy of Failure." It ran in *Esquire* in December, and it set out to define how Americans process, write about, feel about, and define failure. It used four case studies, and one of them was former New York superstar pitcher Dean Tenney, who was the example of a type the writer was unseemly proud of having named: "The WTFailure."

He said that it was one thing to process a failure in which a good idea didn't pan out or a series of unexpected obstacles placed success out of reach. But it was another to see failure, as he put it, "float free of all common sense." He wrote:

> Tenney will be remembered like New Coke. He will be like Edsel, but in human form. He began as a prospect. A physical marvel. A specimen standing for all that we can do. But none of that will matter now. Now it would be better if he'd never succeeded at all. Because now, all that will be remembered is balls sailing past catchers, runners baffled by their good fortune barreling toward home, and teammates straining not to speak ill. If you're watching, there is nothing

to explain any of it or to tell you it couldn't happen to you—not unless you listen to the murmurs of players who believe this is a matter of mental weakness and broken minds unable to repair themselves. Those murmurs are real. And they are real about Tenney specifically.

Tenney is not a pitcher anymore. He is now a bogeyman fantasy. He is a living, breathing worst-case scenario for anyone who has achieved any level of success. This is the story in which all your hard work turns out to mean nothing. This is the story in which your life, for no apparent reason, becomes the draft of a book that's no longer being written, abandoned at a table without even a final word.

In the evening on the Monday in December when these words were published, Andy's car pulled up in Evvie's driveway. Evvie opened the door to two girls bundled up in pink and purple coats, and their father, who shot her a wary look the minute he saw her face. "Those assholes," he mouthed. She nodded.

"Come in, come in," she said to Rose and Lilly, taking their coats. "You guys go upstairs and get in the big bed, and I'll be up in a few minutes."

"Little Mermaid!" Lilly shrieked.

"We'll talk about it. Be nice to your sister, Lill. Slumber party manners, remember?"

"Little Mermaid!" Lilly shrieked again as she and Rose ran up the rest of the stairs.

Andy cringed. "Sounds like you're going to have a lot on your hands. Thanks for doing this. Has he said anything to you?" Andy asked.

"No," Evvie said. "He went into the apartment, shut the door, didn't say a word."

"Okay. I'm just going to take him for a drink, see if he feels like talking." He and Evvie walked into the kitchen, and Andy yelled Dean's name toward the apartment. "Hey, you ready to go?"

"Give me a few minutes." Dean sounded tired.

Andy and Evvie sat at the kitchen table. She raised one eyebrow. "So, how is the new woman friend?"

Evvie knew Andy had taken Monica Bell, a teacher at the high school, out a couple of times since he met her at a party, but he hadn't said much more than that. Now he grinned. "She's fun. We went to the movies, to that thing with the French guy who was in the other one, the one with Jessica Chastain that you didn't like."

"Right, yes. It was Bryce Dallas Howard and the guy is Canadian, but yes."

"Whatever. Anyway, we saw that, and we had dinner at the Fontaine. It was nice. I like her. You'll like her."

"That's good." Evvie could see them in her head, sitting at one of the tables in the corner of the restaurant, walking into the movie theater, sitting together. It felt so intrusive to imagine it down to the dinner forks and where they'd sit in the theater, but she didn't know how not to. "It sounds nice."

"You know . . . you could do that someday." Andy cocked his head at her. "If you decided you wanted to, you could."

"What, take out Monica Bell?" She knew. She knew it was unfairly glib, *and* it was a stalling tactic, *and* it was snotty, *and* it sounded like she was making fun of his new friend. He rolled his eyes, and she held up one hand. "Sorry. I know what you meant. I'm not even thinking about that. At all."

"And you don't have to. I'm not saying that. There's nothing worse than the guy who starts dating somebody and all of a sudden, everybody else has to do it. I promise you, I am not that guy."

She shook her head. "I didn't think you were."

"I'm being your friend."

"I know you are."

"I'm saying you *could*."

"I know I could." She was almost sure she couldn't. She knew he meant it in two ways—that dating was possible and that dating was something no one would judge her for, because enough time had passed. She was quite sure he was wrong about both. In the immortal language of the baseball sex metaphor, she couldn't even imagine getting into uniform, let alone making it to first base. "I'll think about it. It still feels wrong."

"Why?"

"You know. The . . . widow thing. The other day, I was working on this interview—it was that guy Jason I sometimes work for? He interviewed a professor about women immediately after World War II, and they talked about this soldier's *widow*, and I realized that the whole time since Tim died, I've never called myself a widow. Or his widow. I don't walk around introducing myself, 'I'm Eveleth Drake, Dr. Timothy Drake's widow.' I'm the Widow Drake."

"I'm not sure people really do that outside of the BBC."

"I started thinking about it as a word, you know? 'Widow.' It's strange that there has to be a word for 'a lady who was married to someone who died.' But it's real. It's me. I am a widow right now, right this minute. And honestly, I'm a widow all the time. I'm a widow everywhere I go, which explains why I feel like one, *constantly*. I looked it up in the dictionary, though, and if I get married again, I'm not a widow anymore. Even though I still married him and he's still gone."

He frowned. "That's weird."

"Isn't it? It's like the comatose princess who can only wake up if somebody kisses her."

"Well, she's sleeping," Andy clarified.

"Who's sleeping?"

"The princess. Whose name is Sleeping Beauty, not Comatose Princess. I've read fairy tales more recently than you have, so you can trust me, she's just sleeping. But I see your point."

"It's weird," Eveleth told him, "having this thing about me that's because I was married before, and I can't ever get rid of it unless I get married again. Do you realize I can't *ever* just be single? I can only be married or be a widow, *ever*."

Andy thought for a minute, then held up one finger. "What would you be if you got remarried and then you got divorced?"

"Huh," she said. "I think then I'd be divorced."

"What if you got remarried and then it got annulled?"

"Then I think I'd go back to being a widow." She stared down at the table. "I'm horrible. I have to get myself a project or something. When it's cold and I'm not working, I sit around and it's like I can feel all my bones."

"What does that mean? Feel all your bones?"

"I feel my bones. I mean, I get very aware of the fact that I'm lucky I have them, because if I didn't, I would basically be a suitcase worth of muscles and skin and fat and a bag of organs like you get with a turkey."

"Wow, gross."

"Sorry," she said, a little more quietly. "I guess I'm afraid I seem like a sad story, too."

"Well, you don't. I mean, I wouldn't go around telling people the thing about the bag of turkey. But everybody just wants you to be happy. Go get your project, and then they can talk to you about whatever you're doing, and they can stop asking me what to say to you, and I can retire from my job as the Eveleth Whisperer."

"I'm sorry."

"For what?"

"That you have to be the whisperer."

"Can I suggest for your project that you take a class in not apologizing all the time?"

"Sorry."

"Oh, Jesus." He hollered, "Dean, get out here, would you?"

Dean's door opened, and he walked through the kitchen, stuffing his hands into his pockets. "See you, Ev."

Andy shot her a look. "Okay, then. I don't know how late it'll be. Their PJs are in the bag by the door. Thank you again. Text me if Lilly rips your eardrum in half."

"Will do." From the window in her living room, Evvie watched Andy's taillights until she couldn't see them anymore.

By the time *The Little Mermaid* was over, Evvie's room had gone quiet. Lilly had conked out halfway through and was now a tangle of limbs extending across half the bed, while Rose curled against Evvie's side on the other half. When the credits rolled and Evvie shut off the DVD player, she leaned over to peek at Lilly, whose open mouth was smashed against her pillow. Evvie leaned over and whispered to Rose, "Your sister is even more asleep than usual." Rose pushed herself up to peer across Evvie's body, then lay back down. "She's pretty funny," Evvie said softly.

Rose rolled her eyes and returned Evvie's hushed tone. "She's loud."

"She is loud. I think she wore herself out singing along." Evvie smoothed Rose's hair. "Are you getting excited for Christmas?"

Rose shrugged. "I guess."

"You guess? You don't want any presents?"

Rose's one-sided smile was one of the things she'd gotten from Lori. "No, I want presents."

Evvie slid down and pulled the blankets up tighter over them both. "What's the matter, my girl?"

Rose sighed, and it made Evvie think that seven was too young to have a sigh like that in her vocabulary. A sarcastic sigh, yes. An angry-and-frustrated sigh, yes. But not one that sounded like a fifty-year-old diner waitress. "I'm going to my mom's for Christmas, and she says I have to get Fred a present." Fred was Lori's boyfriend, a Charleston furniture designer she had met a few years ago, not long after she and Andy separated.

"And you don't want to?"

"I'm only supposed to have to find presents for my family," Rose said.

Evvie nodded. "Ah." It could only be the first or second year the kid would have picked out her own gifts for anyone, but Rose's quiet picking at her fingernails certainly spoke of a trespass against some expectation. "Well, lots of people buy presents for friends, too, you know."

"Do you and my dad get each other presents?"

"No," Evvie said. "But that's because we're lazy and we hate shopping." Rose smiled. "Your dad would buy me some potato chips from the vending machine and I'd buy him a hot dog at the gas station."

Rose laughed into her pajama sleeve, then she started rolling and unrolling the edge of the blanket. "Fred is so boring. He's nice, but all he talks about is chairs."

"Does he like anything else? Sports? Music? Books?"

Rose turned to look at Evvie and paused, making her eyes as big as she possibly could, before saying, "He *lit'rally* only talks about chairs."

Evvie squinted hard at Rose. "How about . . . golf? Does he play golf?"

Rose shook her head. "He doesn't do anything." She waited a perfect beat. "Just chairs."

"I'll tell you what," Evvie said. "Get him a tie."

"You think he wants a tie?"

"No, probably not. But ties and perfume and candy dishes and stuff have been perfectly okay for hundreds of years when people don't know what to buy. A tie is a nice, safe present."

"I don't know if it's good enough," Rose said.

Evvie grabbed Rose's hand, admiring her long fingers. "You know what? You don't have anything to worry about. Your mom and dad love you, and I'm sure Fred loves you, too. And when Fred sees that you got him something, he's going to be happy, because it's a nice thing to do, and because it's from you."

"Evvie?"

"Yeah?"

Rose squirmed a little, then said, "I don't always want to go to my mom's. I have to pack up all my stuff, and I have to share a room with Lilly. And I just don't always want to go."

"I know. And that's okay."

"I have to go anyway." Rose said it flatly, as much to herself as to Evvie.

"Yeah. Right now, pretty much, you do." Evvie squeezed her hand. "I know you'll be happy to see her."

Rose nodded. "Do you have to see your mom, too?"

"Pretty much," Evvie said. "Not at Christmas, but sometimes. When she's around."

"You probably miss her."

"Sometimes." Evvie smoothed the back of Rose's hand with her fingers.

"I'm not going to be here for Christmas with my dad."

"Maybe not the actual day," Evvie said. "When you get back, though, you can have Christmas with him. And we'll make those snowflake cookies again, and I need you to help me. We'll keep it going. Christmas is not one day. It's a whole thing. There are elves, and there are reindeer, and there's 'Jingle Bells.'"

"*The Batmobile lost a wheel and the Joker got away,*" Rose sang, and then she grinned at herself.

Evvie reached across Rose for a bottle of hand lotion on the nightstand. "You want a little?" Rose nodded, and Evvie put some in her own palm, then rubbed her hands and Rose's together. "It'll still be Christmas when you get back. I double promise."

"I'll get Fred a tie," Rose finally said. "And then I only need something for Lilly and Dad and Mom, and my grandmas and grandpas." She looked up at Evvie. "And you."

"Aw, you're the best," Evvie said, putting her arm back around Rose's shoulders. "Nobody's better than you."

Fourteen

AFTER ROSE WAS asleep, Evvie managed to crawl out of her bed and go downstairs to do the dishes. She had figured that she and Dean would talk about the article once he was home. But when he and Andy got back, they carried the girls to Andy's car, Dean slipped into the apartment and shut the door, and that was it. There was not a kiss on the forehead; there had not been since Thanksgiving. She wondered sometimes if she'd imagined the whole thing.

She was still awake at two in the morning, too sweaty with the extra blanket on the bed and too cold without it. It was winter for real now, close to freezing, and as she lay in bed debating whether to get up and tweak the heat, she heard Dean's truck start. Then she heard him turn it around in the gravel driveway, she heard the careful way he navigated around her car, and she heard him leave.

There were a lot of possibilities. It could be a drive to clear his head. Could be he had to go rescue a friend with a flat tire in the middle of the night. Could be nothing. But she turned onto her side and felt a little hitch in her back, and when she put her hand to it, it was like pressing the play button on a video of all the times she'd seen

Dean rubbing and stretching out his right shoulder. He did it in her kitchen, and when they were walking in town, and when they were having dinner, and he did it when they sat and watched television together. Lots of possibilities for this, too. It could be a nervous habit. It could be an old injury or the cost of twenty-five years of throwing as hard as he could for eight months out of the year. It, too, could be nothing. But in her mind, she saw him throwing a ball until his shoulder ached, and she heard the wind outside. It made her think of when he asked about Dacey Park in winter.

She threw the blankets back and got up, switching on the light on the nightstand. When it was cold, she slept in a soft flannel shirt and checked boxers, so she left the shirt on and slipped into jeans and boots. Downstairs, she pulled on her wool coat and snatched the car keys from the hook by the door.

The Daceys had once owned the newspaper and a charming hotel in town when both businesses were in much better financial condition. There was one Dacey left in town now, and he worked at the bank. But the park that had been built for the Calcasset Braves still carried the family name. Evvie pulled into the parking lot, and at first, she thought she might be wrong. The field lights weren't on; it looked dark, just as it should. But then she saw his truck, tucked up against one of the outbuildings. Evvie was relieved to know where he was, and worried that he was here, and a little impressed with herself for figuring it out.

She got out of her car and walked toward the field, and as she approached the entry gate, she heard the first metal clang that she knew was the ball hitting the fence behind the catcher who, of course, wasn't there. She took a few more steps, and there was another clang, and then she heard him say, almost matter-of-factly, "Fuck."

She stuffed her hands into the pockets of her coat and passed through the gate that stood open, where someone would normally take a ticket. She got closer to the field, and another ball hit the fence, and then she was there, along the first-base line, and she saw what he'd done. He had several big, boxy flashlights, practically floodlights, that he'd set in a line between the pitcher's mound and the plate.

He was looking the other way. She watched as he reached into a bucket for a ball. His leg kicked, and his body rotated, and the ball flew in the dark, and then *clang*. She took a gulp of cold air and watched as it transformed into a white puff of her breath when she said, "Hey."

He flinched, then he turned around to face her. He was breathing hard. "What are you doing here?" His voice sharpened when he asked, "What, did you follow me?"

"I heard your truck," she said. "Then I . . . guessed." She walked down to the break in the fence and made her way out onto the field, onto the winter-nipped grass where she'd only stepped twice: once when her school band performed before a game, and once when her Girl Scout troop was part of the presentation of the national anthem. She stood close to him.

"You guessed that I was at the closed minor-league baseball park at two thirty in the morning."

"I figured you wanted to see for yourself where they ran the cereal-box races." She pointed toward home. "Bree fell right about . . . there." He smiled, but only a little. She looked around, as if there was something to see in the dark. "I didn't know they didn't even lock this place in December."

"They do. But if you ask around and you promise not to break anything, you can find the guy with the key."

Evvie nodded slowly. "I thought you were done with all this. I thought you were moving on and everything."

He shook his head. "I don't want to talk about it. If I did, I'd have told you myself."

"You said 'friends.' You said you wanted to throw out our deal. You asked me about Tim, and the money, and my dad. I'm asking why you got out of bed in the middle of the night to throw baseballs at a fence and swear."

"Jesus," he breathed. "Friends? That's what you think this is? This is private, Evvie. I haven't been able to do anything without people breathing down my neck for a year and a half. Do I look like I want to talk about this right now?"

"Did I look like I wanted to talk about my dad?"

"I came all the way up here so people *wouldn't* stalk me. If I wanted to talk about pitching, I could have stayed in Manhattan. I came here so I could *not* explain myself, so don't ask me to, okay? I am fine. I truly don't want to talk about this."

She didn't even know that she'd expected him to be happy to see her until he wasn't. Now, realizing that she *had* followed him and it *was* the middle of the night, the awkwardness of it crept down her spine. It felt like a kind of involuntary cloning, where a copy of herself stepped away and stared. It saw this man trying to enjoy some solitude in the middle of the night and this crazy lady who showed up in her pajamas without being invited. She could think of nothing to say except "Okay, bye," which she suspected would result in death by human combustion, attributable to humiliation. She felt frozen in place, unable to imagine even a graceful retreat. But then she noticed he was in only a long-sleeved shirt. "Hey, shouldn't you have a coat or something? Isn't this bad for your arm?"

"Yeah." He paced back and forth in front of the pitcher's mound. And then he repeated it: "Yeah, it probably is."

She went over and put her hand on his elbow. "How can I help?"

He looked down at her hand, then met her eyes. "You help."

"I want to help more."

He chuckled and gave that shoulder another rub. "Yeah. I know you do. Honestly, I can't feel the ball anyway." He took off his glove and stuffed it under his arm, and he bent and flexed all his fingers. "It's like I said about pitching in the cold."

She took her hands out of her pockets and put them on his. "Yeah, wow, your hands are freezing."

He looked down and moved just his thumbs, pressing on her hands just barely, just enough for her to be sure he was doing anything at all. And then he nodded. "Okay. Let's go home." They gathered up the flashlights and the baseballs, and she got into her car and he got into his truck, and he followed her right back to the house, where they said good night.

As she got back into bed, Evvie kept thinking about that phantom catcher and kept hearing the ball clang against the fence. Pitching was something he'd been doing since he was a kid. There was only so much to it; he had the same body he'd always had. The same ligaments and muscles and joints. He had the same mind; he hadn't forgotten anything he'd once known. Something had broken, and what was broken could be fixed. That was logic.

Fifteen

A FEW DAYS AFTER she tracked Dean down at Dacey Park, Evvie found a therapist in Rockland named Dr. Jane Talco, whose online profile said she treated anxiety, and who looked trustworthy in her picture. To fix a head case, she figured, you'd start with a head fixer.

When Evvie got there, the doctor was standing at her desk with her back to the door, and she turned with a legal pad in her hand. She was dressed casually, with a pair of glasses pushed up on top of her head. "Hi, there."

"Hi, I'm Eveleth Drake, I have a two thirty appointment."

"Absolutely, come in. Sorry, I was just pushing paperwork all over my desk." She turned and extended her hand to shake Evvie's. "I'm Jane Talco. Have a seat."

Evvie sank into the couch, which was a little deeper than she expected. She smiled awkwardly, examining the placid artwork and the ominous box of tissues positioned on the end table beside where she was sitting.

"So what brings you into the office today?" The sound in the room seemed deadened, like they were in a blanket fort.

She wasn't sure how this was supposed to start. Just jump in, she supposed. "Well, I need some help. I know people always say they're asking for a friend, but I *am* asking for a friend."

The doctor cocked her head. "Asking for a friend. Okay. Tell me a little more."

"Well, I have this friend who used to be a professional athlete. Have you ever heard of the yips?"

"Steve Sax, right?"

"Right, right. My friend got the yips. And he retired. He says that he's fine, but I don't think he is. I'm trying to be a good friend. I know there's a lot of research, and I wanted some expert advice in case it's something like anxiety and I might be able to help."

"Oh, interesting. Can I get some background from you so I know where you're coming from, and then we'll talk about this more?" Dr. Talco said. Evvie wasn't wild about this part, but she figured the fact that she wasn't being kicked out of the office suggested it might be worth staying, so she nodded.

"Are you married?"

"No."

"Are you in a relationship?"

"No."

"Any kids?"

"No." Good lord. This was like talking to Nana when she was still alive, only with fewer ceramic ducks on the shelves.

"Have you ever been married?"

Evvie shifted on the couch. "I was married until a little over a year ago. My husband passed away."

"Oh, I'm so sorry," Dr. Talco said, scribbling on her paper. "How are you doing?"

"As well as can be expected, I guess."

"How long were you together?"

"Since I was fifteen."

Dr. Talco nodded slowly. "That's a long history."

"It is." Evvie cleared her throat.

"So in this last year or so, have you been physically healthy? How do you do with things like sleep? Do you sleep well?"

She thought about her bottle of ZzzQuil and the dreams about Tim pacing and yelling, which showed up every couple of weeks, even now. Sometimes he was in his white coat. Once, Dean had been there. She thought about lying on her bedroom floor in the dark, and about how much she missed lying on the carpet in the apartment. "Yes," she said, "I sleep fine."

"How are your energy levels? Do you feel like they're normal for you?"

"Yeah," she said. She sat up a little straighter.

"Have you had any kind of counseling or anything like that?"

"No. I've had a lot of help from friends and family. That's been all I've really needed." She started to roll the edge of her sweater in her fingers. "I don't really want to spend all my time thinking about my husband and my marriage and everything. It's just complicated. So I'm trying to get out of my head a little. That's why I'd like to help my friend feel better."

"What do you mean when you say your marriage was complicated? Can you talk about that a little?"

Evvie squinted at the doctor's diploma on the wall. "No, not really. It was regular marriage stuff."

"Regular marriage stuff, got it," the doctor said. "How long have you known him? Your friend with the yips?"

"He's my tenant, actually. He rents part of my house. He moved in a couple of months ago."

"Got it." Dr. Talco looked at her notes. "So, let me say this." She fiddled with the end of her pen. "Sometimes, there are people who come into my office, and they say, 'I'm in a crisis, I need therapy.' But it turns out they want a friend more than anything. And I explain to them that therapy is different from friendship. For one thing, friends are free. You know, ideally. So I'm not a friend."

"Okay. Are you saying you think I want to be your friend? Because I don't think that's what I'm asking. I mean . . . no offense."

Dr. Talco smiled. "Nope. What I'm saying is that therapists aren't friends, and friends aren't therapists. And that means you can't be a therapist for your pitcher." Dr. Talco paused to see if Eveleth would get it and seemed to conclude she wouldn't. "If he has problems and he needs support, then you can be his friend, which it sounds like you're doing. But if he needs a doctor, he's going to have to get one for himself. You aren't going to be able to give him that kind of help, as his friend, if that's the case, no matter how much I tell you about anxiety."

"I don't think that's what I was trying to do."

"It's not a bad thing. Believe me, you're not the first person who's had this same idea. People come in and want me to fix a boyfriend or a girlfriend, or a parent, or a kid. And I give them the same bottom line I'm giving you."

"Which is what?"

"That therapy is like a toothbrush. You can't really put it to use for anybody except yourself."

"So wait," Evvie said. "You're rejecting my application for therapy?"

She could tell Dr. Jane Talco came very, very close to laughing. But she didn't. "I am not rejecting your application. In fact, I think there's probably a lot we can do, and it might help you more than you think. But I'd want to talk about you. Losing your husband, especially at your age, is something that I think most people need a lot of help to handle. Complicated marriage or not. It's not a bad thing."

The bad thing, of course, was not the fact that she might well benefit from having her head shrunk so hard that it turned inside out. But what had curled Evvie into a ball on her bed, what had kept her sobbing into the shoulders of Andy's shirts for almost two weeks after he brought her home from the hospital, was more like a bone-deep exhaustion than the grief the doctor seemed to want to unearth. And the last thing—the *very* last thing—she wanted was to talk about it.

She stood up. "Thank you for the advice. I promise I'll keep your card."

The doctor stood up, too, and extended a hand like she was going to put it on Evvie's arm, but she didn't. "Hey. Can you hang around? At least finish up the appointment? I want to help if I can."

"I don't think so, but thank you for listening." Evvie picked up her bag, put on her coat, and let the door of the office latch behind her. When she got into her car, she immediately took out her phone. This was a moment to text *someone* and tell them about the doctor who wouldn't listen, who turned a professional inquiry into some Barbara Walters interview intended to make Evvie cry, as if she needed another person who was obsessed with asking her about widowhood. She sat with her phone in her hand, and she listened to the beginning of a slightly crispy, sleeting rain fall on the windshield. After a few minutes, she put her phone back into her bag and started the car.

Sixteen

ABOUT A WEEK before Christmas, tucked inside, away from an icy wind that now and then made the window frame rattle, Dean and Evvie were stretched out in his club chairs drinking straight bourbon. They were a couple of glasses in. He was slumped down, with his long legs on the coffee table, and she was sitting sideways, her knees bent over the fat arm of the chair, feeling decidedly fuzzy-headed. "Why do they have Christmas every single year?" she asked.

"Oh, boy," he said with a smile. "Where's this going?"

"I think it's a very fair question," she said, tipping the rest of her drink into her mouth and making the little *kuh!* noise she always did when she swallowed liquor. "Nobody has enough time for it. Nobody wants to go through the whole . . ." She waved the hand without a glass in it. "I don't think they need to have it every year."

"How often do you think?"

"Every four years, like the Olympics."

"The Olympics are every two years now."

"Okay, every four years like the Winter Olympics, you *lawyer*."

"So that's your Christmas plan. If you're a four-year-old kid, no more Christmases until third grade."

"It'll be good for them. Some children are horrible. These are the simple truths of Eveleth World."

He nodded slowly. "Seventy-five percent cut to Christmas, zero percent mercy for horrible children."

"Yes," she said. "Zero percent."

"Where does the name 'Eveleth' come from?" he asked, wrinkling his forehead. "Is it a family name? Is it the Viking goddess of lobsters or something?"

She shook her head. "Eveleth is in Minnesota. Way up north, cold as fu-huh-huck. It's maybe forty miles from Canada. It's where my mom was born. Her dad worked in an iron mine."

"They have iron mining in Minnesota?"

"They used to."

"They don't now?"

"Not like they used to."

"How in the hell did she wind up married to a lobsterman from Maine?" Dean asked. He finished his drink, took her glass from her, and poured them both a little more.

"She went to college in Boston, and one summer, she came up here to be a counselor at an arts camp that's not around anymore. He was working as a sternman for a buddy of his, and they met at a bar. It was some kind of . . . infatuation, I guess, and she moved up here and they had me. I'm sure it seemed very romantic to her. Very adventurous. But she missed home, so she called me Eveleth. I am named after my mother's unhappiness." She raised her glass toward him, then took a sip. Normally, she'd hear what she was going to say in her head before it came out of her mouth. Right now, it was the other way around.

Dean looked hard at her, like he might pull on this thread, but he didn't. "My oldest brother, Tom, is an engineer. Mark works for a tech startup that does something with touch screens or some shit. Brian is an accountant. And I, my parents' youngest boy, now have a wrestling move informally named after me. Do you want to know what it is?"

"Probably not."

"Guess what it is."

She scrunched up her face. "I don't want to guess what it is."

"It's choking."

She nodded. "Yeah, I was afraid that was what it was."

Just then, the wind kicked up and the window rattled again. "It's serious out there," he said.

"It's *terrible* out there." She drank, and she sighed. "I want to be in Fiji or something."

"You have a lot of wishes for a lady who wants to give away all her money." He arched an eyebrow. "You could go to Fiji."

"I told you, I don't want the money."

He held up one hand. "No, you told me you *do* want it, but you won't take it. Which I think is crazy. Although you may have read in a few places that I'm also crazy, so take that for whatever it's worth."

"You know what's crazy?" she said. "I can't take it, but I can't give it back. That's why I lied. I can't figure out where to put it. How's that for crazy? I mean, what should have happened is it should have gone to his parents. This whole thing is such a freak show that giving his already rich parents a giant wad of money would be the *right* thing to do. But I can't give it to them."

"Why not?"

Her smile was thin. "How would I explain it? It's his life insurance. I was his wife. They'd want me to have it. They'd never take it unless I explained why I wouldn't keep it. I'm not going to snap them in half after everything they've been through by telling them I didn't love him anymore. I'm not going to tell them that as long as I don't take the money, it's like I left him. And that I want to believe I would have left him."

"Can you give it to your dad?"

Evvie snorted. "There is zero chance my father would take money from me, or that would obviously be the first thing I would do with it."

"I'm still not sure I know why you don't keep it. It came from an insurance company, and you need it more than those assholes. What am I missing?"

She looked down into her glass. "It's just . . . I can't. I can't. It's bad enough I lived off him when he was alive."

"It's how life insurance works, Evvie. People need money. It's for this. It's for this exactly. They're not paying for how sad you are; they're paying for the money he was making that you don't have now."

"So he dies, and I keep the money, and that's how I stay alive, and I drift in and out of all these rooms in this great big house and I get old and I'm just *nothing*—"

Dean sat up and put his glass on the table. "All right, first of all, missy—"

"'Missy'?" She was a little drunk. They were both a little drunk.

"First of all, missy, you're not nothing. You wouldn't be nothing if you put that fucking school-band shirt on and that hairball sweater and moped on your couch until you were eighty, so I don't want to hear that." He took a drink and then said to the bottom of his glass, "Jesus, who *was* this fucker?"

"I should give *you* the money," she said. "You can have it as long as you don't tell anyone I gave it to you."

"I don't need it. I made good money right up until I stopped making any money. And even though I blew a lot of it on startups making engines running on turkey shit or whatever, I have some left."

"What was it like?"

"What was what like?"

"Not being able to pitch."

He squinted at her. "What was it like being married to him?"

"I asked you first." She bobbed one dangling foot up and down.

"It was a lot like being able to pitch," he said, "but if you sucked." She just kept it up with that foot.

"Okay. If I asked you to get up and walk across the room, what would you do first?" he asked.

"I guess I'd . . . get up?"

"Right. And it would happen without you thinking about it, because you know how to get up out of a chair. I mean, what would happen, what would *really* happen, is you'd put your hand down next to you and you'd lift yourself up a little. You'd scoot back and you'd lift your legs up, and you'd turn and put your feet on the ground. Then you'd shift your weight onto them and straighten your legs, and . . . are you getting what I'm talking about?" She tipped her head a bit in response. "You'd *get out of the fucking chair*. You tell your body to get up? It gets up. It knows how. If you pitched for twenty years, same thing. You're not explaining to yourself how to pitch every time. You're trying to hit a spot that's sixty feet away an inch to the left, inch to the right. That's where your work is. And then you wake up one day and it's . . . to you, you're doing the same thing. But all of a sudden, it's like you're trying to bend a fucking spoon with your mind." He took a drink. "It was like trying to pitch with somebody else's arm. That's what it was like."

"Well, hell," she said. "That's sad."

"It wasn't great." He raised his eyebrows. "Now you go."

She drained her glass and tapped her fingers against it. "Let's see. Being married to Tim was like . . . it was like paddling a boat, but for ten years. And you're not getting anywhere, and you're ready to stop. But the farther you get, the more you think, 'Well, I'll just go another hundred yards. In case it's *right* up there. So I didn't take this whole trip for nothing.'"

He nodded. "You know, I used to wish I blew out my elbow or shattered my fucking wrist. So I could point at it and go, 'That, that's why.'"

She turned in the chair to lean over and pour herself another drink, almost feeling guilty about the fact that she could make her body do what she wanted so effortlessly. "Was it a woman?" she asked.

There was that third of a smile again. "Why do you want to know if it was a woman?"

She shrugged as she put her feet back over the arm of the chair. "I'm curious."

"Yeah, but why do you *specifically* want to know if it was a woman? What, you want to know if there's one now?"

She laughed, an incautious whiskey laugh. "Well, you're not supposed to *say* that, haven't you ever heard of subtext?"

"It was not a woman. And there is not one now. Consider that text."

She met his eyes for a second, touched her bottom lip with her thumb, then sat up abruptly. "I should go. I should sleep, I shouldn't . . ." She put the rest of her drink down on the table. "If I drink that, I'll get sloppy."

"I don't mind."

She felt the pink creep into her cheeks, and she got up and turned away from him. She teetered slightly and leaned for a second on the arm of the chair, but she didn't turn back. "Okay, thank you, this was fun," she called back as she crossed over into her kitchen. "Good night, Dean."

"Good night, Eveleth, Minnesota, way up by Canada," he called back.

Seventeen

WHEN DEAN TENNEY was in the minors and living in a rented room in Albuquerque, he and the team had their season-ending party at the home of a local honest-to-God railroad magnate named Fitz Holley. Holley's sprawling Victorian was fusty and untouchable inside, like Colonel Mustard should be bonking Miss Scarlet on the head with a candlestick over by the bar. But in his dark-wood, cigar-scented rec room, there was a restored vintage pinball machine with pinup girls painted on it. The bells rang, the flippers popped satisfyingly, and there was no way to describe the movement of the ball without resorting to noises like *sproing*. Dean loved it. He wanted it, or he wanted one just like it. It went on a list of the things he would get when everything worked out.

Everything did work out for a while, of course, and when he lived in New York, he would sometimes look at listings for pinball machines. But he found that they tended to be pop-culture kitsch—*Gilligan's Island* machines and KISS machines and Michael Jordan machines. He'd bought some high-end dartboards, but when he stopped being able to pitch, something about throwing darts had seemed so ridiculous—even though he found he could still do it, which, *what the hell*—that he gave them to buddies before he moved.

Then in February, while he was living at Evvie's, a friend who lived in Boston tipped him off that a guy he knew was unloading the prized possession of his recently deceased father: a 1956 pinball machine in good condition that could be had for a reasonable price. Really, for a relatively-not-unreasonable price. It wasn't the kind of money he'd be able to spend forever, but it was money he could still spend now. He looked at a few pictures that were in his email, and while there were no pinup girls, it was sharp, painted with race cars. *Sold*. The only catch was that Dean had to come down to Boston to pick it up, which was almost a four-hour drive.

He explained all this to Evvie over coffee on a chilly Thursday morning, and she raised her eyebrow at the pinup girls and laughed about the KISS machines, and she was polite enough not to ask how much he was paying for this pinball machine with which he presumably intended to unleash all kinds of clanks and dings and *brrrrrrrrings* in her house at whatever time of day. "So when are you going to retrieve this thing?" she asked.

"Sunday," he said. "You want to come?"

"To Boston?" she asked.

"Yeah. It's almost four hours each way in my truck, and I've been trying all the podcasts on your list, but I don't think I can listen to that many. That is a lot of close looks at the simple poetry of making manhole covers and shit. You should come keep me company. Besides, you told me you wanted to get out of the house more. This is *way* out. This is get up early, get on the road, get down there, help load a pinball machine into my truck, come back, help haul a pinball machine inside—"

She laughed. "Oh, now I'm *working* on this trip?"

"You bet," he answered. "Hey, you're up to it, you told me you're half iron miner."

"I'm one-quarter iron miner. One-quarter iron miner, one-quarter Minnesotan quilter, and one-half New England lobster people."

"I can't use the quilting, but the rest sounds hearty. You should come."

"If you need company that badly, you could ask Andy."

"You know the music he listens to."

"He's better than I am with the manual labor, though."

"Quit stalling, Minnesota. You coming or not?"

"Will you buy me a cruller at Dunkin' Donuts?"

"There's Dunkin' Donuts here."

"It's not the same. I want Boston Dunkin' Donuts."

"Yes, I'll buy you a cruller at Boston Dunkin' Donuts."

And just like that, she agreed that she'd drive down with Dean on Sunday to pick up the pinball machine he wanted. The widow and the exiled baseball player were road-tripping to fetch a heavy, expensive toy to put in an apartment he didn't intend to stay in that long. And in an isolated moment in her kitchen, it seemed like an entirely logical thing for them to do.

Sunday morning, Evvie slid two eggs over medium onto a plate for Dean and split a bagel—half for him, half for her. "I made breakfast," she called.

Dean came into her kitchen in a New York Giants jersey. She looked at him and raised her eyebrows. "What?" he asked.

"We're driving almost four hours down there and four hours back, and in the middle, we have to pick up a pinball machine. You're going to make time for a bar fight?"

"I'm not going to get in a bar fight. Be glad it's not the Yankees."

After breakfast, she dumped the dishes into the sink, grabbed her coat and keys, and met Dean outside, where he was warming up the truck. She slid in beside him and was seized briefly by the thought of hopping back out and wrapping herself in blankets for the day. She had three DVR'd episodes of *Survivor* she hadn't even watched, and she could choose not to bump along for four hours in a truck for the pleasure of helping a grown man move a half-ton tchotchke. The couch was warm, the truck was cold, Boston was far.

But Dean threw the truck into reverse. "All right, let's do this," he said, and they were crunching over her gravel driveway.

Eveleth had seen Calcasset from what she believed to be every possible angle: she'd stood at some time or another on every corner and looked at every building. But it had been forever since she'd looked at it while leaving. She'd imagined this view quite a bit, not that long ago. She'd imagined herself behind the wheel of her Honda, taking Route 1 to the south, just like they were doing now. But instead of sitting in the driver's seat, she was looking out the window and wiggling out of her coat. And instead of forever, she'd be gone only today.

"So, I have a question." Dean interrupted this line of thought, and none too soon.

"Yes." She turned to face him.

"Will there still be cereal-box races this year? I'm going to be pissed off if there are no cereal-box races."

"There should be. They're eager to restore them to their rightful position as a mundane element of a minor local attraction that's *not* mired in a scandal that involves dirty competition and illicit affairs. Maybe they'll retire the Cheerios box, though. They could hang it from the lights over right field."

"That's about the right amount of dignity," he said.

"Are you going to come to a Claws game with me?"

"Sure," he said.

"I . . . wasn't sure if you hated it or missed it or what."

"You mean baseball? Hell yeah, I miss it. Are you kidding? It's all I did for most of my life. If you think I'm overspending on this pinball machine, you should see what I spent trying to get back into baseball. I would have given them my other arm if they could make the good one work the way it was supposed to."

Evvie hooked her phone up to the truck stereo and put some music on.

The middle part of Maine, all the way from Bar Harbor to Portland, hangs down like stalactites that drip little islands into the Atlantic. It's divided by rivers and harbors with cozy names that sound like brands of bubble bath or places boats sink in folk songs: Sheepscot River, Damariscotta River, Linekin Bay. Route 1 skips down the coast, ducking into tourist towns like Wiscasset and Bath and Brunswick before it almost regretfully meets up in Portland with 95, which stomps down from Bangor and Augusta a little farther inland.

As they approached Freeport, which was a little more than an hour south of Calcasset, Dean pointed at one of the signs. "Hey, we're going past the L.L.Bean store; did you need a tent with a dog door or some boots that are rated for eighty-five degrees below zero?"

"I've been in that store," she said. "It's huge. It's full of men who want to find themselves but will settle for getting poison ivy on their balls instead. Tim was upset they didn't have a wedding registry."

Dean frowned. "What kinds of wedding presents did he want to register for at L.L.Bean?"

"Sleeping bags," she said, "and canteens and backpacks and stuff. He had just moved back up here, and he wanted us to be outdoor people, I think. It never happened. He swore at a bunch of tent poles and that was about it."

About another hour south, they passed a billboard that said, VICTORY TATTOO NEXT EXIT 4 MILES: AWARD-WINNING INK.

"Hey, did you need an award-winning tattoo?" she asked. "We could stop off."

"I have a tattoo," he said.

She turned toward him. "Do you?"

"Yes."

"What is it?"

"I got it when I signed my first contract. I was drunk, though, and even though I was out of college, it's very high school yearbook."

"Where is it? I mean, unless it's—"

He grabbed the right side of his jersey with one hand and, keeping the other hand on the wheel, he yanked it up to reveal a good part of his right side. His eyes were still on the road, so he didn't see her mouth open and then close as she took in his side, his skin, a patch of the belly that drummed against his shirt when he laughed. Something in her knees *answered* this with an appreciative pulse, and it came to her with bell-pealing clarity: *Oh, right,* she thought. *Lust.*

And right over his ribs, there were words inked in black, in simple type: THE DAY YOU QUIT, YOU START TO DIE. She opened her mouth, and what came out was—and one day much later, they'd both agree this was what it sounded like—*"Buuuuuuuh."*

He laughed and pulled his shirt back down, almost apologetically, like she was reacting to the sentiment. "I was into longevity. I didn't expect to set records or get rich. I just wanted to play a long time."

"Oh. That sucks." Surely, she thought, this could not possibly be the best she could do. But as the moment stretched on, it seemed that it was.

"Don't get tragic," he said. "Or I won't show you the one on my ass that says: I HATE LOBSTER."

"I'm not getting tragic!" she protested. "I'm listening to the story!"

"Hey," he said with a nod in an ambiguous direction, "can you grab the address out of that pocket and put it in your phone so we can get some directions when we get closer?"

"You . . . want me to get the address out of your pocket?"

There was a pause, and then he frowned. "Hey. You. Mind in the gutter. The pocket in the visor up there." He shook his head. "Out of *my* pocket."

"I didn't understand!" She laughed and pulled down the visor, which did indeed have a pocket strapped to it, and in that pocket, she found an address in Somerville, which she typed into her phone with her thumbs. "You're the one taking your shirt off," she muttered as the GPS located them and popped up a prediction that they had about an hour and fifteen minutes to go. "Do we know anything about this guy whose house we're driving to?" she asked. "Do we know that he's not going to skin us and make us into lamps?"

"My friend Corey, who I played with at Cornell, works with him at the coffin factory."

"The *coffin* factory?"

"It's not a euphemism for anything, Eveleth, it's a coffin factory. A place where coffins are made. Apparently, Corey does handles and trim and this guy Bill does linings. And his dad, Bill's dad, had the pinball machine that we're going to pick up. It's got race cars on it, you know."

"Yes, you said."

"I'm hoping it has a horn and a siren. You've got to admit, that would be pretty fucking fantastic."

"Why would a pinball machine have a siren?" she asked.

"Probably doesn't, but wouldn't it be great if it did? Keep you up all night long with that," he said. "I just like the sound of it."

"If you're that eager to hear a siren, I can call the police and have them pull you over."

"Oh, big talk, Minnesota."

"You know," she said, "I might not know you well enough to be your navigator yet. I don't know how much time you've spent around Boston, but the streets are designed to prevent anyone from successfully figuring out where they're trying to go."

"We'll take our chances." She kept her eye on the phone until it was time to wiggle the truck through the baffling, jammed, often diagonal *and* one-way streets of Somerville. They found the tall, slate-blue house, and Dean parked in the driveway beside it. They climbed out, and Evvie bent over and hugged the backs of her knees to stretch out her back. She followed Dean up onto the porch, where he rang the bell. The door opened, and a man with half-gray hair and a UMass sweatshirt pushed the screen open.

"Morning, sir, I'm Dean, and this is Eveleth."

"Oh, hello, yes, I'm Bill, come on in." Bill shook both their hands and moved aside, and they found themselves in a mostly empty living room with cardboard boxes stacked in one corner labeled GARAGE

SALE 1 and GARAGE SALE 2. "Pardon the mess, we're still working through my father's things."

"Not at all," Dean said. "I'm sorry for your loss."

"Thank you, Dean. It's a pleasure to meet you, I enjoyed watching you play. If that's all right to tell you."

"Of course, thank you."

"My father did, too, even if he'd sit in front of the TV and call you something not so flattering. He'd have gotten a charge out of you buying the machine." Bill put his hands on his hips and heaved a sigh.

"Well, hopefully he got to see my last few appearances and it brought him some joy."

Bill looked up and gave Dean what Evvie could only characterize as a full-on twinkle. "I think he saw some of it, yeah."

"Happy to help," Dean said, spreading his arms wide.

"I'm gonna overlook that jersey you're wearing," Bill said with feigned sternness. "Was the drive down okay?"

"It was. I still owe Evvie a cruller, but I think we'll make it back home."

"I get paid in pastries," she added.

Bill smiled. "I'm glad you could come down. I've been trying for a couple months to find a good home for this. I wanted somebody to have it who'd enjoy it."

"Dean will *really* enjoy it," Eveleth said. "I think you can safely assume you could not have found a more loving parent for it."

Bill laughed. "All right, perfect." He led them into a game room at the back of the house, where everything else had been cleaned out, but the pinball machine was against one wall. It didn't look new or anything, but someone had dusted it, and, when Bill turned it on, it obligingly buzzed and rang its bells, like an eager shelter dog ready to be rescued. While there was no siren, brightly colored cars decorated both the sides of the cabinet and the backbox—hot cars, in someone's mind, with fins and stripes, being leaned on by girls in full skirts and boys in cuffed jeans.

Dean helped Bill take the machine apart (*he has such nice arms, don't look, don't look*), marking the connections Dean would have to make again later, and Dean and Evvie carried it out to the truck in pieces they'd meticulously encased in bubble wrap and crisscrossed with tape. Back inside Bill's house, she looked away politely as Dean counted out a wad of cash that he handed to Bill with a handshake, and they started back to the truck.

"Not every lady would go for a pinball machine in the house," Bill called out. "You got a good girl there."

"Oh, I know I do." Dean nodded over his shoulder.

Evvie opened the door of the truck and climbed inside, and when he'd gotten in, too, and pulled his door shut, she looked at him, and he shrugged one shoulder at her. "He's not wrong."

She shook her head. "Okay. You owe me a cruller. Let's get to it."

They got donuts instead of lunch, because it was that kind of day, and Dean guided the truck back onto the highway. This time, they mostly listened—to a variety show on the radio and to a true-crime podcast she liked (he kept interrupting and saying "the husband did it," and it turned out the sister did it, but he said he still liked it in the end)—until they were back in Calcasset in the afternoon. When they pulled into her driveway, it was starting to get dark. "I'm starving," she said as he opened up the back of his truck. "I should have demanded you buy me a peanut butter sandwich."

"All right, Muscles," he said. "Grab the other side of this."

They took the cabinet inside, and the legs, and the backbox, and Dean neatly lined them up on the carpet in the apartment. "I am going to put all this together later," he said, walking toward the kitchenette. "I love my race car pinball machine, but I also have to eat." He leaned on the countertop. "Grilled cheese? I want a grilled cheese. You want a grilled cheese?"

"Sure." She dropped down in her usual spot. "Is being a pinball machine owner everything you dreamed of so far?"

"Honestly," he said as he rattled and opened and closed things, "I've thought about this for so long that I'm afraid to put it together. Like the anticipation might be better than the reality. Also, I'm not very good at pinball, and it seems like once I have this set up and working, that's going to be more obvious than it is right now with the thing on the floor."

"I feel like Bill's father is somewhere watching, and he's very excited that you're excited, but he's still upset that a Yankee has his precious."

"At least he probably has a great coffin."

"Whoa, you've gotten dark since you got a pinball machine."

She heard the bread start to sizzle in the pan as he came over and flopped down in the chair next to her. "Can I tell you something?" he asked, running his hand over his short hair.

"Sure."

He pushed his right shoe off with his left foot, then his left shoe off with his right foot. He studied her face for a second.

"What?" she said, reflexively touching her cheek like she might find powdered sugar on it.

"I thought about kissing you a couple times today."

She felt her brows go up, then down. Her mouth tightened, then loosened. *Quick, quick, quick, what does a neutral expression look like again?* "You did." She was shocked. No, satisfied. Maybe gleeful. No, wait, she was just toe-curlingly eager. Also panicked.

"Yeah. I mean, I've thought about it a few other times, but I thought about it a little bit more today. In the truck, and right when we got back and we were going to unload stuff out of, you know, the back." He motioned vaguely with one hand toward the driveway. "I didn't know what you would think, though, and it seemed like it might not be a good thing to surprise you. I mean, surprising you is what I'd normally do. I don't usually hold talks or anything. But it seems like a special case."

"Okay," she said slowly, her brain laboring furiously, like duck feet underwater, while she held her face as still as she could. "Because of the widow thing? Or the landlady thing? Or because we're friends now? Or because you're tight with Andy? Or . . . ?"

He nodded slowly. "Right. All those things. Special case."

"So now you're holding talks."

"I guess I'm offering to hold talks."

She felt like her head was fizzing inside, and she thought maybe, for once, she should just start talking. Open her mouth, see what happened. She was surprised to feel a smile surfacing. "Listen."

He immediately stood up. "Got it."

"Hey, sit down!" she told him, and he came back and dropped into his chair. "It wasn't that kind of 'listen.' "

He held up both hands. "Go ahead. But if you say 'great guy,' there's no sandwich, I'm telling you."

She bit her lip. "I get it," she said. "Right? I mean, I get it. I've been here. You know, I've been *here*." She waved her hand in the space between them. "I haven't missed it. I have . . . I get it."

He grinned at her. "Okay, good."

For a minute, she wished that she had thrown herself into a meaningless fling or two in the time she'd been alone. She wished she'd fed the part of her that wanted someone else's hands and skin and pulse under her fingers. It was too disorienting, too delectable and scary, thinking about this suggestion. Her husband was not the only person she'd kissed, but he was the only person she'd had sex with, and it was like the grown-adult *yes, please* and the high school crush and the hard-won wariness were all trying to squeeze through a door at the same time, and it was chaos.

"I'm not ready," she said. "And I don't want to get into this when I'm not ready, because . . . I'd regret it, and I'd regret . . . regretting it. Do you know what I mean?"

"Sure," he said. "It sounds a little bit like 'maybe later.' "

"I know," she said, cringing with her whole face. "And I would never do that if it weren't a—"

"Special case, no, I get it. Totally fine. But I'm going to assume this is the answer, so if it is 'maybe later,' then later, you're going to have to give me some kind of a go sign if you change your mind."

"A go sign? I have to give you a go sign?"

"Yeah. That'll be up to you, to give the go sign."

She took this in for a beat. "All right, what do you think it should be?"

"The go sign?"

"Yeah."

"I think it should be 'go.'"

"That's the go sign? The go sign is 'go'?"

"That's the go sign."

"All right. Got it. Hey, don't burn my sandwich."

As he stood at the stove, she mouthed it to herself, just to see what it would feel like.

Go.

Eighteen

A COUPLE OF THURSDAYS later, Evvie was watching *Halls of Power* when there was a knock at her door. *Who would be knocking after ten at night?* But she looked out the window and saw Andy's car in the driveway, so she went over to the door and swung it open. "Hey, are you okay?"

"Yeah, everybody's fine," he said. "I'm sorry I didn't call. I was at my mom's, and I came straight here. I need to talk. Is that okay?" His hands were stuffed into his pockets, but she could see a little girl's hair tie around his wrist, meaning someone had taken her braid out over at Grandma's.

"Of course, sure. Come in. Do you need a beer? Or a cup of tea or something? Are you sure you're all right?"

"No, I'm okay, thanks." He sat on her couch, but he sat forward with his elbows on his knees and his fingers laced together. "I need to talk to you about something, and I tried to think of a good buildup, but I don't think I have one."

"You're scaring me," Evvie said, sitting next to him. "What's going on?"

"I'm sorry," he said. "I was over at my mom's, and we got talking about you and how you're doing." Eveleth found this kind of confession mortifying, but Andy kept going. "And we got talking about the night that Tim had the accident."

"Okay," she said, and she started to pick at one fingernail with another.

"My mom told me that one of the things that made her sad was that she realized that you had thought, when you came to the emergency room, that Tim was hurt. And that you'd expected to spend a long time at the hospital with him, which she thought was touching. She talked about how much you had to have loved him to have gotten ready to stay as long as it took. 'That girl packed her bags for the long haul,' is what she said."

"Okay," she said, feeling her mouth dry out. "What made her say that?"

"Do you remember that you couldn't drive yourself home that night? And so I drove you back here? And my mom had somebody drive her to the hospital the next day to pick up your car?"

Eveleth stared helplessly at the carpet. "I don't think I remembered who got the car, it's all sort of a blur. But that makes sense."

"That's how she knew you'd planned to stay. She told me she saw that you'd brought a suitcase to the hospital. To sit by the bed. To wait with him. She told me she looked in the back of your car when she was picking it up, and she saw it. She talked about how sad she always thought it was that you turned out not to need it because he was gone before you ever got there."

Blood started to roar in her ears. She could feel her face flushing, all the way up to her hairline. She was hot, or maybe cold.

"She described to me how she was walking up to your car, and she saw this old blue suitcase with stickers on it." He was trying to look Evvie in the eye, but she fixated on a spot a couple of feet in front of her toes. "She thought you packed it for the hospital. Because my mom doesn't know that that suitcase was your mother's. But I do."

Andy knew this because one night, when they were having beers in her living room and Tim was working late, she'd told him all about Eileen Ashton, who had longed for Eveleth the city but not for Eveleth the daughter. Evvie had opened the hall closet and taken down the beat-up blue suitcase with the stickers that said PARIS and LONDON, stickers that her mother had bought in bookstores. She'd shown him that inside, she kept everything she had that Eileen had sent or left behind: her sunglasses, a cashmere scarf, some letters, a silver bracelet, three faded paperback novels. She'd tried to explain how much she'd missed her mom growing up, and how she sort of dreaded hearing from her now. Dreaded it, but couldn't throw any of her things away.

He went on. "So she doesn't know that there's not a chance that when you got that call from the ER, you took it down, and you emptied it out, and you packed it. My mom doesn't know that there's only one reason you would ever take that bag down out of the closet and put it in your car." He paused. "But I do."

"Andy." Finally, she looked over at him.

"Were you leaving?" He waited. "Were you leaving him?" Again. "Were you leaving him *that night*? Evvie?"

Eveleth had spent the last seventeen months with a squib of dread strapped to her ribs, and now she knew what it felt like to have it explode inside her chest. She thought she might faint, might throw up, might cry, might even burst out laughing. But instead, she said, "I was leaving that night."

"So you were packing the car," he said.

"I had barely started," she said, feeling like her own voice was coming from a recording, or like he'd pulled a string coming out of her back and the words weren't hers, they were playing from a recorded loop. "But I wasn't going to take very much."

"And they called you."

She nodded. And she told him. The car, the suitcase, the phone call, and the doctor with white hair who told her when she got there that her husband was already dead.

Andy had brought her home in his car that night—the same one that was parked in the driveway now with Rose's sweater balled up on the backseat. Evvie had been shaking so hard that when they got to the house, he held her to his side to help her into the house, opening the door she hadn't bothered to lock, taking her all the way up the narrow stairs, and laying her down on her bed, where she turned away from him onto her side and pulled her knees into her chest. Andy had turned on the little lamp on her bedside table, then went into her bathroom and ran cold water onto a washcloth. He had come out and sat next to her on the bed. "Okay," he'd told her. "Here." She'd turned and let him cool her down, like he did with the girls when they were sick. He had dug clothes out of a drawer and waited while she got dressed in the bathroom, and then they lay on her bed on top of the blankets, sleeping for a half-hour or an hour at a time, until it got light outside.

He stayed at her house for thirteen days. Kell kept the girls and brought him clothes, and every day, someone would bring stew, bread, soup, casseroles. Andy would accept it all at the door and promise to give her their love. The school brought in substitutes for his classes. Evvie's father called every day to hear again that she didn't want him to come over, didn't want to see anyone. Andy made Evvie take showers, he coaxed and prodded and bribed her to eat, and although he had a bed in her guest room, about half the nights he slept curled against her, because sometimes she could take Benadryl and doze off with an arm draped over her but not without one.

Tim's parents took care of the funeral arrangements, and Andy brought Evvie. He had her charcoal gray wool dress cleaned, drove her to the church, and held her up again as she received mourners. Mourners who, like him, didn't know she had been packing the car when the hospital called. Every five or ten minutes, he'd lean down by her ear and say, "You're okay." And whenever he did, a fresh jolt of pain went through her. She could have sworn that every time, her heart pumped acid straight to the tips of her fingers. This was the first time the words seemed to bounce around inside her skull: *Monster, monster.*

He brought Evvie back home, and she went straight to bed. She mostly cried and slept and poked at bowls of soup and pieces of toast that he carried upstairs on a tray. After a while, he got her to watch a couple of movies with him—nothing too silly, nothing too sad, nothing with car accidents in it. "I'm so sorry," he'd say. "I'm so sorry, Ev. How can I help you?" And she'd pull the blankets back over her head. After a few days, she came downstairs to eat, and after a few more, they started talking about when she'd be ready to be by herself.

When he reemerged, she knew people asked about her everywhere he went, because he would pass her their best wishes. And she knew how they praised him even when he didn't tell her, because she'd overheard it more than once: "You're so good to her." "She's so lucky to have you." "I don't know what that girl would do without you, Andrew." This still happened, from time to time, even with people who regularly saw Evvie herself. They wanted Andy to say how she *really* was. They wanted him to translate her reticence and explain her absences from places they expected her to be.

"You were leaving him," he repeated. "So all that time afterward . . . it wasn't because you missed him. Or was it?"

Evvie shook her head. "I had no idea what to do."

"Evvie, did . . . did he hurt you? Were you scared of him?"

Does dreading every conversation with him count? Does tensing up when he came into the room count? "No," she said. "I had told him I wouldn't talk about the marriage stuff with you. And I didn't know for sure that I was going to go until I did it, and . . . I didn't say anything. I was going to call you."

He nodded. "You were going to leave town," he said. It was not a question. He would know she couldn't have been planning to leave Tim and stay in Calcasset. She had to have intended to go farther away than that.

"Yes," she said. .

"You weren't going to say goodbye to me, or your dad . . . my girls."

"No, I wasn't." She almost explained that she was leaving notes for them, but it seemed like it would make it worse.

"Evvie . . . I would have helped, I would have helped you find somewhere to live. I would have taken you anywhere."

She shook her head. "I didn't say anything to anybody."

He never raised his voice, not the whole time. "You were the first person I told that I was getting a divorce. I told you before I told my own mother. I can't believe I had no idea."

She was sure Andy was watching a slideshow in his head of those days bringing food to her bedroom upstairs, and of himself at Tim's funeral leaning down by her ear, and of the two of them at the tree-planting ceremony, and she knew he was changing the captions on all those pictures. He'd told her over and over that he understood everything she thought was strange, wrong, bad, ill-suited to the circumstances. The loss explained all of it, he thought. The grief did. But now he had to take all those pictures out again, and it felt inevitable to her that as he searched for new tags to place on them, sooner or later he'd get to *Here is a picture of her lying*. "I didn't want to answer questions about it," she said. "I thought everyone would blame me."

"You thought I would blame you?" He didn't have to tell her how unfair it was or that he'd never given her reason to think anything like that. He was right, and it didn't change the fact that she had intended to leave him nothing but a note, after which he'd have spent the same thirteen days comforting her father. She could argue, but it was true: she'd been ready to walk away from all of them with no goodbye. She'd have visited. She'd have called. But being really gone was what she had intended. Being really, really gone.

"No," she said. "No, of course not, of course I knew you wouldn't. I don't know what I thought." It was the two of them, and the faint *pick-a pick-a*, and the furnace kicking on. "I'm sorry."

He nodded, but what he said was "You don't have to be sorry."

She looked down and noticed for the first time that she still wore her ring, and he didn't. He'd taken his ring off two months after Lori moved out. Andy had been married and was now unmarried, de-married. She was differently married, but forever.

"I want to know we're okay."

He nodded. "Of course. Of course we're okay." He turned to her. "It's a lot to think about."

"Yeah." She rubbed her eyes.

Andy looked at his watch and said, "I don't want to keep you up. And to be honest, I should get home. I have work in the morning. It's been a long day. I just didn't want to go to sleep with it out there."

"Okay," she said. "I'm glad we got to talk." They stopped at the door. "Andy, I'm sorry that's how you found all this out, and I'm sorry I didn't tell you."

"No, I understand." He jangled his keys in his hand. "Maybe I fell down on the job."

"You didn't. I didn't want anybody to know. So nobody knew."

He nodded slowly. "Yeah." He repeated it—"Yeah"—and walked toward the door.

"See you Saturday?" she asked as he stepped out onto the porch.

"Sure."

"I love you."

"I love you, too, Ev." He went down the steps to his car and waved, and she shut the door behind him.

Nineteen

ON FRIDAY AFTERNOON, Evvie was reading in the living room when she got a text from Andy: *Hey—have to cancel tmrw AM. Wknd plans with M. Should be back next wk. okay?*

She stared at it for a minute, then hit reply. She typed, *Sure, have fun.* Then she backed up and changed it to *Sure! Have fun!*

Well, that looks sarcastic, she thought, and changed it to *Sure. Have fun!*

The next morning, she was puttering in the kitchen doing the dishes when she heard the distinctive rings and bumps of the pinball machine. She poked her head into the apartment. "Can I watch?"

"You can as long as you don't make fun of me," he said without looking away from the game. "Wait, it's Saturday," he said over the bells. "Aren't you supposed to be out with Andy?"

"He canceled," she said as she walked over to the machine and leaned on the side. "Girlfriend plans."

"Ooh, the other woman," Dean said. "How do you feel about that?"

"Well, it means I have to make my own pancakes, which is a drag."

"I don't think *that's* what I was asking."

"No, I know it wasn't. I'm happy he's happy. I wish he didn't have to cancel, but I don't blame him. Or her, or whoever. If I were dating him, I wouldn't want him to have a standing commitment every Saturday morning. I'd expect him to be able to go out, or go away, or . . . stay in. Or whatever."

"Or whatever," he repeated. "Everything's okay with you guys?"

"Don't do that."

"Don't do what?" He swore gently and let a new silver ball go.

"Don't expect me to be jealous, it's such a cliché. She's not the first person he's dated in the last four years; she's just lasted the longest."

"I thought maybe you didn't like her."

"I don't know her very well. I mean, I know her, and she was at his birthday in February, but I haven't talked to her much."

"She's probably terrified," Dean said, as he knocked the machine with his hip.

"I think that's cheating, if you bump into it," Evvie said. "And she's terrified of what?"

"She's probably terrified of you."

"Why would she be terrified of me?"

"Seriously? Evvie, how many people, since she started dating Andrew, do you think have told her that they thought he was dating you? Or waiting to date you? Or trying to date you? You live here; you know all this bored-ass gossip. I get you guys—you know, sort of—but if I were Monica, I'd think you would be like . . . some crazy combination of his mother, his ex-wife, his older sister, and his manager. You've got to admit, it's . . . you know."

"No, what?"

"Intense."

"Well, I don't think she's going to have to see much of me anytime soon, so she's got that going for her. And what do you mean by you get us 'sort of'?"

"I'm saying it's unusual."

"What's unusual?"

"This platonic soulmate thing you do is not something that most people do."

"No, I know." A buzzer went off. "It just ... it happened, you know?"

"Fate?"

"Domestic necessity," she said. "When he got divorced, Lilly was a baby and Rose was a toddler. And Lori was . . . poof." She made a motion with her hands like a magic trick. "Did you know she took all the spoons? For some reason, when she set up her new place, she wanted more spoons. He wanted it to be over, and he wanted it to be easy, so he told her—even though, for the record, I told him not to—'Take whatever you want.' So she took all the spoons from their kitchen. I went over there one morning a week after Lori moved out, and Rose was trying to eat cereal with a plastic fork."

"Kell didn't order five of everything for him?"

"He didn't tell her. But he told me. So I brought him some spoons. And I bought him a cookbook. I stayed with them when he had to go out. I was staying with them the night Lori called and said her mom had died, and I rubbed Rose's back until she fell asleep. I taught Andy . . . well, I tried to teach him how to braid their hair."

"He told me you saved his life."

"He did?"

"Yeah." The ball Dean was playing rolled down into the depths, and he looked hard at her. "And all I'm saying is: that takes up space. He's got kids, an ex, a mother, he's got his regular friends. And he's got you, the totally no-big-deal platonic woman friend he tells everybody saved his life." He reached over to the nearby coffee table and grabbed a sip of coffee. "All I'm saying is that it could be intense."

"Point taken. You really have seen a lot of psychologists. So, what are you up to today besides this?"

"Well, there's some conditioning work with the team, and then I'm supposed to talk to this reporter." At her surprised look, he nodded as he shot a new ball. "I know. I like this one, though. He wants to write about what guys do after they're done. He said he wanted to profile somebody who didn't retire voluntarily. That was his expression. 'Didn't retire voluntarily.' It's a fuckin' polite way of saying 'crashed so hard you left a crater they turned into a swimming hole.'"

"And you're sure you want to talk to him?"

"I wouldn't say I'm sure, no. But at some point, I have to figure out what I'm doing besides living in your house and bumming around with a bunch of high school juniors. I'm going to have to stick my head out eventually and see whether it's six more weeks of winter out there or what."

"Mm, I'm afraid you already missed Groundhog Day."

"Well, then for St. Patrick's Day, I'll stick my head out and see if there's six more weeks of not-Irish idiots throwing up on the sidewalk."

"There you go."

Watching Dean try to play pinball turned out to be a pretty decent way to blow a weekend morning. Still, she missed the coffee warmups, and the bacon, and she missed sitting across from someone who found a babysitter every single weekend, so they could sit around and talk about nothing in particular.

The following Thursday, Andy texted her: *Can't do Sat. Can you get together Sun.? Crazy busy wknd w/M & Lil & Ro.*

She wrote back: *Busy here too. Let's regroup next weekend.* Then she deleted the text she'd drafted and saved and never quite sent, which said, *Can't wait to see you Saturday. Sorry we've been missing each other, hope we can talk.*

The article Dean had been interviewed for appeared in the second week of March, during spring training. It was the first spring training he hadn't been part of in eleven years. The piece was supposed to be published online at ten o'clock in the morning on a Tuesday when it was raining in Maine but undoubtedly gorgeous in Tampa. Dean stayed in the apartment with his iPad and his coffee and a bagel. Upstairs with her laptop, Evvie refreshed the site and watched a few movie trailers—she hadn't been to the movies in almost two years. Knowing he was downstairs waiting, she also waited. Nothing doing right at 10:00. 10:02. 10:05. But at 10:07, she saw it at the top of the column of stories: "After Baseball: Eight Players on Having Free Time, Paying for Drinks, and Moving On." Six of the guys had retired after long careers, and one quit young to focus on his family. And then there was Dean, whom the writer called "at first glance, perhaps the most famous washout in twenty-first-century sports."

But in the piece, Dean talked affectionately about the town where he now lived (he called it "the opposite of New York in pretty much every way") and the boys on the teams he was coaching ("You miss a bunch of bozos giving you shit once it's gone, so I'm lucky I met these bozos when I did"). The magazine article version of Dean could easily have been in the running for Mellowest Man Alive, explaining that "the team did everything to try to help" and "sometimes you have to know when you're not an asset anymore" and "I'd be pretty ungrateful to complain about eleven seasons of professional baseball and three trips to the World Series. I was lucky. I'm still lucky." He talked about the trip to Boston to get the pinball machine, which it seemed he'd showed the reporter during a visit Evvie didn't realize had even happened. The reporter had even talked to Somerville Bill, who said that Dean was "a good fella, for a Yankee."

Dean had not told the reporter he sometimes sneaked off to the local minor-league field to pitch at two in the morning, clanging the ball off the chain-link, ringed by flashlights. He didn't describe hurling pinecones at her fence until they exploded when he went to take out the trash. He didn't tell the reporter he had felt like he was pitching with someone else's arm. Instead, he showed the reporter a well-adjusted, super-relaxed Dean "They Named Choking After Me, But It's Fine" Tenney. The King of Chill.

Then, at the end, the reporter wrote this: "Sometimes, Tenney reaches over with his left arm to rub his right shoulder, like he still uses it every day. I ask him at one point whether it bothers him. 'I'm just a creaky old man,' he tells me. 'Though it could always be my arm telling me to get the hell off the couch and go do my job.' He smiles and adds, 'It's one of those.' I'm not sure whether he's kidding."

Evvie got to the end of the article and stared at a picture of Dean, credited to a staff photographer. In it, Dean, dressed in a warm coat and a Yankees cap, sat on a stack of lobster crates on a boat called the *Second Chance*, which she knew belonged to one of her dad's friends. He had offered the photographer a mild squint, a slightly scruffy face that spoke of hard times and intrigue. And sex, though maybe only to her.

She could imagine how elated a photographer must have been to take Dean out for a shoot and find a boat called the *Second Chance* for him to sit on. It might as well have been called the Floating Blunt-Force Metaphor. It was exactly what Andy had always said—that someday, the press would long for Dean to fight his way back. They'd want to forgive him, and it wouldn't be because they were merciful. It would be because the flavor had gone out of hating him like it goes out of cheap gum, and now they needed to taste something different.

She closed the laptop and went down to the kitchen, where she made tea and waited. When the kettle whistled, he appeared. "Hey."

"Hey," she answered, dropping her teabag into her cup. "The piece is nice."

"He's a good guy," Dean said, resting in the doorway on one shoulder. "It's honest. I recognize myself."

"It was funny about your arm," she said. "What you said about how maybe your arm wants to pitch."

She knew without turning around that he was tilting his head like he didn't have the slightest idea what she was talking about. Like he hadn't just read it. "I didn't say my arm wants to pitch."

She didn't turn around. "You said maybe. You said maybe your shoulder hurts because your arm wants to do its job."

"I was kidding."

"So you don't want to get back to pitching." She turned around and sat down. Then she reached under the table with her foot and pushed out the chair opposite her.

Dean sat. "I don't understand the question. You know what happened. It's not a question of what I want. This is how it is now. I'm okay with it."

She tapped the side of her mug with her fingers. "Why do you go out in the middle of the night and pitch in the cold? Why did I find you out there throwing at nothing like a crazy person? What are you *doing* out there?"

"Well, you found me out there because you followed me," he told her in a tense, measured tone. "You found me out there because you got out of bed at two o'clock in the morning in your pajamas and drove around looking for me. I mean, maybe we should talk about that. You want to explain why you're driving around in the middle of the night looking for clues like you're on fuckin' *Murder, She Wrote*?"

"I'm trying to be your friend. I'm trying to understand. You tell me you're fine—"

"Look, sometimes it feels good to do something normal. You have a ballpark, I don't have a job. When I got here, I didn't know anybody except Andy. I like fields. It feels familiar, that's all it is. You're making too much out of it. I'm not going to be able to explain how it feels that I can't pitch, no matter how many times you ask me."

"What about pinecones?" she asked. "Do you like pinecones? Is that familiar?"

Again with that same look. "What are you talking about?"

"I saw you out there, picking up a pinecone off the ground and pitching it at the fence over and over until you blew it up. Do you do that everywhere? Do you walk around throwing things? Is *that* why you rub your shoulder? Because you can't stop throwing at nothing until you hurt yourself?"

Dean fired back, but not quite the way she thought he might. "What's with you and Andy? Why haven't you been meeting up on Saturdays?"

She shook her head like she had water in her ear. "What are you—what does that have to do with anything?"

"Who knows you?" he asked.

Eveleth stared back at him. *Am I going to faint? Because that would be weird.* "What do you mean, 'who knows you'?"

"You want to be my friend, you want to ask me about things you saw when I didn't know you were looking, but who knows you? I don't. Andy doesn't, your dad doesn't. I'm thinking your husband didn't. I live in your house, and you say we're friends, but I don't think I have the first fucking clue what's going on with you. Now you want to quiz me about what happens in the middle of the night? Forget it. You want me to deal with my shit, you know what I say? You first."

She felt her pulse in her head. She looked down at her cup and saw that the fingers resting on its handle were shaking. She stood up and walked over to the upper row of cabinets. She swung one open and took out one of the china plates with the little yellow flowers. The ones that looked like they'd be at home in a dollhouse. She turned back to Dean and held it vertically so he could see it.

"It's a plate. What?"

She lifted the plate until it was about even with her forehead, then, without taking her eyes off him, she opened her hand and let it fall. Time seemed to catch for an instant, the way a word catches in your throat before you say it. But when the plate hit the ground, it exploded with a percussive glee.

Dean jumped in his seat. "What the fuck?"

"I live here," she said. "Right? I live here. My dishes. That's what you said. You said if I don't want them, I should get new ones." She turned back to the cabinet and took out a cereal bowl. This time, she didn't drop it—she flung it at the tile floor, where the pieces broke harder, skittered farther.

He didn't say anything. He just stared.

She took down another plate. Used both hands. For some reason, when this one hit the ground, it didn't break. She threw it right—

threw it wrong—and it landed flat, and it survived. She bent down, picked it up, and looked at him.

"I get it," he said, holding up one hand. "You don't have to break them. I get it."

She pulled her arm back and plowed the plate into the side of the kitchen table, where most of it broke away, leaving her holding a piece in her hand. She dropped it on the growing pile by her feet.

"Eveleth, Jesus," Dean said, standing up and pushing his chair back from the table.

She turned around and took the rest of the plates—the other six—down in a stack, which she set on the counter. She broke them, one by one, smashing some against the counter or the table before letting them land on the kitchen floor, and Dean stood and watched with his arms folded. She threw one while she thought about the time Tim called her an idiot when she couldn't find her keys, and the bits of it slid and skidded across the kitchen floor until they were under the refrigerator and beside the dishwasher.

When they were all dashed to pieces—every plate she'd ever eaten dinner on at nine thirty at night after she'd given up on Tim coming home, every plate she'd put in front of him for his birthday breakfast with a candle in a stack of French toast—she stopped. She was hot and dizzy and her heart was pounding, and Dean was still silent. Then he walked toward her, kicking broken dishes out of the way, clearing himself a path to where she was standing. He got right next to her, until she recognized the smell of his laundry detergent.

He reached behind her, over her shoulder, and she wondered if she was about to feel his hand on the back of her neck. Fortunately, before she could close her eyes or otherwise behave like a person transparently hoping to be kissed, she saw that he'd pulled down a bowl, which he finished off with a snap of his wrist—a snap that had once been worth many millions of dollars a year.

In a movie, they'd have wound up laughing, and maybe even tickling each other. There would have been joy in it. But they just stood by her sink and smashed eight dinner plates, eight cereal bowls, and eight salad plates. When he handed her that last plate, she held it straight out in front of her, almost reverently, and she uncurled her fingers and just let the weight of it not rest in her hand anymore. The plate broke into such little pieces on the floor that it stopped *being*. The sound crested and stopped, and then they were alone together, standing on a little tile island in a sea of broken yellow flowers. She lifted her left hand to push a scraggle of hair away from her pink face, and he cringed. "Ah, you're hurt."

It wasn't a surprise that surrounding herself with shards of broken dishes had given her a cut between two of her fingers. It was more surprising to confirm, as she turned her hands over, front and back, that there wasn't more blood. She ran her hand under cold water and washed it, and Dean got a clean paper towel and pressed it to the cut. "I've got it," Evvie said, taking over, but he put his hand on top of hers.

"Make sure you press down," he said. "It'll stop."

He was so tall that she should have anticipated the sheer size of his hand, but how stumpy her fingers looked under his made her chuckle. "You have paws like a Great Dane puppy," she murmured.

"Yeah. You know, they still do some things well," he said.

She looked up at him. There was a little scar over his eyebrow. Almost definitely, she figured, it was the result of having been hit with a ball. A cut must have opened up. Maybe he had been little, like she'd been when she fell on a piece of glass and got four stitches in her knee. Maybe not. For as long as it took to blink, she could see herself in her mind, fastening a bandage over his eye.

He peeked under the paper at the cut. "I think you're going to live."

Evvie kept looking at his hands, and she slid her eyes up his arm to his shoulder. In there somewhere. In there somewhere, was the answer. "You should teach me how to pitch," she said.

He laughed. "What?"

"You should teach me how to pitch," she repeated.

"What for?"

"So I'll know how it feels to pitch."

"What for?" he repeated.

She shrugged. "So I'll know how it feels not to pitch."

He nodded slowly. "But you know that I can't actually pitch myself. You know that's sort of my thing."

"I know. But you can teach me how to."

"How good are you trying to get?"

"Let's say . . . to where I wouldn't be laughed off a Little League field."

Dean squinted. "What age group?"

She thought for a minute. "Twelve-year-olds."

"They're pretty good by the time they're twelve," he cautioned. "Don't overcommit."

"I want to learn."

He smiled, just a little. "Okay. You want to start now? I assume you're a righty, so that hand won't be a problem."

"No, just someday. I have stuff to do today."

He raised one eyebrow. "Anything good?"

She leaned on the sink. "Clean the kitchen and shop for dishes."

SPRING

Twenty

ONE THURSDAY IN early April, Evvie was up in the bedroom packing away her winter sweaters when her phone buzzed in her pocket. She pulled it out and saw Andy's picture with a text: *Can we do Saturday breakfast? Sorry we've been missing each other. Lots going on, but it would be great to see you.* Relief instantly lowered her shoulders an inch.

Ever since they'd talked about the night that Tim died, he'd felt far away. He had this new girlfriend, he had kids, he was busy, he had work. But she couldn't quite convince herself he wasn't angry that she had let him try to soothe, for weeks and for months, an injury she didn't exactly have. She'd seen him a few times, and it had been distressingly cordial. She'd pulled out her phone to text him over and over, but she hadn't.

When a few minutes had passed, she reached into her pocket again for the phone. *Hey!! Great to hear from you. I'd love that, yes. Been missing you a lot.*

She heard back right away: *Me too! OK if Monica joins?*

She assured him that this was fine, and that she was looking forward to it, which she didn't quite mean.

She took out her phone again and texted Dean. *The good news is I'm having breakfast w/Andy on Saturday.*

He came back: *& the bad news?*

And before she could answer, her phone vibrated again. *Bringing the gf?*

She sent him back the emoji with the tense, grimacing mouthful of teeth. The one she always thought of as Mr. Okaaaaay.

Still glad you're going, he answered. *It'll be ok. She's great. Promise.*

She sent him a yellow heart. All the hearts were different to her, shaded and pleasantly oblique and sent in a language only she spoke—which maybe meant it wasn't a language, just a diary hiding in plain sight. The yellow heart was for gratitude.

Evvie got to breakfast first on Saturday, and it was finally getting to be spring, so she sat at their table with her coffee and turned her face toward the big window with her eyes shut, letting her cheeks get warm in the sun. She turned at the sound of Andy laughing as he guided Monica into the booth across from her. "Hey, sorry we're running late," he said.

"No problem at all," Evvie said. "It's good to see you."

"You, too," Monica said with a smile. "I appreciate your letting me barge in on your tradition. I know it's a special thing."

"Hey, I'm glad Andy could make the time." *No, no, no, that's not what I meant to say.* "The more the merrier," she added, which didn't sound right either. This made her 0-for-2. "I recommend the blueberry pancakes, even though Andy is a sucker for the ham and cheese omelet."

"Oh, believe me, I know," Monica said.

Just then, Marnie came by the table. She set down a cup with a teabag in it and a little pot of hot water in front of Monica. "Good to see all of you here together!" Marnie said. "Food order's in for all of you, be a few minutes," she said as she filled Andy's coffee cup.

"Sorry, I didn't know you'd been coming here, that was dumb,"

Evvie said, straightening the napkin in her lap. Andy was looking at his phone.

"Andy's a creature of habit," Monica put in on his behalf. "I wanted to tell you, by the way, we drove by your house the other day and I couldn't stop talking about how great-looking it is. I think your porch is glorious."

Eveleth laughed. "That's very nice of you. You should come sit on it sometime." She squinted. "That came out weird."

"No, not at all. Please come sit on mine, too, although it's considerably less attractive." Andy reached over and threaded his fingers through Monica's.

"How've you been, Ev?" he asked.

She reached for that rope. Really reached for it. "I've been good. I finally watched some of *The Americans,* by the way."

He smiled. "Was I right about it?"

"You were, you were." Evvie nodded slowly.

"You don't think it's 'propaganda'?" he asked, his eyes flickering over to Monica's.

"Oh my God," Monica broke in, rolling her eyes, "I'm sorry I didn't like your show. Talk to Evvie. She liked it." She playfully yanked her hand away, but Andy kissed it and then pulled it, clasped in his, somewhere under the table. "He is a baby about television."

Eveleth smiled. "I know. How are the girls?"

"Ah, they're good," Andy said. "Their mom is marrying Fred, by the way."

"Holy shit," Eveleth muttered. "She's finally marrying him?"

"Fortunately, the girls like him all right these days. It would be way dicier if they didn't. It's one of the reasons we waited a couple months before they met this one." He tipped his head to the side.

"Oh, so you have been getting to know them," she said to Monica.

"I have," Monica said. "They're great. But you know that better than I do. They're not happy it's been so long since they got to spend time with you." Her eyes flicked toward Andy, and his answered, a little.

A couple more silences, a couple more volleys of nothing, and Marnie brought the food—Eveleth's pancakes, Andy's omelet, and something for Monica that looked like a veggie scramble. She did seem like a veggie scramble kind of person—very sensible. Very healthy. Not some cottage-cheese showoff, just a person who was more grown-up than anyone at the table who might be eating, for instance, pancakes.

They ate and talked: Eveleth and Monica talked, and Monica and Andy talked. And when most of the food was gone, Monica excused herself. "I'll be right back," she said, bumping Andy's shoulder so he'd get up and let her out of the booth. When she was gone, Evvie picked at a blueberry on the edge of her plate. "She seems amazing." She rested her chin on her hand and looked at him. "It's good?"

He smiled. "It's so good, Ev. I mean, it's still early. But yeah, she's great, I'm happy. And I'm sorry I haven't been around. I've been, you know. I'm trying to be a good boyfriend. Weekends are busy, it's been a lot. I felt bad. I was afraid you'd think I was upset about the thing we talked about at your house, about the suitcase and everything."

Evvie felt her cheeks get pink. "I wondered, yeah."

"I'm sorry. I admit it blew my mind a little bit. I don't know."

"I didn't mean to do that," she said. He laughed nervously, with one narrow strip of his voice, and Evvie felt so sharply the distance that had opened that there was a stinging in her eyes and her throat got slightly tight and, just, *no*. She coughed instead. "Dean's going to teach me how to pitch."

"Oh, really?" Andy laughed. "It seems like you guys are having fun."

She knew it was an opening; the right time to talk about the go sign and the dishes. But those things, for now, were her only secret that faced forward instead of backward. If she told, it would shatter the slight mischief of it, like drinking bourbon from a coffee mug. Besides, she couldn't think of a single thing he could say in response—*go for it, be careful, tell me everything*—that she'd know how to answer. So she said, "You were right; it's nice to have the company. It keeps me from sitting around by myself."

"Just don't try to fix him. I know how you are."

"How am I?"

"You're very . . . caring. Literally. You took care of your dad, you took care of Tim, you took care of me when Lori left. I just don't want you to take in strays for the rest of your life. You're the kind of person who winds up with a two-legged dog that you pull around in a cart."

"That's not a kind of person."

"It's absolutely a kind of person. It's a person who ends up running a doll hospital and putting tiny little toothpick splints on birds with broken legs."

"Well, I promise I will not open a doll hospital."

"What do you think you do want to do?"

She put a strand of hair behind her ear. "Work. Or maybe school. I don't know. I'm thinking about it. Nona's been sending me messages; she's got a new book. You know how much I love to work with her."

"That would be fantastic," Andy said, sitting up. "I just think you should have something." She could see the precise moment he heard himself say it. "I don't mean you don't now. I mean something that would be fun and great and different." They looked at each other.

At that moment, Monica appeared beside the booth and pushed on Andy's shoulder, so he scooted in to make room, still looking at Eveleth, still wondering exactly what had happened. "Did I miss anything?" Monica asked.

"Nope," Eveleth said. She picked up the check that Marnie had slipped onto the table and stood up. "I'm going to get this. It was great to see you guys, though."

"Oh, Evvie, thank you," Monica said, reaching over and squeezing her elbow. "Next time's on us, okay?"

Evvie put her hand over Monica's. "Absolutely. Next time." She slid the tip money under the edge of her plate, then she went up to the counter to pay the check. Andy and Monica waved to her on their way out, their fingers casually tangled together, and then they were gone. Standing by the cash register, she felt eyes on her. They wouldn't be used to seeing her cleaned-up on a Saturday morning, they wouldn't be used to seeing her leave this early, and they wouldn't be used to seeing her standing by herself. They'd be used to seeing gossip that continued out the door, and then the hug by his car. Not today.

Twenty-One

THAT AFTERNOON, EVELETH again climbed into Dean's truck, and again he said, "All right, let's do this."

This time, he took her to the soccer field at the high school. "Dean, I am not a sports person, particularly, but I do know this is not a baseball field," she said as they walked across the grass.

"That's true—that's your first win on your first official day as a pitcher. As it happens, there's a JV game on the baseball field, and all you're doing today is throwing a ball. You don't need anything except a ball and a glove." His right hand came up from between them with a baseball in it. "So take this."

"Is this, like, a sacred thing, taking a baseball from you? Do I have to promise to uphold the laws of the—?"

"Take the ball," he said, and his voice got sort of low and sandpapery. He turned and stood right in front of her, holding the ball between them, so close it almost touched her ribs. She took it, and he reached into a duffel that was over his shoulder and produced a black baseball glove with hot pink lacing.

"You're joking," she said.

"Take it."

"It's pink," she said, not touching it. Leaning back a little to not touch it.

"It's not pink, it just *has* pink."

"I'm not wearing it. I object."

"Why?"

"I think . . . the patriarchy."

"Evvie, I'm not doing that well with the patriarchy myself. I got chased out of New York by guys on the Internet who spell 'loser' with two O's. Would you please put on the pink glove?"

"It's not pink, it just *has* pink," she groused as she slid it onto her hand and tentatively fit the baseball into it. "And I don't think you understand the patriarchy."

Dean gestured with the beat-up glove on his left hand. "I probably don't. Okay, walk backward until I tell you to stop. And don't fall over."

"Is this part of your coaching? 'Don't fall over'?"

"Absolutely. I say it in a really wise way, though. With the benefit of experience," he said as he held up a hand for her to stop. "Okay. Now, don't think too hard about it, just throw me the ball."

She turned her left shoulder toward him, remembering with her body a lesson her father had once given her. She took a step as she threw to Dean. It sailed a little and he reached across his body to his left and caught it. "That's a good start. Do it again." He flipped the ball back to her, and as he did, she couldn't help thinking about poor Mackey Sasser. She turned the glove palm-up to make the catch, cradling the ball as it reached her. "There you go," he said. "You have talent."

"Really?"

There was a pause. "You could have talent."

She laughed. They did this a few more times—she threw reasonably consistently for a person who never threw anything except maybe crumpled-up tissues into a garbage can, and she caught what he gently lobbed in her direction about half the time. "Okay, I want to show you something," Dean said, and he walked over to her. He came and stood right behind her until she felt heat coming off him all up and down her back. "If I handle you a little while I show you this, is that okay?"

She turned and looked him in the eye over her shoulder. "Yeah, it's okay."

He might have winked. He might not have. It was a tough angle. But he put his hands on her arms and repositioned her with her left shoulder facing the target again. "You have this part right. But then when you throw, lead with your elbow, and before you release the ball, I want you to flop this wrist"—he grabbed the wrist of her right hand—"flop this wrist back like this before you throw. Palm up. Like you're about to raise the roof."

"Raise the roof?"

He put his palms up and pumped his arms. "You know."

"Oh my God, forget I asked. If the kids you coach see you do that, they're never going to listen to you again."

"All right, Muscles, are you ready to get serious?" She felt him pull a couple of inches away from her, and she smiled.

"I'm ready, I'm ready." She cocked her arm behind her.

He was against her back again. His left foot crept forward and nudged her left foot a few inches forward. "You want a little more space here." He curled his right arm along hers, right up to the back of her hand, where he rested his palm. Five seconds passed. Five more. "What are you doing?" she finally asked.

"I'm hanging out," Dean said, directly into her ear.

Eveleth had always hated how blushing felt. It was accompanied by such a miserable desire to cease to be, utterly, to turn into a fog that could be waved away. This blush, though, was like blooming, like she might look down and see petals flutter from her own shoulders. She sucked in her breath and they stayed like that. She started to worry that he could feel her pulse in her wrist, because she could feel it in her temples and was afraid her whole rib cage might be going *thmm-*

thmm-thmm. Before she could even try to inch away from him, he reached up and laid two fingers against the side of her throat. "I'm checking your heart rate. You know, making sure you're nice and relaxed. It's part of my system." *Thmm-thmm-thmm.* "Wait," he said. And he blew on her neck. He blew right on her neck, which made her whole arm break out in goosebumps. He looked down at her skin and said, with a mix of curiosity and satisfaction, "Huh."

She looked over her shoulder. "You blew on me."

"Yes," he said.

"Because?"

"You had a bug on you."

"Oh, please. Get back to work, *Coach*," she said firmly.

"Suit yourself," he said. "Next time I see a bug, I'll let it crawl down the back of your shirt."

"Great. Next time you blow on me, I'm going to elbow you in the gut."

He laughed from somewhere in his chest, somewhere pushed up against her shoulders. "So, you're going to turn as you throw. Like I said, you're going to lead with your elbow." He moved his hand up from her hand to her elbow. "That's going to go first. Then as you throw, you're going to pick up this foot"—he reached down and tapped her right hip with one finger—"and wind up facing forward, right? So you're going to turn your body front."

She looked over her right shoulder again and narrowed her eyes. "I feel like this isn't how you teach high school boys to throw."

"It's not. They smell terrible."

"You know this is incredibly transparent," she said.

"Hey, I'm working a method here. Take it or leave it."

"Carry on," she said.

"So here, take your glove hand"—he bumped her glove with his—"and put this elbow up. Point it where I'm going to be. Then you're going to flick your wrist, follow through, come around with this leg, and that's . . . that's throwing a baseball."

"Now I can throw like you do?"

He stepped away from her. "These days, yes, you can probably throw exactly like I do."

She scrunched up her face. "I didn't mean it like that."

"I know you didn't." He jogged away from her a little, then he slowed and turned back. "Okay, hit me," he said, punching his glove.

She turned so that her body was perpendicular to him. She scooted her feet a little farther apart. She pulled her arm back with the ball in her hand, and she aimed her left elbow at Dean. *Weight forward, elbow forward, flick, follow through, rotate.* She threw the ball directly at the ground. "Oh, uh-oh."

He ran forward to pick it up, laughing. "No, no, it's a lot to remember."

"I want to watch you throw. I feel like it would help."

He stood up with the ball in his hand and seemed to weigh it. "You were just watching me throw."

"Throw for real," she said.

"Eveleth, I don't think that's—"

"Not at me, you goofball, you'd kill me. Throw it at the fence." She gestured with the glove that had pink.

He eyeballed the gray fence that bounded one side of the soccer field. "I don't know, Ev."

She walked toward him until she was close, and then she folded her arms. "It'll help. Just let me observe."

"Fine." He turned toward the fence, stepped, and she watched his body operate. She felt like she could see every muscle and bone and tendon that he arranged, pulled taut, and then let go like a slingshot. His shoulders rotated, his hips twisted—she even saw something shift in the back of his neck. The ball flew and made a sharp bang against the fence. He turned back to Eveleth, who nodded a little.

He opened the bag on the ground next to him and turned it sideways, and ten or so baseballs rolled out. He threw them one after another, *bang, bang, bang,* first looking like a guy who knew how to throw, but then looking like a pitcher. He fiddled with the brim of his Calcasset High School cap. He rubbed his hand against his hip. By the time he threw the last one, he was fully kicking his leg in the wind-up, and Eveleth even saw him sneak a look at a first base that wasn't there.

He was out of breath at the end, and a pile of baseballs had accumulated at the base of the fence. He stood with his hands on his hips. Evvie stood next to him for a minute, mimicking his stance and his forward gaze. Then she walked over to the fence and gathered up the balls, dropping them into a little pouch she made with her shirt. She came back and dumped them on the ground in front of Dean. He nodded. He picked one up. *Bang.*

They hit at what looked to her like a very consistent spot. After a while, she could see the marks where they were hitting, and they were close together, grouped like a basket of peaches. But mostly, she watched Dean. His forehead got a little damp, until a little swirl of hair stuck to it. There was a story in it for him somewhere in there, somebody to beat, and once, she heard him whisper what she was pretty sure was "Yeah, there it is, fucker."

Dean threw like big cats pounce in nature documentaries. She could know it was coming, she could watch him settle, she could watch the twitches while he waited, but every time it happened it was still surprising how merciless it was and how silently it was done. She gathered up the baseballs and brought them back and put them at his feet, but this time he stopped with his hands on his hips and said, "How much of this do you need to see?"

She shrugged. "I don't know, how much of it do you need to do?"

He smiled and shook his head. "Nah, this is for you, Minnesota."

"You sure?"

He looked at her, a little out of breath. "Why are we out here?"

She walked over to the fence with her hands in her pockets and peered at the marks on it. "This doesn't look to me like you're throwing all over the place," she called over to him. "What am I missing?"

"Fuck's sake," he said, looking at the bright blue sky. "Evvie, it's *inches*, pitching. It's *inches*. The fact that I'm not throwing it over the fence into the road doesn't mean anything has changed. Why are we talking about this again?"

"Because if I could do anything as well as you do that, I'd want to keep doing it as long as I could. And I think you do, too. I've seen what it looked like when it wasn't going well. You weren't doing that." She pointed at the little cluster of marks on the fence. "So something's different. You're not even curious?"

"I quit. It's done."

She walked toward him. "If it's done, why did you sit on a boat called *Second Chance* and let them take your picture?"

He shifted on his feet. "It was a photographer. It was his idea. It was that or the *Natural Booty*."

She shook her head. "Don't do that. You know what I'm talking about. You know what you said in that interview, you know that you go out in the middle of the night—"

"I don't want to talk about that," he told her firmly. "If I'd wanted to *talk* about it, I'd have *told* you about it, like I said the last time you *asked* me about it."

"I don't think you're ready to give up. I think that's why you sneak around."

"Evvie . . . do you ever quit?"

She was right in front of him again, and she rested her hand on his pitching arm. "There's a game every year, an exhibition game, between the Claws and this team from Freeport. They play, they raise money, the money gets split between their PTA and ours, with a bonus for the winner. Sometimes there are guests who play on one of the—"

"Are you kidding me? Fuck, no," he said. "You want to bring a hundred reporters here to write about how sad it is that I'm pitching in a charity game? These people are just now getting bored with me; I'm not giving them anything."

"We're not going to announce it," she said, moving fluidly into the future tense. "We'll tell the team. It'll be a surprise for everybody else.

The kids you coach are going to love it. And you can see how it goes. You'll pitch an inning."

He still had a ball in his hand, and he kept running his fingers over the stitching. "You're not listening," he said.

"I know."

Twenty-Two

THE CALCASSET CLAWS and the Freeport Explorers played an exhibition game they called the Spring Dance every year on the last Sunday in May. They alternated between the two ballparks, had a carnival beforehand in the parking lot, and, every year, the host team tried to top the year before. There was laser tag in Freeport one year; there was a virtual reality room in Calcasset the next year. There was a dog show in Calcasset one year; there was a bull rider in Freeport the next year.

This was Calcasset's year, and the organizers were understandably enthusiastic when Dean Tenney sidled into their temporary office at Dacey Park a couple of weeks ahead of the game to tell them that if it was okay with the team, he wanted to show his gratitude for how he'd been welcomed by pitching an inning. Freeport might have had a vertical wind tunnel last year, but Calcasset was going to have a news story. It would remain a secret until he walked onto the field; that was his only condition.

When Dean had closed the deal with Liza, who ran the whole thing, he exited the office and stepped into a cinderblock hallway. The way he'd come, to the right, led back out to the lot where he'd parked his truck. The other way led to the field where he'd only ever been at night. He went left. As he walked, he took out his phone and texted Eveleth. *They went for it,* he wrote. *Now I have to do it.*

She sent back a blue heart.

He opened a gate with a squeaky latch and stepped onto the field. The first baseball field he'd ever been on was in Lansing, Michigan, where he was born.

He used to lie under the bleachers when his brothers were playing and listen to the ball instead of watching. It was the sound of it hitting the catcher's mitt that had hooked him. *Thump.* For so many guys he knew, it was the sound of the bat. They'd loved to hit, growing up craving first the *clang* of the Little League aluminum bat and then, if they made it that far, the gunshot sound of the major league wooden bat. But for him, it had always been the ball hitting the mitt. He firmly believed that good pitches sounded different from bad ones, and when he had started to fail, he had craved that good sound, that satisfying sound of the pitch that was where the catcher wanted it.

The last time he'd walked off the field at Yankee Stadium, the crowd had been happy to see him go and unhappy not to be given the opportunity to drop an active beehive right on his head. He'd known—he'd *known*—that he might never pitch again. Walking onto the field in Calcasset was going to be his first pitching gig since he'd handed the ball to the Yankees' pitching coach and walked into the dugout, accompanied by a guy he heard, clear as day, yelling, "Get the fuck out, ya fuckin' head case!"

He walked out onto the grass, crossing from the dugout through the infield until he was on the pitcher's mound where Evvie had once found him surrounded by flashlights. With his hands on his hips, he stood and stared at the plate. He thought about her, and about smashing the dishes in her kitchen. She'd been so calm and so determined, one plate leading to the next and the next, and he hadn't been sure she even knew he was there at times. He'd looked down and seen her bleeding, and for a second, he'd known what to do and been able to do it.

He kicked the dirt once and walked off the field, thinking about the way he had peeked at the back of her neck when he was standing next to her at the sink, pressing down on the cut on her hand.

The next few weeks were an exercise in plotting. Liza spoke to the manager of the Claws, and he in turn spoke to the team about Dean. One or two of them expressed surprise that he wanted to do it, but who could resist the pull of a comeback story that would get written up *everywhere*, that might happen on their own home field? To a player, the guys who had met Dean liked him, found him funny and surprisingly smart for someone who'd been talked about like he was a bit of a nut.

They made Dean a uniform that said TENNEY on the back. They asked him whether he wanted his old number, but he said no. Instead, for luck, he asked them for 26, because Evvie's address was 26 Bancroft Street. When he got home and he showed the shirt to Evvie, she said, "Hey, look. That's my house number. Maybe it's lucky."

He'd folded it up, saying, "Maybe."

The weather for the Spring Dance could not have been better. There was a lazy breeze, and there were almost no clouds. People packed blankets into car trunks for lawn picnics and threw in light jackets for when it got cooler later. In the parking lot, it already smelled like hot frying oil, girls were trying on earrings that a woman in Camden made from recycled plastic, and they were setting up the speakers by the stage where the band—brought up from Boston— would be playing before the game.

Back in the kitchen at 26 Bancroft, Evvie packed a canvas tote bag with her sunglasses and her Claws seat cushion and a long-sleeved shirt Dean had loaned her after he noticed that the zipper on her jacket was broken. He had his door shut, and after putting her ear close to it and hearing that he was still listening to one of the podcasts she was trying to hook him on, she opened a side cabinet and took down the champagne bottle by the foil at the neck. She put her hand on the label and closed her eyes for luck, then swiftly moved it into the refrigerator, hiding it behind a pitcher of iced tea.

As she was getting ready to make herself something to eat before she left, he emerged from his apartment in jeans and a green Henley, with his duffel over his shoulder. "Okay," he said. "I'm taking off."

She put down the tote. "You feeling all right?"

"Sure, yeah." He hitched the bag up on his shoulder. "Little nervous, I guess."

She nodded. "You're going to be great."

"I hope you're right," he said. "It's going to be a real shitshow if I'm not."

"It's a fun game to raise money. It's not that different from coaching. You're doing what you know how to do."

"Everybody's kind of forgotten my sad ass," he said. "I don't know if reminding them is that smart."

"I chased what's-her-face off the porch, didn't I? I can do it again if I have to."

"You're ready to be the muscle, huh?"

"Whatever it takes."

He narrowed his eyes. "You're fantastic. I just . . . feel like you should know. I don't know if you know."

She leaned back against the sink. "So are you. And as scary as I know this is, all you have to do is the same thing I've already seen you do."

"If I fuck it up, it's going to be the biggest flop this place ever saw."

She waved her hand. "That's not true. You'd be way behind a second-grader falling on her face, dressed like a box of Cheerios. That's the great thing about failing here. You're still beating the elementary school students who face-plant for our amusement."

He laughed and rubbed his jaw. "Hey, can I ask you a favor?"

"Sure."

"It's going to sound . . . I don't know how it's going to sound. But they told me it's general admission. Could you try to set up behind the plate?" He made a straight-ahead gesture with his hands, like he was helping to park a plane.

Her first thought was that he wanted her to be able to see whether the pitches were good. Her second thought was that he wanted her to have a good seat. It took three thoughts to get what he meant.

"I can. You want me to wave or something? I don't know if you'll really be able to see me."

"I won't," he said. "I'll know, though. Who knows? It might help. I'm ready to try anything."

"That's sweet. I think I'm honored."

"I should get going," he said, not going. He stood with his keys in his hand, fiddling with them, dangling the ring from different fingers. "I'm fucking nervous."

Her intent when she took the first step was to get some kind of perfect, knee-melting hug, where he smelled her hair, where she smelled his neck, where they lingered in a strange, suspended, secret clutch. But as soon as she moved, he looked right at her and dropped the bag from his shoulder. It slid down his arm and went *bump* on the floor. It pulled his shirt to the side, and she saw his collarbone. And a step later, he let his keys go from his fingers, and they clattered on the tile. Just as she got to him, in one motion, he grabbed her Claws cap by the brim and tossed it behind her.

All she could think as she finally, finally kissed him was *finally, finally*. She crossed her wrists behind his head and felt his hands on her, his fingers digging into her hip bones. He made a surprised little noise, or maybe they both did.

It was a little sloppy and imperfect, or maybe perfect, because they'd never done it before. Toothpaste, scruff, breath, Dean's hand creeping an inch under her shirt at her waist, a joint in his shoulder that popped like a cracked knuckle when he shifted his arms to hold her tighter. That was all that really registered. That and *finally, finally*.

They pulled apart slowly, and she stepped back. She put her hands in her hair and realized he'd halfway dislodged her small ponytail. "I forgot to give the go sign," she said, leaning her hands on the table behind her.

He grinned and rubbed one hand over his cheek. "It's okay, I got it."

She reached down to get her cap, then looked at him with a little flash of concern. "Oh my God, I know you have to go. I know it's a big day. I didn't plan that or anything. I didn't mean to . . . do something confusing."

He picked his keys up off the floor and hoisted the duffel onto his shoulder. "Evvie, that was . . . not confusing." He started out the kitchen door, and before he went, he turned back around. "Lotta things. Not confusing." He paused, then added, "I'm sorry if I messed up your hair." He winked and left.

Twenty-Three

EVVIE MET UP with Andy and Monica and the girls on the way in, so they could sit together. When she saw Lilly's hair in two neat French braids, Evvie leaned down to inspect it. "My lightning bug, it looks like your dad finally figured out your hair."

"My dad can't do anything," Lilly said matter-of-factly. "Monica did it. She did my best braids ever."

"Ah, of course she did." Evvie stood back up and gave Monica a thumbs-up, marveling at the way a kindergartener could deliver a shot to the solar plexus without even looking up from her cotton candy.

Of everyone in the stands except some of the players' wives and girlfriends and a couple of people on the Claws' staff, only Evvie and Andy and Monica knew that Dean Tenney was going to come out of the dugout and pitch the fourth inning. They'd picked the fourth because the game would be underway, but he wouldn't be responsible— well, any more responsible than necessary—for how it turned out.

The Claws were leading 3–2 when the Explorers came up in the top of the fourth. Between the third and fourth innings, Gloria Rubia, the principal of Calcasset High, came out and read a list of Top Ten Cafeteria Improvements We'd Like to See, written by the senior class. ("6. Skee-Ball.")

Evvie shifted in her seat, adjusted her cap. Andy looked over at her. "Are you gonna be okay whatever happens here?" She nodded, and he smiled. "Okay."

Over the loudspeaker: "Ladies and gentlemen, with a very special announcement, please welcome the owner of the Calcasset Claws, Ginger Buckley!"

A roar. Ginger was a straight-up eccentric dowager in the best sense, the heir to her late husband's Kentucky-based whiskey empire. In the mid-1990s, after he died in his early fifties in a small plane crash, she'd packed up and left the South because she'd grown up out East and missed the ocean. Now she lived in a decommissioned and renovated lighthouse all the way at the end of a jetty, with three rescue greyhounds and a constant stream of freeloading grandchildren she adored. In 2009, she'd bought the Claws, as she put it, "for my adopted hometown to enjoy forever and ever." She came to every game, often putting a papery silver space blanket over her bright red hair when it rained, and now and then, she took to the field to deliver important news.

"Welcome, welcome, welcome to the Spring Dance!" she said into a microphone with pink baubles around the handle that was reserved for her alone. A roar. "How's everyone enjoying it so far?" Another roar. "Well, you ain't seen nothin' yet." Another. "Sometimes we like to invite very special friends to play in this game, and we bend a few rules"—she leaned teasingly to one side—"to make it possible." She glanced over at the Claws' dugout. "We are very pleased that this year, we can welcome one of our recent arrivals in town"—the first gasps were here—"to take a turn pitching. Calcasset, give your warmest welcome to the assistant coach of the Calcasset High Hawks and our good friend, Dean Tenney."

Eveleth saw him jog out of the dugout, and she heard the cheer that got so loud it was almost a buzz in her ear. At the pitcher's mound, he shook Ginger's hand, and she walked off the field, waving her pink microphone in the air and pumping her other fist. The catcher, Marco Galvez, who also worked at the Honda dealership in Thomaston, set up behind the plate, and Dean looked down at the ball in his hand. "It's warm-ups, it's fine," she muttered to herself. "Just breathe." All she heard was hollering, but her mind was still enthusiastically replaying the memory of his fingers finding the skin on her back.

He wound up. He rotated, and the ball left his hand, and 2,500 people knew that whatever this was, they could say they were there for it later.

It went *thump* into Marco's mitt, and a cheer went up. Marco lobbed it back. And by the time Evvie looked up again, she saw a sea of phones in the crowd, held up, some briefly to catch a photo and then back into pockets with something like shame, some documenting with video. And some, she assumed, would soon be streaming it live, and one of those streams would be spotted and shared by someone famous, and people would stand at bus stops and sit in restaurants and pause games on their computers and mute the television because there was live streaming video of Dean Tenney, who might be about to embarrass himself by being unable to put the ball over the plate at a game where the national anthem had been sung by the seven-woman, two-man glee club from a local senior center.

She looked at Andy next to her and took a deep breath in. He reached over and squeezed her arm. Monica mouthed, "Good luck." Evvie watched Dean successfully take a few more warm-up pitches, and then she was almost sure she saw him look into the stands. *Should I wave? I definitely should not wave. Should I stand up? Should I have worn brighter colors?* She rubbed her hands on her thighs and leaned forward as if to whisper in his ear. *You can do it, you can do it, you're fine.*

The batter was Brian Staggs, a compact Freeport outfielder with a squatty stance and a caffeinated or otherwise sloshed cheering section. The program said he was nineteen. That meant that as a fifteen-year-old high school freshman, he had probably been watching Dean pitch for the Yankees. If he came from around here, there was a good chance he was a Red Sox kid. He might be batting against his adolescent mortal enemy. A lot of them might.

Staggs twitched the end of his bat. Dean held the ball at his chest. Evvie sucked her breath in and held it. There went the leg, the body, the arm, the ball. And there went Staggs rotating *his* shoulders to swing, and there went the bat in an impotent swat, and there went the ball smacking into Marco's mitt. A fat, deep, punishing punch of a sound that would have sounded great from under the bleachers. Andy bellowed beside her, Rose and Lilly clapped their hands, and Evvie exhaled.

It was one pitch. Just one. Even at his worst, he'd sometimes been able to get off one decent pitch—he'd told her so. He'd even had a couple of passable games. But he'd also told her that very often, right away, even before his problems started, he'd known whether he had his stuff or not. He talked about it as this feeling, like the way you know someone is watching you or the way you know you're getting a cold when you feel the first dry tickle in the back of your throat. She wondered whether he knew now.

The crowd had gone from revelers at a local charity event to aspiring witnesses to some flavor of history. They'd have been even louder if half of them weren't texting or tweeting or using one finger to write *Dean Tenney* in bright blue chicken scratches and draw an arrow on a grainy eight-second video of Dean getting the ball back from Marco.

And it was not just one pitch. A crowd that regularly watches good minor-league pitchers can tell when it's suddenly visited by very good major-league pitchers. Dean threw hard. Like, *hard*. His fastball was rude, thrown at guys who could only either watch it as it passed or swing at it when it already had. Staggs, Carlos Stanfield, and Mickey Cudahy all struck out. Four pitches, three pitches, and four pitches. Cudahy had been kicking around for years, and he'd even batted against Dean once years before. When the last of the four pitches to him was called a strike, Evvie saw him smile at Dean and point at him with the bat.

Dean Tenney, who had walked off the field in New York being called a fuckin' head case, walked off the field in Calcasset, Maine, being figuratively lifted onto the shoulders of 2,500 people cheering and who knew how many glued to their phones. Marco ran out and leapt at him for a righteous chest-bump that was perfectly captured by Charlotte Penney, a ninth-grader in the front row on the first-base side. Charlotte tweeted the video, which was passed on by her cousin Brenda, then by Brenda's boyfriend Steve, then by Steve's dad Rick, then by Rick's college roommate Michael McCasey, a sports journalist at a very small news site, and then by Walt Willette, a sports journalist at a very big news site. This all took four minutes.

The team surrounded him as they left the field. They patted his back, they shook his hand, and Evvie could see that they were chattering and thanking and marveling. They'd been afraid they were going to get whatever he had turned into that hadn't been Dean Tenney, but they'd gotten Dean Tenney, at least in the fourth. Brett Bradley, who played first base, leaned over as they walked toward the dugout and said something that made Dean laugh—and laugh hard, clapping Brett on the shoulder. Just as he was about to leave the field, Dean turned and looked right toward where she was, like he could see her, even though it seemed like he couldn't have. Monica leaned in front of Andy and put her hand on top of Evvie's. "Well, we couldn't have hoped for much better than that." She raised her eyebrows. "He looked amazing out there."

"Yeah, he sure did," Evvie said.

The most-shared tweet labeled #DeanTenney carried the video and said, "A very nice moment for a nice guy who's had a very bad couple of years." The second most-shared tweet carried a photo of the team around Dean, congratulating him. It said, "Congratulations, fuckwit u have 4 world series wins. u struck out 3 scrubs in an exibition [sic] in bumblefuck MAINE."

Dean spent the rest of the game in the dugout with the Claws where Evvie couldn't see him. She held Lilly on her lap for a while, she ate a pretzel, and she received a few visitors who wanted to lean over and goggle their eyes at her about whether she'd known this was going to happen. All she'd tell them was, "I had a feeling he might show up." She took out her phone and saw that Dean's name was trending pretty much everywhere, that his surprise appearance was in the list of headlines on SI.com, and that ESPN had decided in its first version of the story that Dean had been living as a "recluse," which would be news to the high school athletes whose backs he'd been slapping for the last six or seven months.

All in all, she was pretty sure that if he popped out of the dugout right now, she'd leave an Evvie-shaped puff of smoke behind as she Road-Runnered down to the field to climb him like a tree.

Andy leaned over. "You look happy," he said.

She smiled. "I am."

"I'm glad." He went back to explaining the backstory of Ginger's lighthouse to Monica, who was dividing her time between listening to that and shelling peanuts for Lilly.

Evvie picked up Dean's shirt and scooted her arms into it, pulling it tight around her and sneaking a sniff of the collar while she pretended to look at a spot on the ground. The sun was starting to slip away and leave an orange thrum behind it, and the lights in the park glowed white. A breeze blew her hair back from her cheeks, and she closed her eyes and licked pretzel salt off her lip. *Oh, that's right,* she thought. *I remember having good days.*

Twenty-Four

WHEN THE GAME was over, Evvie said good night to Andy and Monica and the girls and went and waited by Dean's truck, leaning against the driver's side door, trying to look busy on her phone. By now, the Portland paper had sent their sports reporter up, and it seemed like there would be others. Tomorrow, the motel in town would be fully booked, there wouldn't be a rental car to be found any closer than Brunswick, and she'd be back to shooing reporters off her porch. Only this time, they'd be here to take it all back. Maybe Ellen Boyd would show up with her little leather notebook to say she was sorry and apparently Dean *wasn't* drinking and maybe they *hadn't* been having an affair and maybe she *didn't* know anything. Maybe Ellen Boyd would admit that nobody called Tim Doc, and that Evvie had never threatened her, and that there was nothing wrong with Dean at all. Maybe Ellen Boyd would fall down Evvie's steps and land with her face in the flowerbed.

"Ma'am, you're leaning on my truck."

She looked up. He was the absolute picture of *hoo boy howdy* in his jeans and his Henley and a brand new Calcasset Claws jacket. She stuffed her phone into her pocket and ran toward him. "Holy shit, holy shit, holy shit," she said as she hurled herself at him. He grabbed her and she felt her toes leave the pavement, then he set her down and gave her one quick smooch right on the mouth. "I cannot believe how good you looked," she said. "I can't believe it. You looked amazing. How do you feel?"

He put his hands on the back of his neck. "I don't even know."

"Well, you should know. You should feel amazing. Those guys got up there, they never even saw it coming. I almost felt bad for them, they looked so *pitiful* and—"

"You know this was for charity, right?"

"They were *pitiful* for charity. Charitably pitiful. Nobody got close to anything you threw the whole time."

"You know it was eleven pitches, right?"

"Yes, I know it was eleven pitches. But it was eleven *great* pitches. You had your stuff, I couldn't believe it. Everybody was so excited, and so happy for you, and—"

"And we won the game."

"Right! We won the game! I forgot we won the game! I'm very happy about that, too." She bounced up and down on her toes. "I'm so proud of you. I'm *so* proud of you. Oh! And I have something for you at home."

He raised an eyebrow. "Yeah?"

She laughed and held up her index finger. "Not what I meant."

He leaned down toward her. "Okay, but can we still make out in the kitchen a little bit more? I barely got your hair messed up and then I had this thing I had to do."

"You mean . . . pitch like a superstar? You mean . . . make all these fools look like fools? You mean . . . confound the sports think-piece industry? That? That thing?"

He bent and laid his forehead against hers. He took a deep breath— the deepest, it seemed like—and sighed. "It felt good."

"To me, too," she whispered.

"It was only one inning."

"One thing at a time."

He straightened up. "Meet you back at the house?"

She nodded. They walked past each other, and as he went to the truck and she went toward her car, they both turned and looked over their left shoulders.

In the car, Evvie cranked an Avett Brothers record she hadn't listened to in almost two years. Technically, the song was about dying, but it sounded like hope: *When I lay down my fears, my hopes and my doubts; the rings on my fingers and the keys to my house; with no hard feelings . . .*

She was still in Dean's shirt, and even though the night had a clipped chill to it, she left the window halfway down as she made her way out of the parking lot. She could smell the bay's salted fog from here, and when the music was quiet, she could hear the buoys and horns, sounds of the water where people worked. It was where her dad had come every day for so long, up so early and back so late sometimes, with muck on his boots and his back so sore that he'd asked her to walk on it in her fuzzy pink socks up until she went away to college. She'd gone out on the harbor so many times that she could pick everything out on the shore from far away—the houses right on the water, the restaurant, the dock where the boys she knew had dangled their legs and fished with poles while they drank Cokes and ate Doritos.

She turned up Cherry Lane, which led her to Bancroft, and she saw Dean's truck in her rearview mirror, and she smiled. She saw her house, her wide porch with the light she'd remembered to leave on, and the driveway, where she pulled in and stopped. She could barely see Dean in the dark, and he whispered "Hey" as he got out of his truck.

"Hey yourself, ace." She leaned back against the tailgate, and he put one hand on either side of her.

"It's noisy," he said, leaning toward her.

"It's crickets."

He kissed the corner of her mouth. "Crickets and what?"

"Crickets and . . . frogs, I think."

"Let's go in?"

Evvie nodded, and he followed her up the steps. "So," she said, "I told you I had something for you." She walked through the living room to the kitchen. Opening the refrigerator, she moved the iced tea aside and took out the bottle of champagne. "In honor of your victory."

He grinned. "Aww, thanks." He took the bottle from her and looked at it, then back up at her. "What were you going to do if I bombed?"

She made a face. "That was never going to happen."

He started to unwrap the foil. "You were a fucking lot more confident than I was, then." He balled up the foil and threw it at the trash can, where it bounced off the side. "Ignore that. That doesn't count."

"Hey, could you see me? When you were pitching? Tell the truth."

"I tried, but I couldn't find you," he said, coaxing out the cork. "I knew you were there, though. I figured you were busy punching people in the face who were saying they'd heard I was crazy." There was a pop and a misty curl went up from the bottle. He filled two juice glasses.

"Well, here's to eleven pitches and lots more like them." They clinked their glasses and drank.

"So," he said.

"So."

"What made you think I wasn't going to bomb?"

Evvie shook her head a little. "I'm not even sure. I just knew."

"You know that even at my very worst, I still knew how to occasionally throw eleven decent pitches in a row, right?" He looked down into his drink.

"How often did you throw eleven that were that good? After things started to slide, I mean."

"Almost never." He took another drink.

"Well, there you go. Don't get me wrong, I believe in all the stuff they had you do. But sometimes, it's all about the intangibles."

"The intangibles, huh?"

They looked at each other. This time, she raised an eyebrow. He rubbed the back of his neck. "Oh, boy, I'm going to regret the thing I'm about to say."

Her eyes widened. "What's the matter?"

He chuckled. "Nothing's the matter. But I have to tell you the truth. I'm tired. I need about a month under a hot shower before my joints are going to work. And it sucks, because I really want to . . . hang out."

She nodded slowly. "I see. You want to hang out."

"Ev, I just . . . this was a big deal for me, you know? I feel like it might not be smart, mixing up the things that I care about not fucking up. The other thing, we have more than one day, you know?" He leaned on the sink. "Oh, boy, I'm going to regret it."

She'd woken up this morning with none of this to consider. None of it had seemed real, and now it all did. It was too much at once. "If I'm completely honest, I'm a little bit relieved." She felt the muscles in her back relax. "This was so slow, and now it's so fast, and I'm not sure I should give all the go signs on the same day." She drank the rest of her champagne and put the glass down on the table. "I mean, I married my high school sweetheart."

"I know."

Eveleth leaned forward. "And he died."

Dean looked confused. "I know. Did I say something wrong?"

"Nope." She tapped her fingers on the counter behind her.

"Ah," Dean suddenly said. "You're saying just him."

"Just him."

He shrugged. "Okay."

She pressed on. "So, I'm just saying."

"You're just saying what?"

Eveleth looked all around the room—ceiling, floor, stove, sink, cabinet, other cabinet, table—and then at him. "No warranties. Satisfaction not guaranteed."

He busted out laughing. He put one arm around her waist and pulled on her until she stepped right to him. She was very aware that he seemed to look at her hairline, then her ear, then her cheek, and then her mouth, before he looked her right in the eye. "I'm not worried," he whispered. And then he kissed her. The first one had been crazy, the second one had been quick, but this felt like the one that had been coming since they met. Kissing Dean was a lot like talking to him: it was easy. Well, it was easy and it made her want to rip her clothes off. So, still similar.

"Maybe we should have a date," he finally said.

"We already live together," she said, looking at him sideways. "I don't think you can go on a date with someone you live with."

"We don't live together," he said. "You're going up there"—he pointed—"and I'm going in there." He pointed again. "That is not living together. Let me take you out."

"Out where?"

He thought for a minute, tapping his finger on her hip. "Just dinner. Like regular people. Wherever you want."

"That's a good offer," she said. "But maybe we should stay in. I don't want everybody to gossip. It's weird. You know I hate . . . people talking. We can order in. You usually hang out in the kitchen. We'll eat in the living room."

"I can do better than that," he said. "What if we go out of town? Someplace where nobody's going to care?"

"You're pretty hot news right now. I'm not sure where that place would be."

"I'll figure it out. Someplace small, someplace we can drive to." He pushed a lock of hair off her forehead. "Let me take you out," he repeated.

She looked up at him, at his green eyes—gold flecks, thick lashes, such a stupid abundance of good genes—and that little scar he had. She said, "I would love that. When should we go?"

He smiled. "Good. I have to run practice after school Monday-Tuesday-Wednesday, so how about Thursday? Thursday dinner. We'll leave at five since we're going on the road." She nodded, and he reached out and kissed the tip of her nose. "All right, Minnesota.

Thank you again for everything. Fuck Freeport, and back at it Thursday."

She frowned as he headed for the apartment. " 'Back at it'?"

He called out, "Or whatever," and he shut his door. Apparently, a sense of mystery now had to be maintained.

Twenty-Five

THE NEXT DAY, Evvie called her father and asked if she could bring him some take-out chowder for dinner from Sophie's. She'd spent the morning reading amazed news reports about how noted failure Dean Tenney had emerged in some tiny hamlet in Maine and pitched, for at least one inning, like he used to. Ellen Boyd had weighed in, as a matter of fact, referring to Dean's reappearance as "miraculous, grading on a curve of Major League Baseball to exhibition games to raise money for the local PTA." Eveleth hated the word "bitch" and tried to never use it herself, but she understood in occasional moments why other people liked it.

Her dad, of course, was delighted to have a visit, and when she pulled up a little after six, she saw him standing behind the screen door before she even got out of her car. Paper bag in hand, she climbed out and walked up the cracked stones to him. "Hey, Pop."

"Hello, sweetheart." He opened the screen door, and she leaned in and kissed him on the cheek.

"I got soup," she told him, holding up the bag.

"Well, I got an appetite."

He still ate at the kitchen table in the same house where she grew up. He wasn't much of a decorator, so his house was a collection of old things, new things that replaced old things when they finally gave out, and new things that he sometimes allowed Eveleth to give him without objecting. He'd said nothing to her as often as he said "Keep your money" once Tim became a doctor.

"Did you have fun at the game yesterday?" Her dad had been with buddies in a row of lawn chairs by left field.

"Are you kiddin' me? Best Dance I ever went to. Weather was perfect."

"The weather *was* perfect."

"Won the game." He waited for her to nod. "Didn't expect to see Dean out there throwing."

She smiled as they sat down across from each other. "No, that was sort of a surprise. I'm sorry I couldn't tell you. It's tricky, with all the attention, and with the press and everybody. He wanted to give it a shot and see how it went."

"He's feeling good about it?"

"Sure, yeah." She was trying not to smile too much. And not in too telling a way, not that her father was especially likely to notice.

"Well, he's lucky he's got you rootin' for him. And I'm glad you've got company in that big house. I don't like you being by yourself so much."

She blew on a spoonful of thick, salty chowder and popped it into her mouth. Sophie's had opened only a few years ago, but it was already in all the magazines that wrote up the region for summer tourists. "Well, you know, I don't like you being by yourself so much either," she said.

"I'm an old man," he said, opening a plastic packet of oyster crackers and dumping them into his bowl. "You're a beautiful girl. I don't want you rattling around that place forever. And if you pardon me saying so, Tim wouldn't want that for you either."

She stopped with her spoon in her hand and looked at her father's freckled hands, decorated all over with little scars. Over his shoulder, on the counter, she could see a tray with his bottles of pills for back pain, for blood pressure, for high cholesterol. Her own hand was soft and pale. "Pop, did you ever think about getting married again? After?"

"Married? No. I met people, of course."

She remembered no one. "You did?"

He looked at her and raised his eyebrows. "Your mother left when I was thirty-three years old. What'd you think I did? Talk to the lobsters for twenty-five years?"

"But nobody special?"

"I didn't say nobody special. I said nobody I thought about getting married to. You gotta remember, sweetheart, I was working on a boat every day. We didn't have a lot, and it didn't leave a lot of time for dates."

Eveleth smiled, but then her mind flashed on a picture of herself and her dad that had been taken when she was about nine. She was holding a fish, her hair in pigtails, while he crouched with his arm around her waist. "And you had a daughter."

"Sure," he said. But then he looked up at her expression. "You listen, though, that had nothin' to do with it. You were my best part. You still are. Don't get any ideas."

"Still," she said, "it would have been a lot for anybody to take on, probably."

"You're talking crazy," he said. "What kind of a nut would want to live with me and not you? It's more likely my fault you never got a stepmother." He took a bite. "I've been happy. Lucky and happy my whole life. That's how I want it for you."

"I know, Pop. I'm trying." She put down her spoon. "Can I ask you a question? It's a little personal."

"All right."

"How did you know what to do after she was gone?"

He got quiet. Eventually, he folded his hands in front of him and looked at her. "I guess I kept gettin' out of bed. At first, I felt a little bit like how you feel. I know it's different, Tim being really *gone*. But I got up and I went to work, and you went to school. I didn't sit around and think about it. Might have been good I was busy, I suppose. And then I'd get home, and we'd eat. We couldn't stop, so we kept going."

"Did you know why she left? I mean, did it help at all?"

"Your mom was never happy up here. She wanted to be someplace bigger, I think. With more people. But she never told me she was thinking about anything like leaving on a Tuesday before we were awake, if that's the question. The only thing I know is it was nothing about you. She loved you."

This, Eveleth firmly believed, was his training kicking in. Somewhere, he'd read how important it was to reassure her that it wasn't her fault, and he'd never stopped, and he never would. *Nothing about you, nothing about you, nothing about you.* But this, she had always feared, could not possibly be true. Her mother had decided that Calcasset with her daughter was not as good as Florida without her daughter. It meant *something*.

Eileen had left on a Tuesday, and when Eveleth had awakened that morning, she'd sat down at the breakfast table to find her father making eggs instead of her mother, when normally he'd be gone already. He'd been wildly excited the night before, because he'd finally bought the boat he always wanted. His very own boat that he could work himself. His own business. It had seemed like something was starting. But now, he looked gray and drawn.

She'd asked where Mom was, and he'd said, "She went for a walk." It was years before he told her that on that day, when he woke up, there was a letter on the bedside table next to him, and that it started with the words *Dear Frank, I'm sorry but*, and that it had taken him hours to decide to read the rest.

That night, "she went for a walk" became "she went away for a while," and after a week, Frank told his daughter that Eileen had decided that she should live in Florida, and they should stay in their house. Evvie only knew Florida as the place where Walt Disney World was. So to her, this meant her mother was going to be at Walt Disney World all the time, and who could argue with that?

At first, she asked often when they were going to see Mom in Florida, or when Mom was coming to see them. She thought of them as a family with two homes, as if Pompano Beach were her parents' pied-à-terre. It took two months of not seeing her mother before she fully absorbed the idea that she now lived with her father the way Heidi, in a book Frank had begun reading to her at night, lived with her grandfather in the Alps.

The first time she'd heard that it wasn't her fault that her mother had left was on her tenth birthday, when she first asked whether it was. After she'd blown out the candles on a cat-shaped birthday cake from Specialty Sweets and pulled the red paper and white ribbon off a box with a new winter coat from her father in it, she'd picked up the card that Eileen had sent. She almost never got mail, so she loved seeing her own name written above their address, and she knew the handwriting from reading and rereading a long letter her mother had sent her about her abandoned ambitions, which Evvie had barely understood. It said things like "I was a very talented dancer! But a lot of things can get in the way of that, and that made me sad. I knew that if I was an unhappy person, I couldn't be a good mom!"

I am named after my mother's unhappiness.

On the front of the card was a Scottie dog, and when Evvie opened it, on the inside it said, "Hope your birthday is through the woof." Eileen had written, "Love, Mom." Just "Love, Mom." This card had been in the blue suitcase on the night of Tim's accident, when Kell saw it in the back of Evvie's car.

Evvie had shown the card to her dad and said, "She didn't even write 'Happy birthday.'"

Frank had taken the card from her and looked at it all over. "No," he'd said tightly. "She sure didn't." But then he pointed to the pre-printed writing. "Well, it says 'birthday' there. Maybe she didn't want to say it again." He squeezed Evvie's shoulder.

"I think she's mad at me," Evvie told her dad, laying the card on top of the coat.

"She's not mad at you," Frank had said evenly. "I promise you, you hear me? She's not mad at you."

Evvie had felt herself starting to cry and dug her fingers into her palms. "Then why doesn't she come home?"

He'd led her into the living room and they'd sat down next to each other on the beat-up green couch. "Your mom," he started, "is down there thinking about a lot of things. But she loves you, Eveleth. She didn't leave because of you." He put his hand on his daughter's cheek. "That's important."

Eveleth had looked down and said to him in something of a choked voice, "I'd never leave."

"Me neither," Frank had told her. Then he tapped her under the chin so she'd look him in the eye. "Hey. Me neither."

Her fortunes were a mixed bag: widow with a huge house, no real job, a semidetached best friend, and what seemed to be an appointment in three days to have sex with one of the best pitchers of the last twenty years. But she was smart enough to know that maybe her most important lucky break was one of her first: that when he'd told her "me neither," he meant it. And now, looking at him eating a bowl of good chowder, ignoring the sore back she knew he had almost all the time, she could only hope to be as good to him. "I love you, Pop."

He reached over and squeezed her fingers. "I love you, too, honey."

Twenty-Six

O N THURSDAY, EVVIE gave Dean a cup of coffee in the morning and he kissed her goodbye on the forehead. And then, as he headed out the door, he said, "Five o'clock, right?"

She nodded. "Five o'clock."

"Be ready to go."

"I'll be ready. I hope you picked out someplace good."

"Oh, I did. Bring a bag in case we stay over. Also, I have a proposition."

Evvie snorted. "I'll bet."

"You have a dirty mind," he said in a low voice. "What I meant is that I propose that this dinner is back on old rules. No husband, no baseball."

"All right, agreed."

"So anything you have, get it out of your system now."

"Okay. Wait: my husband was a jerk."

"Well, sometimes I watch myself strike people out on YouTube."

"All right, good enough. Now go to school. Teenagers are waiting for you to mold their character."

When he was gone, she went upstairs and into her closet, where she'd stashed a white bag with elegant black letters that said CATHE-RINE'S. This was a lingerie boutique that, in fact, Monica had recommended to her via text after being sworn to secrecy.

Weird question: do you have a favorite place for pretty lacy things? I'm looking to upgrade and I haven't shopped in ages.

YES. Go to Catherine's in Bangor. Worth the trip. Beautiful not trashy, good for everyday and special occasions. There was a winky face. She couldn't blame Monica for the winky face. She deserved the winky face.

Thank you. PLEASE don't tell Andy I asked you about this.

Monica had texted back the smiley face with the zippered mouth.

Well, it certainly qualified as a special occasion, if being a special occasion had anything to do with having been neglected for so long on this front that she'd pretty much forgotten whatever moves she'd ever had, not that she'd ever had much call for moves. She'd picked out a pink two-piece set, a red set, and a black set, and she'd handwashed them all in the sink in Woolite the previous day, then hung them to dry and put them back in the bag in the closet, as if she were quarantining their wickedness away from the rest of the apparel, lest her sweatshirts be scandalized. She picked out the black ones and laid them on the bed.

In the afternoon, she sat in the tub, shaving and trimming various zones with a precision she'd previously associated with building ships in bottles, then slathering everything with lotion. Wishing she'd had a pedicure, she scraped at her softened heels with a pumice stone and sprayed her feet with a peppermint foot spray.

Out of the tub, she wrapped up in a robe and went downstairs, where she ate a peanut butter sandwich in her bare feet and tried to relax. In September it would be two years since Tim had died, which meant she hadn't had any sex of any kind in even longer than that, and she hadn't had any with anyone except Tim, ever. She hadn't thought about it all that much until recently—it was part of widowhood, part of not being a wife anymore, and it was all wrapped up with her other questions about what she should do now that everything she'd planned originally and also everything she'd planned as her escape had evaporated.

She remembered wondering in that first December whether this meant that she would never have sex again. What if nobody else had any interest? What if she just didn't feel like it, forever? What if there was a rule she hadn't read that required her to abstain until Tim's parents died? What if the town passed a resolution to encase her in glass and prop her up in front of the post office as her late husband's memorial installation?

It was sometime after the peanut butter sandwich when she decided to do something stupid. She opened her laptop and googled "Dean Tenney girlfriend." Then she clicked on "Images."

"Oh, fuuuuuuuuuuuck," she said softly. She'd known about Melanie Kopps, the actress he'd been seen with right before the end of his career. She was a redhead, with super-pale skin and eyebrows that looked like she won them playing poker with Audrey Hepburn's ghost. In one picture, she clung to Dean's arm in a green dress that plunged almost to her waist, which was to say almost to what there was of her waist. But here, too, was a picture of Dean with a professional surfer, who was blond with powerful shoulders and a splash of freckles. And then Dean with a singer named Bev Bo, who was famous for mixing gentle vocals with an electric cello. She was also really, *really* beautiful, with dark skin and gorgeous black hair.

Evvie slammed the computer shut and went to the bathroom mirror. She had two acne scars on her forehead. She had one slightly dark spot of undetermined origin on her cheek that a dermatologist had assured her was not lying in wait to kill her. Her nose was slightly crooked, and her front teeth were, too. Through the robe, she poked herself in the softness of her belly with all her fingers. She put her hands on the sides of her waist and sucked in her breath. She had tree-trunk legs, according to a girl who'd been briefly in her class in ninth grade, and while she'd always been reasonably satisfied with her boobs, they already weren't quite as satisfactory as they'd been when she was twenty.

Evvie leaned in close to the mirror. She picked up tweezers from a little silver tray and squinted. As always, tweezing her left eyebrow made her sneeze, but she cleaned up the space between her brows, the parts where little straggler hairs kind of disorganizedly wandered toward her temples, and some that just didn't belong where they were, like calves somehow separated from the herd. She rubbed her face with a cream cleanser, hoping it wasn't the kind with plastic beads that were bad for dolphins or turtles or whatever it was, and she followed it with a moisturizer that promoted itself as "revitalizing." She hadn't yet turned to "anti-aging," but she figured "revitalizing" was for over thirty and under forty, "anti-aging" was for over forty and under seventy, and then when you were seventy, you just told everybody to fuck off. She put three drops of an eye serum under each eye, because eye skin was apparently not made of regular skin, and she slicked her lips with a balm she suspected was secretly made in the same factory as ChapStick, but at the end of the mixing process, instead of pouring it into a tube, they poured it into a little round plastic thing, added a drop of vanilla, and sold it for sixteen dollars.

Her hair had a natural curl to it, which she'd battled intermittently for a few years in high school after she overheard her grandmother Ashton telling her exhausted father that he ought to do something about "that rat's nest." Aw, Gran, rest her soul, preferably in a highly judgmental salon waiting area forever and ever. Sometimes Evvie blew her hair out straight when she was dressing up—back when she dressed up, that is—but if she did it now, it would look like she was trying too hard, wouldn't it? The idea here was to look like she *happened* to be a sex goddess, not like she spent the *entire day* on it. So she settled for a curl-taming lotion and hoped for the best.

And then, to the closet. She picked through a drawer full of jeans until she found her nicest and darkest ones, the straight-leg pair that she considered the most flattering. She put them on the bed and started sifting through hangers in her closet. She had a black slouchy top with a ribbed waistband, and a black wrap top that tied at the side, and a lightweight short-sleeved sweater. Without knowing where they were going, it seemed awfully hard to pick. The idea was to achieve a result that was only possible with sustained effort, but without giving the appearance of any effort at all. She could not look like she was not trying. She could not look like she was trying.

She pulled out the sweater and laid it on the bed. But what about a whole different approach? What if she wore her Decemberists concert shirt? Wouldn't that be casual? Wouldn't that be effortless? He'd come home, and she'd be padding around the kitchen in her—no, that would be different jeans, and not nice enough for dinner, and *for the love of God,* she thought, *just pick something.* So she slipped out of the robe and shimmied into the black underwear and wiggled everything that belonged in it into the black bra, and then she slipped on the jeans and the sweater and gave her hair a toss. She was almost done. Almost.

She went back into the bathroom and took out her little makeup bag. Foundation would be too much; she'd look made-up. She wasn't sure Dean had ever seen her in a whole made-up face before; what if he thought it was weird? She was pretty sure this was a sex date; what if something got on the pillow? How old was this bottle, anyway? No, no, just a little powder and a little blush, and a little mascara. Oh lord, how old was this mascara? She probably shouldn't use it, because she had definitely not bought mascara since her husband died (a handy but grim way to date her perishables), but she dabbed it on anyway and promised internally that she would buy new eye makeup before the next time she had sex.

"I'm an adult woman," she said to herself in the mirror. "This is stupid."

She wandered downstairs and into the living room, where she plunked down on her sofa and pulled the *Sports Illustrated* out of the pile of magazines next to her. She noticed that, up in the corner, there was a little square of the photo of Dean and Marco chest-bumping, and a headline across the top that said, "Not So Fast: Is There Life in Baseball's Exiled 'Head Case'?"

She found the little article inside, which included a shot of Dean sitting in the dugout three years earlier. His elbow rested on his knee, his cap was in his hand, there was a little bit of sweat on his forehead. She leaned down close to it to look at his eyes. The piece referred to him as "troubled" and "once-brilliant" and "dynamic." Searching his face, having known him for all these months, Eveleth could think only about how *hot* he was.

Oh, *boy*, he was hot. He was . . . he was smart, and he was sharp and funny, and he'd been so kind to her, and he was a good tenant, and he was a good ballplayer, and he was good with Andy's kids and Andy's mom and Eveleth's dad. He was supportive of the town, and he had helped Evvie's neighbors shovel their driveways once when it snowed a foot and a half overnight in January. He made good French toast (his new specialty) and a solid grilled cheese, and he was . . . well, he was getting better at pinball. But God almighty, he was hot. When he'd kissed her the other day, it was like everything between her chest and her knees made that noise she'd made when he showed her his tattoo: that noise, *buuuuuuuh*.

She went into the kitchen and took down a bottle of wine that she'd picked up the day before while driving back from Catherine's (which she'd been calling Catherine's House of Presentable Brassieres in her head for the last twenty-four hours). She peeled away the foil and dug out her corkscrew. It took a little wiggling, but she got it open and glugged a little into a glass. She was leaning on the sink, the glass to her mouth, when she heard the key in the side door. It swung open and he stepped in with a duffel on his shoulder.

"Hey," he said with a grin. "You look cute. Ready to go?"

They drove about an hour and a half, until they pulled up in front of the Stafford Hotel, tucked into one of the high-end coastal pockets of wealth nestled in between the working marinas and former factory towns. Inside, the hotel restaurant was quiet and dark, but not stuffy, and they slid into a dark-leather booth. "This is nice," Evvie said. "Who hooked you up with this place?"

"You know how I hate the Internet?"

Evvie nodded. "I know it well, yes."

"It's pretty good at restaurants."

A waitress dropped off menus. "I have to ask you," Evvie said, "whether it's a coincidence that this restaurant is in a hotel."

Dean squinted at her for a minute. "I have no idea what you're implying."

There was bread on the table, and some kind of acoustic indie music hanging in the cozy and mostly empty dining room. And as she dipped a hunk of bread in olive oil, he poured her a glass of red wine from the bottle he'd asked for. "So school's almost over," she said. "Are you sad it's ending?"

"Very," he said. "Did I tell you that Krista Cassidy is going to Purdue on a track scholarship? I ran into her the other day and asked her how she was, and she lays this on me. I never liked high school kids when I was one, but I'm going to miss these guys."

"Well, they'll get to tell everyone they know you, which I have a feeling is going to become a pretty good perk."

Dean raised his glass. "Okay. To . . . all the great things we're going to do."

Her glass dinged against his and they drank. "And to the fact that if modern technology helped you find dinner, it can't be all bad. Maybe you'll invent a restaurant-finding app for people who don't want to run into anyone they know."

"God, please punch me if I ever tell you I want to build an app. Punch me if I tell you I want to give somebody else money for an app. Or a start-up of any kind. My dad made me promise I wouldn't give any more money to anybody in a hoodie."

"Why?"

"I used to be a real sucker for guys who were going to make the world better. No-carbon-footprint vegan chicken tenders, recycling plastic bottles into raincoats, just . . . you name a guy whose fuckin' tech idea has a green logo or whose business plan says he can turn shit into not-shit, and I probably gave him money."

"Why?"

"It beat buying cars. It was a different time, I guess."

"You know, speaking of that, I have to tell you something," Evvie said. "I googled your girlfriends."

"Ah," he said. "You have questions."

"They were all very pretty."

"That's not a question."

"No, it's an observation."

"So," he said. "You saw Melanie Kopps, she's the redhead. An actress. My mom mentioned her. She was a very nice girl."

"Woman."

"Exactly," he said. "Very nice woman. That was my most recent relationship. I dated her for about two years, and we broke up right at the end of my career. Bad breakup, unfortunately."

Evvie frowned. "Because of the career stuff?"

Dean shook his head. "Not directly. It wasn't the best time in the world to be spending a lot of time with me. I was doing all these treatments, I was a grump all the time. Plus people blamed her, and I couldn't do anything about it. But I liked her very much. Who else do you want to ask me about?"

"You dated a surfer."

"Lindsay," he said. "That was a while ago. She was an athlete, so she got some of the weird stuff about me that women sometimes didn't. Liked her a lot, too. That one had a very normal ending, right when I went to the Yankees. She was religious; it was a huge thing with her. And I grew up, you know, as a Christmas and Easter Presbyterian, and we couldn't pull it together. It was only going to get worse if we got more serious."

"And you dated Bev Bo."

"That was about a year, year and a half, but on and off. That was before Melanie. Bev was just getting established. She was touring a lot—not high-end touring back then, but more like back-of-a-van touring. We'd meet up for these very hot weekends, but then we'd go off in different directions. That relationship got me through my first year in New York. She might be the smartest woman I ever dated. She majored in music theory in college."

"Did you learn anything?"

"About music theory, no. But come to think of it, I did learn that dirty texting is too fuckin' embarrassing for me. I know everybody does it now, but I swear, the most boring things you do during sex sound totally deviant if you type them out. You've done something all your adult life and when you write it down, it's like, 'Who would *do* that?' I remember trying to describe how I would kiss her shoulder— her fuckin' shoulder!—and I felt like a farmer talking about how to knock up a horse. I might just be bad at it, though. Describing, not kissing." He paused. "Are you blushing?"

"No," she said. "I'm paying close attention."

"Very wise, very wise," he said. "Have you ever transcribed dirty talk?"

"I don't know what you consider 'dirty,'" she said. "I transcribed an interview with a guy who was studying the female orgasm, but he had a way of making it sound like a . . . like a red wine."

"Hm. Tell me more."

"I'm not sure he was exactly a scientist. He had all these descriptive words for, you know, orgasms. He called different ones 'hearty' and 'vibrant' or 'light' and 'superficial.'"

"With oaky undertones," he said.

"Right? It was very odd to me. But I wrote it all down. Weirdos are gonna weirdo. They're part of the job."

"I bet you read a lot when you were a kid," Dean said, tilting his head a bit and, she was sure, picturing her as a funny little nerd, which she had, after all, been.

"I did," she said. "But to be honest, my other big thing was the radio. My dad was out fishing six days a week for a lot of the year. He'd be gone from maybe five in the morning until dinner. Including all summer when I wasn't in school. And once my mom left, that meant I was by myself a lot. We didn't have cable, and we didn't get very good reception, so I didn't watch a lot of TV. I loved the radio, though. I didn't even listen to things that were that good. I'd listen to this medical advice show, and people would call in and ask about things I didn't know *anything* about, like bunions or goiters. I remember asking my dad what tennis elbow was when I was maybe ten, and he didn't know either. I just listened, even if I didn't really understand. Which is why, by the way, when I was in sixth grade, I wrote a story about a girl named Chlamydia. None of it meant anything to me, but every time there was a new person on the radio talking, it was like they could say anything. Anything could happen. There was a psychologist who would talk about grieving or divorce, which I thought was totally interesting but didn't get. And I listened to a lot of news. All this public affairs stuff, local news. I liked hearing people talk."

"And you still do," he said.

"I never thought about it that way, but yes, I guess so. And I learn a lot. When . . . well, when I lived in California, I transcribed exam review sessions for this guy who was studying aging skin. I practically bathed in sunscreen for the next five years."

"Well, your skin looks good to me."

She squirmed, and then she frowned. "I'm normal, you know. I hope you're not expecting that I'm secretly an actress or a surfer under here."

"Evvie?"

"Yes."

"I know who you are. I have for sure given some thought to what's under there, but I do not wish you were an actress or a surfer."

"Have you dated a normal person before?"

"You mean ever?" he said. "Yes. Of course. I have dated a good number of what I think you would consider 'normal people.' Google might not know about them, though. But you're right that I've dated some women who are better known in the last few years."

"Is there a rule that once you're famous, you can only date people who are also famous?"

"There is not," he said slowly. "It's more like . . . once I was a public person, it got harder being around a lot of people who weren't. That makes me sound like such a jerk—it's not because I was so cool or awesome or anything. It's just because it was weird being the only person there who everybody knew about. Once you can't walk into a room and assume people don't know who you are or what you do, it's easier if everybody else is in the same position. I didn't like being in rooms where somebody would ask eight people in a row what they do and then say, 'Well, I know who *you* are.' So the way it worked out, even though I'd rather have been, I don't know, hanging out with friends and watching TV, I'd wind up at a vodka launch party. And at a vodka launch party, you meet a particular kind of a person."

Evvie leaned forward. "A what party?"

"You know. 'We're debuting our new, whatever, peanut butter vodka, and we're having a party at some club that's going to be dark and loud as fuck, and everybody's going to be screaming in each other's ears, and it will take ten minutes to get a drink at the bar and you'll be behind some walking wad of grease trying to sell a screenplay, but the good news is that all your booze is free as long as you drink our new vodka, which probably tastes like Mr. Peanut's back sweat.'"

"Is there really peanut butter vodka?"

"If there isn't, it's not because it's too stupid for somebody to launch with a party."

"I think of parties as a good thing. That doesn't seem to be your experience."

"In, I think, 2014," he said, "I went to a St. Patrick's Day party in a warehouse that was so crowded that a woman poured an entire green beer down my back. I'll bet whatever you were doing up here was a lot more fun than that."

Evvie looked at the ceiling, trying to remember. "I think in March 2014, we were negotiating the bill for my dad's back surgery so he could keep his house."

It was quiet. Dean put down his glass. He put one hand on his chest. "I am an asshole. I'm sorry."

"You are not," she said, reaching over and resting her hand on his wrist. "That wasn't fair." She sat back up. "We've just lived differently. I mean, I'm not particularly glamorous, Dean. This is . . ." She looked down at herself. "This is about as good as I get."

"Are you trying to talk me out of being into you?" Dean asked, fixing her with a stare. "Because it's not going to work. I'm *very* into you right now. Very."

Buuuuuuuh. "Good," she managed to say.

"Speaking of which." He produced from his pocket a key on a ring with a round brass tag. He laid it down on the table. "This is for Room 208, which is upstairs."

Evvie leaned forward to look at the key but didn't touch it. "Wow, a real key. I thought everybody used plastic cards now. Very classy." She didn't know if she was supposed to say more. "I bet it's nice."

"Well, that's not for you," Dean said. "I'm in 208." He reached into his pocket again. He slid another key onto the table. "This is 204. Across the hall."

Evvie raised her eyebrows. "You got separate rooms," she said. "You're serious. You seriously got separate rooms."

His eyes flicked around the restaurant, and he fidgeted with his key. "I—I get that we're not nineteen or anything," he said. "But I figure I'll hang out, and I'll wait. And, you know. Consider yourself invited over."

She looked at a strand of his hair that curled against his ear. "You got separate rooms," she repeated.

"It seemed like it was going to be slick when I first thought of it," he muttered toward the table, and then he looked back up at her. "Now I'm not sure. This feels like a weak move. Is this a weak move? This is a weak move, right?"

Evvie picked up her key and turned it over in her hand. "No, I think it's hot."

They looked directly at each other, and Evvie briefly considered grabbing both keys off the table, hooking her fingers through Dean's belt loops, and dragging him upstairs so fast that he'd still be holding his wineglass when she ripped his shirt off. But just then, the waitress reappeared, and she realized that neither of them had given a moment of thought to what they were going to eat.

Twenty-Seven

EVENTUALLY, THEY ORDERED, and they ate, and the place got a little bit more crowded. Evvie avoided anything with too much garlic, out of courtesy. After Dean paid the check, they sat and stared at the keys that were on the table. He reached out and pulled 208 toward himself. She did the same with 204. "You go up," he said, "and I'll bring your bag in from the car, okay?"

"Deal," Evvie said. There was a wide staircase that went to the second floor, and her room was a few steps from the top of it. The lock clunked open satisfyingly, and she swung the door open. A king bed, a dresser, a TV on the wall, and a desk with a vase of roses. She went and lay on the bed, not even slipping off her black flats. She waited to be uncertain, but she was just twitchy, jumpy, waiting for him to knock.

And then he did. "Oh, hello," she said as he extended her bag toward her. "Thank you very much. Excellent service."

He looked around her room. "Very nice."

"Thank you for the flowers."

"I know they're a cliché."

"For good reason." As he stood in her doorway, she was struck once again by how tall he was. "You didn't have to do this."

"I know," he said. "But now it's going to be very exciting for me when you knock on my door in a few minutes."

"You seem confident."

He leaned down until he was only maybe an inch from her. *His eyes are as green as a spring leaf* flitted across her mind, unbidden and brutally corny and completely true, as he looked lazily at her mouth. "I'm . . . an optimist."

She went up on her toes to kiss him and then looked up and down the hall. "I'm not going to make out with you in the hallway," she said, "because people will stare at us. Now you get over there. And don't fall asleep."

"You have to believe me, Ev. I'm not going to fall asleep." He pulled away from her and disappeared into the room across the hall, and she closed her door.

In the bathroom, Evvie brushed her hair. As she leaned into the mirror and reached up to swipe a speck of something off her cheek, she saw the glint of her rings. Her simple gold band and her diamond solitaire had rarely budged since her wedding. When she tugged on them, they eased over her knuckle and left a ghost stripe across her finger. For a minute she looked down at her hand, her own plain hand, looking like it had when she was eighteen, give or take fifteen years of sun. She set the rings on the vanity and slipped off her shoes. Barefoot, she opened her door and sneaked across the empty hall to 208. She knocked twice.

"Who is it?"

"You know who it is."

"What's the password?"

"Advice and consent."

There was a pause. Then, through a grin she could hear in his voice, he said, "It's open."

She went into the room and closed the door behind her, then leaned back against it. Dean was sitting on the bed in his white

T-shirt and jeans, with his back against the headboard and his bare feet stretched out in front of him. "Hi there," she said.

"Oh, hello, nice to see you," he said.

She grinned and moved fast, crawling up onto the bed beside him and wrapping her arms around his neck, kissing him in a way that made her feel greedy and great. She couldn't count the times she'd managed to touch his shoulder, his back, his elbow, his hip—all innocent in theory, but all because she wanted this, this very thing. She slid her hand up under his shirt and he obligingly peeled it right off, demonstrating nothing if not a dexterity that made her instantly grateful for the otherwise kind-of-boring world of professional sports. His fingers crept under the edge of her sweater, but then he paused. He pulled back from her, slightly out of breath, and gazed into her eyes. "What?" she asked. A beat, then another. He kept looking at her. Suddenly, she clapped her hand down on his bare shoulder so hard that it sounded like a slap. "Oh!" she said. "Go. Yes. Go, definitely. Definitely, go."

He smiled, looking almost shy, and she helped unbutton the sweater and push it back off her shoulders until it fell. He picked up her hand, and he looked down at her fingers, at the ghost stripe, which he kissed. When he let go, she reached out and rested her hand on his right shoulder, where he always rubbed it like it hurt. She let it rest there, then drew her hand down his arm until their fingers tangled together.

When she would think about it later—and she did—it was like someone had spliced together a second or two of a movie at a time, perfectly clear but disjointed and maybe not in order. He had kissed the palm of her hand at one point, which had surprised her. She had pulled off the last of her clothes awkwardly, lying on her back, getting her foot stuck in the leg of her jeans and yanking at them while he teased her: "Get back here. You can leave that if you want. I can work around it."

"This is going to go slower if you make me laugh."

Evvie had expected to be self-conscious, feeling air and breath on all of her skin, knowing he was mapping her for the first time, but she wasn't. She managed to keep her mind inside her body for once. Maybe even briefly subservient to it.

She could remember she heard herself gasp, and that she reached up to wipe sweat off his forehead. She remembered seeing her hair slide across his bare shoulder. Eagerness bred clumsiness: she got him in the thigh with her knee, he accidentally elbowed her in the stomach, and when he did, she laughed and he kissed her brow bone.

"Is your stomach gurgling?" "Did you crack your knuckle?" "Do you have enough room?" "Are you okay?" "Definitely okay."

It was different, that was for sure.

She never messed up the sheets in 204. They fell asleep, and when they found they were both awake at three in the morning, they lay with their faces inches apart and whispered about a dream she'd had about *Halls of Power*. She said she was cold, and he found his T-shirt and gave it to her. He smoothed her hair, and they dozed off.

She woke up again a little after five thirty, and she turned over to find Dean flat on his back, dead asleep, visible by the slivers of street-lights coming in through the slats in the blinds. She would not be one of those women who watched someone sleep, she thought. It was creepy. So she closed her eyes and listened instead to the inhale and the exhale, the trading of air for air without effort. She synced her breath to it, and she went back to sleep.

The next time she opened her eyes, it was light outside and he was awake, staring at the ceiling. She stretched, and he turned to look at her. "Hey."

"Hey," she said, sitting up in bed to lean toward her toes and stretch out her back. He scratched lightly between her shoulder blades.

"Did you sleep okay?"

"Yeah."

He extended his arm behind her, and she curled up and settled back down, resting on his chest with her arm across his ridiculous abs. It was not a terrible place to lie down, all things considered.

"So," she finally said.

"So." He picked up her hand that was resting on his tattoo and idly played with her fingers.

"I think I hurt my hip," she said.

"Seriously?" He froze. "Are you okay?"

"No, no." She laughed. "I'm fine, stop. It's just . . . have you ever worked out with a new trainer?"

He looked at her. "I don't know how I feel about you forgetting I was a professional athlete at this particular moment."

"Good point," she said. "Anyway, I think it's like that."

"It's absolutely not like that. What gym are you going to?"

"I've been working out alone, mostly, if you get my drift."

"Well," he said, throwing an arm over her, "I appreciate you leaving it all on the field. I hope it was worth it."

"Yes, completely worth it," she said. She looked gravely into his eyes. "Hearty, with oaky undertones." They laughed in their barely awake hoarse voices, and she kissed him on the shoulder. "What time is it?"

He checked his phone. "8:27."

"So, what now?"

"Checkout time is eleven," he said. "I need a shower. They have breakfast downstairs, I think."

Evvie turned her head to look at him. "That's not what I meant."

"Ah," Dean said.

"I mean, I'm not trying to start a status conversation. No big status conversations before everybody's got their clothes on and had coffee—I feel like that's a good rule. I'm just not sure even where you want to sleep tomorrow and stuff like that, that's all I mean."

There was a pause. It might have been the longest pause ever, she thought. It felt like tides went in and out, planes took off and landed, buildings were built before he talked. "I like you a lot," he said.

"Well, good, I like you a lot, too."

"And you live here, and I live in New York."

"Right."

"I've got to admit, I haven't thought about it much farther ahead than that."

"Sure," she said. *What does being completely chill sound like when you don't have any pants on?* She sat up and swiveled around so she was lying back on her pillow. "I do think it might be better if we kept it between us."

"You don't want to tell Andy."

"I don't want to tell anybody. You're not staying. And my dad and Kell and Andy and whoever, if they know all this, they'll think that you're staying, or that I'm leaving. I think it's . . . better to skip it all. Besides, right now, there's not anything to tell except, you know, this. It's not like you're my prom date."

"I could bring you a corsage next time."

"Hey, don't make promises you're not going to keep." She stretched her arms straight up in the air. "I have weird fingers. Do you see how they're crooked?"

He scooted his head over next to hers on the pillow. "They look like fingers."

She folded her arms back over her body. "You don't know what it's like being a mortal."

"Hey, you should see inside my elbow. It looks like everything looks at the beginning of *WALL-E*."

"*WALL-E* the cartoon?"

"Yeah, when the whole world is trash and bent metal and beat-up shit. That's what the inside of pitchers' elbows looks like. I had an MRI once and the doctor said, 'I have good news and bad news, and the good news is that your bones are still attached everywhere they're supposed to be attached. The bad news is everything else.'"

She paused. "What do they do if your bones aren't still attached?"

"They do surgery. They use a tendon from your leg and tie your arm bones together."

"You're lying."

"I am not lying. If that doesn't work, they use part of a dead body."

"They do not."

"They absolutely do. They do it on teenagers."

"Wait, how do you tie a bone to something?"

"They drill a hole in it and loop it through."

"Oh my God."

"Oh, it's disgusting." He rubbed his elbow just thinking about it. "You ever broken a bone?"

"When I was eight, I jumped off a picnic table and broke my arm."

"Why did you jump off a picnic table?"

She turned her head toward him. "Because John Cody said I was afraid to jump off the picnic table."

"Your badass phase."

"Indeed."

"When I was fifteen, I broke my collarbone skiing," he said, pointing to it. "My dad was so pissed. 'You're supposed to be going to college for baseball, and you're going around with these idiots and hot-dogging.' I hadn't told him we were going. I wasn't supposed to go. I went anyway."

"What did he do?"

Dean laughed. "Nothing. He didn't want me to let my knucklehead buddies toss me off a mountain in a hang glider. I come home in a bucket and he can't send me to college. And he wanted me to go to college."

"What did you do in college besides play ball?"

"I was a chemistry major."

She turned to look at him. "You're kidding."

"Oh, I get it. You thought I took bullshit classes? Just a lot of Running Laps 101 and How to Tape Your Ankles?"

"No, of course not. I didn't know." She stared at the ceiling. "What did you like about chemistry?" she asked.

"I got to do things," he said. "You mix this with that, and if you know how it works, you can make it turn blue or heat up or blow up.

It was crazy shit, but it was predictable crazy shit. You could make something give off green smoke or turn into foam, but it did it the same way every time. And then you record it, and boom, that's your result. It's the same thing with baseball. It looks crazy, but it's all physics. It feels like there's no logic, but there is. I mean, except when there isn't, obviously."

She turned on her side and sat up on her elbow. She reached out with her ring finger and ran it along his brow bone. "What's the scar here?"

"Ball to the face junior year at Cornell," he said. "Blood pouring down. Just pouring. Remember the normal people I said I dated? I had a girlfriend then, Tracy, who was at the game, and she fainted. Just, boom, like that. I felt so bad. From what I heard, she took one look at me and she slithered right down in her seat like in a Daffy Duck cartoon. Her friend revived her with a face full of ice and Diet Coke."

"Oof, that's a hard way to wake up."

"Then they took me to the hospital and glued my face back together."

"You didn't have stitches?"

"No, glue. When I called home and told my mother I got taken to the ER and fixed up with glue, she hung up and called the hospital. My dad says it was all 'You glued my child together,' 'This isn't an arts and crafts project,' stuff like that. But then they told her that it wasn't glue, that it was called artificial skin. And she's just 'Oh, okay.'" He pantomimed hanging up the phone.

"Is it really called artificial skin?" she asked.

"No idea. She felt better, though. Have you ever had stitches?"

"Once in my knee, and then once a couple years ago when I stepped on a broken glass in the living room."

"Ouch."

"Bled all over the place. It was really gross."

"I bet."

Almost without realizing she was doing it, Evvie used her toe to feel the scar on her other foot where the ER had stitched her up. It had been Tim's broken glass. He'd been angry. But she'd told the nurse she broke the glass in the kitchen. "Slipped right out of my hand," she'd said.

She trailed her finger down from Dean's temple to his jaw and jumped at a deep red mark above his collarbone. "Oh, damn, I think I got you right here. You have a bruise."

He sat up in bed until he could see himself in the mirror over the dresser, and he tipped his head to the side. "That's not a bruise," he said, feeling it with his fingers. He turned to her and lowered his chin until he was looking at her through his impressive eyelashes. "You gave me a hickey." He repeated it. "You gave me a *hickey*."

She squinted at it. "Wait, when did I do that?" And then she remembered. "Ohhhh, I did do that." She smiled and gritted her teeth. "Sorry?"

"Don't be sorry. Shit, this is almost enough for me to get on Instagram. I'll just write, 'Having fun up here in Maine.' Then put up the picture—*ka-pow*!" He reached for his phone. "I'm taking a selfie."

"You are not." Laughing, she reached for it, too, but she was hopelessly overmatched by his considerable wingspan, and she wound up lying on top of him, inches from his scruffy face, as he held the phone out of reach. "It doesn't hurt," she whispered, "does it?"

"No," he whispered back, smiling. "It doesn't hurt."

Twenty-Eight

L ATER, AS DEAN'S truck bumped along Route 1, they passed a billboard for the Compass Café that had been there for ages, at least since Evvie was a teenager. "I wonder if the Compass is going broke now that you guys don't sit around for six hours every weekend," Dean said.

"It wasn't six hours." Evvie kept looking out the window. "Maybe two."

"Are you ever going to tell me what that's all about?" he asked.

Evvie looked over at him, the way his once-disobedient arm rested on the wheel. What was broken could be fixed, and she took a breath. "So, the night that my husband died . . ." She paused and took a deep breath. "I was leaving him. Like, I wasn't thinking about leaving him. I was in the process of leaving him."

Dean was still. "How close were you?"

Now she looked back out the window. "I was standing in the driveway when they called me. I'd packed one suitcase, and some money, and my birth certificate."

"But you hadn't told Tim?"

"He would have argued. I wouldn't have left. And the next day, he would have been sorry."

"Of course."

"Anyway, Andy's mom saw the suitcase in my car at the hospital. She mentioned it to Andy. He figured it out. He was upset."

Dean frowned. "But he wasn't upset that you were leaving."

"No. I think he was upset that I was going to leave without telling him. Without telling anybody. Upset is the wrong word. Hurt, maybe."

"Why *didn't* you tell anybody?"

"Because I wouldn't have left then, either."

"You really know how to hold your cards close."

"I promised Tim I wouldn't talk about marriage things with Andy. Which seemed reasonable enough."

"When did you decide to go?"

"Oh," Evvie said. "Well, there was this night when he said he was going to bring pizza home for dinner, but when he got home, he didn't have it. I say, 'What happened to bringing pizza home?' And he says, 'I never said that.' It was so . . . *so bizarre,* the idea that I would have imagined an entire exchange with him where he told me he was going to pick up pizza for dinner on the way home. I remembered specifically that he said he was going to get pepperoni and mushrooms, because I don't like mushrooms, and I'd decided to pick them off. I remembered. And I told him, 'Why are you trying to act like I'm crazy instead of saying you forgot to pick up dinner? Who even cares?'"

"What did he say?"

"He said, 'I just spent ten hours taking care of sick people while you sat at home doing nothing. I'm not your delivery service.' I walked away. Before you lived in your apartment, it was sort of where I went to get away from Tim. So, I go there, and I lie on the floor, and of course I'm *starving,* because I waited for him, and there's no pizza. And I start thinking maybe I'll run out and grab something to eat.

And then I think maybe I'll take a drive. And then I think maybe I'll stay overnight at this nice place in Rockport. Just stay away for a night, watch TV, be by myself, call it a spa night, or maybe fib and tell him I had to go stay with my dad because his hip was acting up or something."

"Did you do it?"

"Nope. I went out and I got pizza, and I brought it back at ten thirty at night. Mushrooms and everything. Argument over. But practically every day after that, I'd go back in and I'd lie on the floor and I'd add something to this story I was writing in my head. I wasn't going to do it. It was just this idea. What if I stayed away a weekend, where would I go? Did I have enough money to go to Boston for a week? What would I need? What would I take? How long could I go? And I don't even know what he had said to me, but there was some night when I was lying in there listening to the ceiling fan rattling, and I thought, 'What if I left and I never came back?' And that's when I started having these fantasies about where I would go, that I'd go live in the mountains. I'd have some little cabin, and I'd have a dog, and I'd have a job. I had these fantasies where I turned into a new person nothing had ever happened to."

"Like the 'I Married an Asshole' division of the Witness Protection Program."

"Yes! That's exactly what it was. And every time I thought about what my dad would do if I left, or what Andy would do, I shoved it out of my mind. I thought about making dinner or doing my hair or painting a wall without anybody telling me I didn't know what I was doing."

"And then what?"

"I went on like that for months. But then one night when he was out, I took a pack of playing cards—I sometimes play real solitaire with real cards—and I put them into this backpack that I had. And that was it. That was the beginning of packing. It was real, and I was doing it."

"And you didn't talk to anybody."

"I still felt like I was rehearsing it, to see if I wanted to do it. I still felt like I'd choke at the end. I figured I wouldn't go through with it."

"But then you did."

"Yeah." She chuckled a little. "Well, I started packing the car, at least." Evvie briefly put her hand over her eyes. "I sort of had a target date. And then a few days before he died, I told him it bugged me that—well, we'd made this trip to Bangor to have dinner with a couple doctors he knew. And when they asked what I did, he'd said, 'She makes me happy.' I told him, 'They wanted to know what I do. You should have told them I work. You should have told them I work with journalists, I have a business,' all that. And he said, 'I was trying to protect your feelings. I didn't know how you'd feel if I told a bunch of doctors you were a typist for somebody's book about trees.' "

Dean's mouth went slack.

"The day came, and I packed the car. Maybe I would have gone. Maybe I would have chickened out, I guess."

"You would've gone."

"I hope so," she said, and even though she knew she was imagining it, it felt like the sound of those words bounced around the truck. "I keep having plans. I thought I was going to marry this guy and be happy and be done with everything that was hard by the time I was twenty-five. And then I thought I was going to pack all my stuff and get in my car and get a divorce. Go back to my maiden name and get a job and live in some little house in the mountains, and it's just . . . nothing turned out."

"Well, that part sounds familiar to me."

"Now I'm on Evvie Drake, take three."

"You think you'll ever change your name back?"

"I can't, really."

"Of course you can," he said, frowning.

She raised her eyebrows. "Give back the name of my husband who's going to wind up with a wing at the clinic named after him if his mother has anything to say about it? Tell his parents I don't want it anymore? I don't think that would go over very well."

"So you're going to drag around his name for the next fifty years so nobody gets their feelings hurt?"

"Eh. Maybe. I don't know." Evvie's fingers went reflexively to her pocket, to the ridge where her rings pushed up against the fabric from inside. "It's only the first day."

"Of what?" he asked.

"You know," she said. "Whatever."

SUMMER
TO OPENING
DAY

Twenty-Nine

IN EARLY JUNE, Evvie was putting off making dinner and reading a diary from a 1912 textile strike in Massachusetts when she heard Dean's truck pull into the driveway. She kept the book open and kept her eyes pointed straight at it, but really, she waited to hear his key in the door. She knew how long it should take, the way you know how long someone who goes underwater should take to come to the surface, and when she didn't hear anything, she went to the window and looked out. He was sitting in the truck, both hands on the wheel. She watched him sit very still until she felt more self-conscious watching than she would barging in on his reverie, and she finally stepped out the door into the dry, warm early summer.

Coming up to the truck, she tried not to wonder what was wrong. *Someone died. Someone called. He met someone else. He's leaving. Whatever it was, I broke it.* As she came up to the window, he looked over and saw her, and he motioned for her to come around the other side. When she slid into the front seat next to him, she could see that his face wasn't in a state of traumatized paralysis. It was in a state, instead, of uncomplicated disbelief. "What's going on?" she asked, pulling the passenger door shut.

"Do you remember I told you about my buddy Dante, who was so jealous that I had the pinball machine?"

"With the two girlfriends?"

"Yeah."

"Sure."

"He texted me today, right before I left school."

Dante played for the Phillies now, she was pretty sure. Or the Nationals. Their uniforms were similar. "What did he say?"

Dean kept his voice even. "Well, their pitching coach is Alex Laramie, who used to be with the Yankees. And Dante said that Alex saw the tape of me at the Spring Dance and I should call him." Finally, Dean looked over at her.

"And?"

He looked straight ahead. His hands hadn't come off the steering wheel. "And so I called Alex. He wants me to come down to a facility they have in Connecticut. They've had a couple of injuries, they're feeling a little desperate, and he's trying to figure out if there's anything to, you know, pursue. With me."

"You mean he wants to know whether you can pitch. He wants to give you a chance to pitch. Major league baseball. To major league baseball players."

"Evvie, it's just to see. He wants to see how I look, bring some of the other coaches, see what the situation is."

"I know what the situation is," she said, poking him in the side. "The situation is that you're going to pitch again. Which, I want to point out, I always knew you would."

"You did, huh." He finally took his hands off the wheel and put them on the back of his head. "That's interesting, because I'm fuckin' shocked."

"You should have more faith. Like I do."

He reached one hand over and put it on the back of her neck, under her hair. He kissed her a little, then pulled away and said, "Wait. I don't have to make out with you in the car. I'm not sixteen. I can make out with you in the house."

"You can," she said. "That's very true." Even in the car, she managed a sassy hand on the hip. "Do you want to see my room? It's got all my cool posters and Trapper Keepers and stuff."

"Of course."

They got out of the truck and met up again by his door, closest to the house, where she kissed him again. Here were the irregular gray paving stones that Tim had picked out during their landscaping project after he told her the terra-cotta bricks looked "ordinary." Here were the steps he'd rebuilt with a buddy in the crushing heat of summer while he was going through a "handy" phase, which lasted as long as it took for him to realize he was too accustomed to being good at everything to start over as a novice who couldn't make a corner perfectly square.

Here was the front door she had opened, laughing, while being carried into the house on the day of the closing. Then the wood floor she'd once scratched with her suitcase wheel, for which he called her "so damn careless." Here was the wide doorway into the kitchen, where on one occasion Tim had kissed her with unexpected urgency, pushing his hand under her shirt while she tried to scratch his shoulder enough to prove she, too, was trying. Here was the kitchen table where they'd agreed that they'd just have a baby if they had a baby, and they wouldn't try one way or the other, which was a terrible lie since a doctor would know what it meant when, from time to time, she'd say, "Rain check?" Here was the sink where she had once put a rose down the garbage disposal—given too late for a birthday Tim forgot, which he'd made up for the next day by having six dozen fresh roses delivered to the house.

Here were the stairs where she had slipped two weeks before Tim died and put a big bruise on her hip. She fell; she wasn't pushed. She wasn't hit, she wasn't punched. But she was hurrying down the stairs in her socks on the way to her hideout only because she was so tired of listening to him yell, so, as she said only to herself, *you tell me*.

And in the bedroom, here was the dresser that had carefully been coaxed through the door. It would later play a central role in the first of the fights she was sure would be their worst until another proved her wrong.

Why am I upset? I'm upset because you pushed me into the dresser, Tim.

I absolutely did not.

You did this with your shoulder, like this, and you knocked me into the dresser. I'm going to have a bruise. You want to see it tomorrow?

I was leaving the room so you could calm down. What did you step in front of me for?

I didn't.

Evvie, you don't need to be so dramatic, okay? We need to get going. My parents are going to wonder why we're late.

This had been six months after they moved into the house. She had indeed had a bruise on her back the next day, where she'd fallen—fallen?—against the edge of the dresser. She'd told nobody, and when Tim had noticed it on her back when she was undressing a couple of days later, he'd said, "Ouch, how'd you get that?" She wasn't sure if he honestly didn't know, but she'd said, "Playing freeze tag," and even though she thought it sounded sarcastic enough not to miss, he just nodded and kept looking at his phone.

And here was the bed where they had sex, but not very often, and not very well, and not for very long. She'd hardly ever regretted that her best friend was a man, but part of her mourned the fact that she'd never felt comfortable disclosing to Andy how precisely she could clock sex with her husband at nine minutes. If it started at 9:51, she'd be able to watch *Halls of Power*, and she never missed the beginning.

And now, here was Dean, tall and broad and slow-moving as he lay next to her in his jeans and bare feet. He always smelled like freshly mowed grass, and she wasn't sure whether it was because of something he wore or washed his hair with, or because he spent so much time on baseball fields, or because she was imagining it, the way she always expected a lobsterman to smell like the ocean, whether or not he actually did. But she could not inhale enough of it, and when she'd find a spot, a hollow under his jaw or a span along his side, where she especially noticed it, she'd linger there trying to memorize it for when it was inevitably gone.

There was something about fooling around with clothes on that—no, it was not better than the sex, but the voluntary frustration of it thrilled her. It was like they were sneaking around in her own house, collapsing on her bed and tugging at each other, letting snaps and buckles slow them down. But finally, she cracked: she sat up and pulled her shirt over her head, and his fingers threw shadows on her skin in the sun through the bedroom window.

Later, as they were dozing between acknowledgments that they should go downstairs and eat something, she said in a shared waking moment, "I'm excited. Do you want me to come to Connecticut with you?"

"No, you can't," he said. "It's a work thing. They're going to test me out, try things, put me in situations and see what happens."

"I'll give you a lock of my hair for luck," she said, pulling a strand away from her head with her fingers.

"I'll settle for knowing you'll be here when I get back," he said, gathering her up with his arm and curling up against her.

Thirty

DEAN AND EVVIE decided one night while they were a little bourbon-drunk that before Dean went to Connecticut, they ought to have Andy and Monica—going strong after six months— over for dinner. Evvie and Monica had texted a few more times back and forth after the Great Lingerie Advisory: a conversation about what to get Rose for her birthday; a story Monica shared about Mama Kell calling her Eveleth and then, while apologizing, calling her Lori; and their discovery that someone had written some very elaborate fanfic where Dean fell in love with Jennifer Lopez. (They agreed that it wasn't bad.)

So Dean texted Andy with the invitation for a Saturday, and Andy texted back that they'd be "stoked" to come—a word, Evvie noted, that he had to have picked up from Monica, as she'd never heard it from him before. When the day came, it was warm and dry, so Dean took a steel brush to the gas grill in the yard, which had been dormant for two years, and picked up a bottle of propane. Evvie spent more than she usually would have on steaks and fat sausages from the butcher, and she loaded a basket with bright green, unblemished farmers' market lettuce she could build salads on. She fell to the temptation of some wild local mussels—much tougher to find than they'd once been—and bought a bag of those as well. In the afternoon, she baked brownies from scratch and let them cool while Dean made a run for beer and wine. Red with steaks, she figured, but white for summer, so she told him to grab some of both, and some beer, and she threw in a bottle of vodka, because, hey, you never know.

Just after he got back, while he was in the backyard starting the grill, her phone vibrated in her pocket, and when she took it out, it said, "Unknown." Probably a wrong number or a marketing thing, or possibly the people doing the survey about Maine's public lands, which she'd gotten two or three times already. She slid her finger over to "Ignore." But when it vibrated again a minute later, she realized whoever it was had left a message. She poked the button to listen.

"Hello, Eveleth!" *Oh, God.* "It's your mom. I'm going to be in Portland in September, and I was hoping we could get together. I haven't seen you in ages, and I hope you're doing well. By the way, my friend Foster saw your name in the paper in a story about your friend who's a baseball player. It sounds *very* exciting and I can't wait to hear all about it. Bye-bye, honey, call me back."

Evvie put her phone back into her pocket. Perfect. A headache started to kick in almost immediately. Eileen Ashton was coming to Portland. Eileen, who had seen Evvie maybe five or six times in the last twenty years, wanted to meet up. The last time they'd seen each other had been the second time her mom met Tim. The first time had been while they were dating as teenagers and Eileen unexpectedly showed up at Eveleth's high school graduation party. The second time had been after they were married, when Tim insisted on a visit once, when they took a vacation to Florida. It had been tense and anxious for her, happy for her mother, and obligatory for Tim. Since Eileen had missed the wedding, it seemed only right she'd missed Tim's funeral, too, but at least she'd sent cards for both. Evvie decided to think about it later. For now, she had a Bluetooth speaker she kept in the kitchen, so she put on a mix she liked and opened the windows as it started to cool down outside.

The side screen door opened. "Grill's working, and I didn't burn down the house or blow myself up, so I'm feeling pretty goddamn great about myself. Got my hands a little dirty, but I'm giving myself a win." He went by her on the way to the sink as she was drying the lettuce in a spinner, and without touching her, he bent and kissed her shoulder, at the edge of her stretchy, sleeveless bright blue dress.

"I see you're getting out ahead on the booze," he said, noticing the half-full glass of white wine that was already dewy on the outside.

"Hey, if I have to work this hard, I might as well be in a good mood," she said, dropping cut tomatoes and cucumbers into the bowl. Just then, she heard the doorbell, and Dean finished drying his hands and said, "I got it, you do this." When he was out of the kitchen, she reached over and picked up the glass and finished it off in a couple of hearty swallows.

By the time they got into the kitchen, her glass was full again. "Hey, welcome, glad you could come," she said as Andy leaned over to give her a hug. "Dean's going to go burn stuff on the grill, it's going to be very exciting. Can I get you something to drink?"

"Yes. Monica's driving, and Lori has the girls for the weekend, so I will take a beer."

"Oh," Evvie said. "I didn't know Lori was taking them this weekend."

Andy sighed. "Yeah, me neither. We'll talk. Hand me some of that raw meat I see over there." Dean and Andy went out back with the steak and sausage, and Evvie put on the pot to steam the mussels open, and poured wine for Monica. They sat at the table with their glasses, talking about the girls and about Catherine's House of Presentable Brassieres, and at one point laughing so hard that Dean hopped up the back steps and stuck his head in to make sure they weren't yelling—not that he said this. What he said was "Are you two getting in trouble in here?"

It wound up being a table you could only call "bountiful." Monica had brought a round loaf of thick-crusted bread with a cracked top and crisp edges just shy of turning black. When she handed it over,

Evvie had felt that it was slightly warm, and her eyes widened. "Did you make this?"

Monica held up one hand and counted off on her fingers. "Flour, water, salt, and yeast—that's all that's in it."

The bread sat between a white ramekin of soft garlic butter and a big bowl of steamed mussels, popped open, all salty and lemony. The sausages were beaded with grease, and the steaks were comically macho, perfectly seared and so big they hung off the edges of the platter. Evvie had put a pungent, mustardy vinaigrette on the salad before they sat down, and the little plates, too, seemed overmatched by the task. They ate and they ate. And they ate.

"To friends," Dean said, raising his bottle of beer. Glasses and bottles clanked together. Evvie already had a sheen of wine sweat on her forehead, and it was getting dark, so they closed the windows and turned the air conditioning on.

"So tell me more about this trip to Connecticut," Andy said. "What are you doing down there?"

"I'm not even sure," Dean said. "Fuckin' out of nowhere, they want to see me. They already did everything but put a chip in my brain, so God only knows what this is going to be. Probably throw in front of some guys, throw to some batters. They'll put a clock on me, which didn't happen at the Dance. And I'm assuming they're going to want me to pitch while a few cereal boxes run around the bases to make sure they're re-creating the optimal conditions."

"Are you nervous about it?" Monica put in, earning a tiny squirm from Evvie. There was no point in *asking* whether he was nervous. It would only . . . make him nervous.

"Of course," Dean said, picking at the label on the neck of the beer bottle. "I spent two years trying to figure all this shit out. I pitch one good inning against—no offense—guys who aren't that good, and everything's wide open again. I'm trying to figure out if I'm going to regret it."

"You're not going to regret it," Evvie said, staring directly at her glass. "It's going to go great."

"Wow, that's a bold promise," Andy told her.

"I'm a bold girl," Evvie said.

"All right," Andy muttered.

"Okay, you two," Dean said as he sawed off another piece of sausage. "Monica, what's new with you?"

Monica talked about her classes and the turmoil in her book club, which had been infiltrated by someone who was very unhappy that nobody ever read the books. Most recently, the book had been *Infinite Jest*, and Monica ran her hands over her hair in aggravation as she explained that of course they didn't read *Infinite Jest*, and the point of book club was socializing, and if you had something to say about the book, that was perfectly fine, but you can't come in and inflict your own rules on everyone. "I honestly think they're going to blow up the whole book club and instead of having a book club where you don't read the book, they'll have a knitting group."

Dean nodded. "Made up of people who can't knit."

"Perfect," Monica agreed.

"Maybe you could take Evvie," Andy said. "She could use something to do."

Evvie leveled her eyes at him. "What does *that* mean?"

"You said you wanted a project," Andy said, slathering butter on another piece of bread. "What happened to all that? You don't want to do that anymore?" He threw his third bottle cap into the sink, where it clattered to a stop.

"I didn't say that."

"You used to talk about going back to school. You still thinking about that?"

"I don't know. Things take time. Apparently it only takes six months to be the guru of active social lives, but—"

"I didn't say I was the guru of anything. I said you keep talking about it and you're not doing it. You'd say the same thing to me if I were sitting around my house all the time."

Evvie had never considered herself any good at comebacks. Tim had caught her flat-footed all the time, saying things that left her shocked and stubbornly silent, if stubbornly anything at all. Growing up, she'd never had a thing to say to the kids who teased her about her small house or her too-short jeans. But on this occasion, with the belly full of food and the tongue loosened by pinot grigio, she looked at Andy and found precisely the right combination of ice and taunt and tart and sweet when she said, "Oh, I'm keeping myself occupied right here at home, Andy, don't worry about it."

She, of course, was the one who had said she didn't want to tell him. And she hadn't, but of course, she had.

Andy's eyes flicked from her to Dean and then to Monica, whose look was hilariously transparent: *Well, what do you want? I told you.* "Well, I'm glad to hear it," Andy said, and he went back to eating his steak.

"Evvie, I can't get over how great your house is," Monica said, grabbing the conversational wheel and pulling as hard as she could away from the ditch as the tires squealed. "Like I said, I've always thought you had the prettiest porch in the entire town, but the rest of the house is just as gorgeous."

"Thank you. I can't take credit for very much of it; my late husband bought the house without even telling me, so." Evvie could feel the sway now, the way she knew it would take her a minute if she tried to stand up. "But it all worked out," she quickly added.

Andy went to empty his mussel shells into the big pot on the table and he frowned suddenly at his bowl. "Hey, what happened to the flower dishes? I haven't ever seen these, I don't think."

"I put them away," Evvie said quickly, pouring more wine. "They're in the basement." She was pretty sure Dean was looking disapprovingly at her, but she ignored it.

"Did you get tired of them?"

"Yep. Just wanted a change. I like these, they're simple."

"Boy, out with the old and in with the new over here, huh?" Andy said.

"What's that supposed to mean?"

Dean jumped in. "Okay, that'll do, Tipsy McGee, Buzz Lightbeer. I say we go sit outside now that it's not so hot. I'll bring the brownies, because I'm going to stuff about ten of them down my throat."

Evvie grabbed the wine bottle she'd only just started on, and indeed, when she stood up, she reached out and steadied herself against the side of the table. "You good?" Dean muttered. She nodded and winked at him.

Out in the dark, they lit a candle and sat around the metal patio table. Monica slipped her shoes off and put her feet on Andy's lap, and Evvie looked at the candle flicker reflected in her wine when she held her glass in close. "This is cool," she said, her words beginning to slur.

"I'm not sure you want to be too close to an open flame right now," Dean said, scooting the candle away from her. "And don't breathe on it either. We're going to get a flamethrower situation."

"Do you remember the guy," Andy said, "from high school, the guy who lit vodka puddles on fire with a lighter? And somebody said he had done it at home and he burned their toolshed to the fucking ground?" He took another drink. "That was nuts."

"I have vodka," Evvie said. "I could light puddles of vodka on fire."

"No, thank you," Andy brayed at her. "You are not the kind of girl who lights shit on fire." He gestured at her with his beer. "Although maybe you are now, I've lost track of a lot. Dishes, everything."

"Yeah, well. It's funny how little information you get when you stop speaking to me."

"I didn't stop speaking to you. We stopped having breakfast together every single week because I got busy and you got busy."

"Busy?" Eveleth almost knocked her wineglass over with her animated response to this one. "You weren't busy, you were cutting me off."

Andy wrinkled his brow. "I'm pretty sure you cut me off first, even if I didn't know it at the time."

Evvie was shaping every word with her mouth like it wasn't responding the way she expected. "Oh my God, what is your problem?

I'm sorry I didn't tell you about the dishes. Why are you obsessed with every detail of my fucking life?"

Andy's beer clanked inelegantly against the table as he leaned forward with it in his hand. "What are you talking about, I'm obsessed?"

"You're picking at me about everything I do. You're mad that I didn't talk to you all about my marriage, you're worried about what plates I'm using, you're on me about school like you're my dad, you're telling me not to help Dean. I don't get it. I don't get what your problem is."

"You're not making any sense. Have some more wine, would you?"

"Did you not want me to meet anybody, Andy? Is that why you're mad about everything I do without telling you? Or are you mad it wasn't you?"

Now Dean, who had been watching and hoping all this was going to sputter harmlessly like a birthday candle, the way his teammates' drunk arguments always had, leaned forward toward her. "Hey."

"No," she said. "I'm serious. He's pissed off at me all the time, and the minute you moved in, he decided he was ready to start dating again. What is your issue, Andrew? You have something you want to tell me about why you're acting like a jealous boyfriend? You want to explain it to her?" She tipped her head toward Monica, whose feet were still in his lap.

Andy, even with the hoppy aroma currently wafting from every word he said, was now still. All he said, when he finally said anything, was "What?"

Dean stayed right by Evvie's ear. "Listen to me. Listen, listen. You have had a lot to drink. You trust me, right? You trust me. I am telling you that you have had a lot to drink. This is a bunch of things you don't mean. You're upset, and you're very drunk, and in the morning, this is already going to be an unhappy situation, so listen to me and let me help you and take you inside so you can go to sleep. Let's go to sleep."

She didn't answer him. She was looking at Andy, who seemed to be getting the same whispered advice in his ear from Monica that Dean was trying to give to Evvie.

"We're going to take off," Monica said. "Long night. I have a big to-do list tomorrow." It was hard to say precisely who was the target of this politeness, under the circumstances, and who was supposed to be getting cover, but Monica pulled Andy up by the elbow. "Come on. Come on, we're going."

As Andy got up, he turned to Eveleth, pointed one finger at her, and said, "You're crazy."

Now Dean stood up, looked at the friend he'd had since elementary school, and held up one hand. "Goddammit, you are both drunk. Enough. Go the fuck home and I will talk to you tomorrow."

But Monica at his elbow and Dean across the table weren't enough to move Andy. He stayed where he was and he looked down at Eveleth, who was now refusing to meet anyone's eyes at all, and he said, "Glad you found a project. If you decide to break up with this one and take off in the middle of the night, let me know this time. I'll water the plants."

"Go fuck yourself," Evvie said, finally looking at him.

"Fucking crazy," he muttered again as he pushed his chair out of the way and followed Monica through the side yard toward the car.

Evvie was sitting with her forehead resting on her hand, and Dean blew out the candle, then leaned down to her. "I'm going to go say good night to Monica, okay?" She muttered her agreement.

Dean found Monica putting Andy in the passenger side of her car, going so far as to lean over to buckle him up. "Hey," he said to her. "You all right?"

She closed Andy's door and came around to the driver's side. "Not the most fun I ever had."

"You know she didn't mean that," he said. "You know that was just the biggest bomb she could think of to throw."

"Oh, I know that," Monica said. She opened the door. "Make sure she falls asleep on her side and get her to drink some water, okay?" She shrugged. "I was an RA in college."

Dean nodded. From the front seat, Andy declared that he wanted to go home, so Dean put his hand on Monica's shoulder, and she smiled, and Dean returned to the backyard, where Evvie had now put her head down on the table. While she slept, or cried, or whatever was happening in there, he took the bottles and the glasses inside. He pulled her up gently, scooting the heavy metal chair, which screeched across the stone. "Okay, come on. I've got you, come on." They walked a few steps before he decided it wasn't worth the trouble of trying to get her to walk, and he picked her up and carried her up the back steps and into the house, through the kitchen, up the stairs, and into her bedroom. He brought her a glass of water. "Hey. Drink this, okay? Evvie? Drink this and then you can go to sleep."

He took off her shoes, got her to wriggle out of her dress, and coaxed her into a T-shirt. He put the plastic trash can from the bathroom right next to the bed. "Evvie, if you feel sick, this is right here, okay?" She gave him a noncommittal "mm," but figuring it was about the best he was going to do, he maneuvered her under the covers, made sure she was lying on her side, and pulled the sheet and the blanket up over her.

Dean stripped to his boxers and folded up the rest of his clothes on the chair by the closet door, then he slid into bed next to her. There was an imposing mess waiting in the kitchen downstairs for the morning. Food that would be bad, wine that would be stale, dishes with everything dried onto them, and everything smelling like garlic and drenched in leftover booze, none of which was going to be good for Evvie if she woke up feeling the way he suspected she would.

Just as he shut off the light next to the bed on his side and adjusted the pillow under his head, he heard her voice, still slurred but easy to make out. She chuckled sort of lazily, slowly, and then she said, "I knew I should never have tried to be happy."

When Evvie woke up in the morning, she could hear Dean downstairs cleaning up in the kitchen. It took a minute for her to reconstruct her evening. There was this great dinner, there was this friendly chat, then they went out onto the patio and, and, and . . . it would have been one thing if she didn't remember it. But she remembered pieces of it. She remembered Andy looking shocked, like she'd punched him in the eye. She knew she'd said "Go fuck yourself," and when she'd been awake for about five minutes, her mouth sour and dry and her head swimming every time she moved even a little, she remembered Andy sticking his finger out at her and saying, "You're crazy." She couldn't remember how it started. She was pretty sure she'd announced to him that he was secretly in love with her. In front of his girlfriend. As hard as she searched her memory for a full-length video, she could find only a little stack of photos and a few snippets of sound.

Evvie sat up in bed as slowly as she could, and it took a minute for everything to stabilize, and for her stomach to make the first of several unsettling writhes. Realizing Dean couldn't have known he was putting her in an old shirt of Tim's (*a perfect capping-off of that particular evening,* she thought), she stripped it off in the bathroom and stepped into the shower with toothpaste and a toothbrush in one hand. Under the hot water, she brushed her teeth and set the brush in a cup, then she stood and let the water hammer her. Nothing felt good; she just wanted something to feel different.

When she started to cry, the upside was as it always was: the shower cry takes the logistics out of it. Crying has to be dealt with—it makes a mess, it swells up your face, it creates a little pile of tissues that are a tell. But the shower cry is the superspy's cry, Evvie had always thought. It was between you and the tile walls, and everything that hurt turned into water, and the water went away.

Thirty-One

FOUR DAYS LATER, Dean put his duffel bag into the truck and came back into the living room, where Evvie was curled up on the couch, flipping through *The New York Times* on her tablet. "Okay, I'm taking off," he said.

She went over to him and put her arms around his waist. "Text me when you get there?"

"I will. Like I said, I think I'll be back Monday night. They might keep me pretty busy, so don't worry if you don't hear much for a couple days."

"You worry about showing all those guys your stuff, don't worry about me."

He looked down at her and hesitated a little, then he said, "I still think you should call him."

She dropped her arms to her sides but stayed where she was and groaned. "I know."

"Somebody has to pick up the phone."

"Maybe it can be him."

"Maybe it can be you."

She sighed. "I told you, you can call him yourself. Have lunch, play *Madden*, do whatever. I promise, I don't mind at all. I'm not ready to get into it."

"Okay. Up to you. Either way, I have to get going, so I'll talk to you soon." He kissed her and whispered, "But call him."

She smiled and rolled her eyes. "Good*bye*," she said as he pulled back and turned to go.

Evvie finished her reading with her feet tucked up under her on the couch, sipping iced tea and listening to what sounded like a very spirited argument between two birds outside the living room window. One bird, she fantasized, had taken a prized fluff of cotton that the other one *really* wanted for her nest. She made herself laugh squawking their dialogue into her empty house: " 'You take everything, Florence! You got the stick, you got the yarn . . . ' 'Fuck you, Maurice, I already told you that Horace has that yarn!' "

She wandered into Dean's apartment, where she'd been sleeping maybe half the time for close to a month now, and she lay down on the bed. He made it up every day, which he told her was a habit his mother had instilled in her boys that he'd never abandoned. Even when traveling with the team, he told her, even though he stayed in high-end hotels and was fussed over by eager managers and officious liaisons of all kinds, he made his bed before housekeeping could do it.

Down here, she slept on the opposite side from the one she slept on upstairs. She kept a water glass beside the bed, and her spare phone charger was plugged in with the cord dangling over the corner of the table. On Dean's side was a book about Lyndon Johnson that he'd been reading, with a receipt from a coffee shop holding his place. She had learned that he took a long time to fall asleep, but once he was out, it took a lot to rouse him. She'd learned that they had roughly equivalently murderous breath in the morning, so sometimes they'd wake up and pick a couple of mints out of a tin first thing, sometimes not. He slept in soft flannel pants unless it was hot, and then he slept in boxers. She liked it a little bit cooler at night than he did, so sometimes she stuck her bare feet out from under the covers, and sometimes he put on a long-sleeved shirt.

While she was lying on the bed, she noticed that on top of his dresser, Dean had set the trophy that he'd taken home when Calcasset High baseball came in second in the regional tournament. She got up and went over to look at it. Cheaply made with glue and plastic, with the etched plate stuck on crooked and the baseball player alarmingly loosely attached, it said, COACH, CALCASSET HIGH, SECOND PLACE. And right beside it was his World Series ring. Well, his first World Series ring. Right now, he was on his way to what some tickle in her mind told her was going to be another.

She lay down on the floor, staring at the ceiling. She could call Andy. But he hadn't called her. If she called, what would she say? She couldn't just say she was sorry, the way she had when she closed his fingers in the door of her car. Because as sorry as she felt, she couldn't stop remembering *You're crazy,* and even more, the way she eventually remembered he'd thrown it in her face that she'd tried to leave. Every time she had thought about calling, texting, maybe showing up at his door, she'd remembered him saying *crazy,* and she'd frozen.

Monica had texted her once, two days after the dinner: *Are you OK?* She had responded: *Yes, OK. Thanks for checking.* And she'd added a smiley face, which was almost as ridiculous as Monica herself claiming she was dragging Andy away because she had things to do in the morning. Evvie didn't even know who the smile was for, or who might be convinced by it. It seemed like the thing to do. Or at least like a thing to do.

She hated to admit it, but it still meant everything to be able to close her eyes and picture the moment when Dean's first pitch thunked into Marco's mitt. She'd felt it in the crowd—their surprise, their relief. It meant hope, like it had meant hope for her. It was possible for things to get better when it felt like they couldn't. It was possible for things that seemed doomed to be revived. This was why people kept rooting for the Red Sox and the Cubs until they finally won. It was why people who didn't care about speed skating knew about Dan Jansen, who fell at the Calgary Olympics after he found out his sister had died. People rooted for him until he won a gold medal six years later, simply because they wanted to believe there was hope.

She could see Dean in her mind right now, and she could imagine what he'd be like later at what she imagined this meetup with coaches might look like. She knew how he'd pace at the hotel where they were putting him up, rubbing his shoulder. Would he think about her? Maybe. In case he did, she closed her eyes and focused as hard as she could on the words *You can do it, you can do it*. This was a thing she did not believe in at all, as she would admit if she were pressed. But the feel of it was wonderful—the feeling that she could package her feelings and put them to use, wrapping them up, and no, of *course* she didn't believe in telepathy, but what was "best wishes" on a birthday card, after all, except the idea that your good thoughts might matter?

She breathed in and out in the quiet, ignoring the rumble of her stomach. The room felt so different with someone living in it: his book by the bed, his shoes by the door, his peculiar collection of nutritional supplements that he sometimes made into what she called Hulk Smoothies ("They make you strong *and* they're unnaturally green," as she'd told him) lined up on the kitchenette counter next to the blender. She had more room on her countertop in the big kitchen, she thought, than he had in here. He could move the whole smoothie operation for as long as he decided to stay. And she had room in the living room where her TV was to set up his Xbox. Maybe her bedroom upstairs could be the guest room. Maybe they could build a big walk-in closet out of part of the apartment. Maybe the pinball machine would go in the living room if they moved the sofa in here. If he decided not to leave.

Of course, she thought, if he went back to pitching, he'd travel a lot. He'd be gone all the time. All over the country, different places, big chunks of the year. Could he be based here? If he wanted to be? Did other people travel with the team? Did wives? Did . . . whatever she was right now? What if it turned out that he pitched better with her there, the way he had at the Spring Dance when they'd made sure he knew she was in the stands. Maybe it depended on what team. If he spent time in the minors, she supposed that might wind up being anywhere. She didn't know. But they'd talk. They'd figure it out. If he decided not to leave.

Evvie didn't hear much from Dean during the trip, but then, he'd warned her about that. She texted him *Good luck!* and a red heart on the first full day he was gone, and he texted back, *Thanks, Minnesota. Keep things warm while I'm gone.* She had laughed at this and blushed, but she had taken the request seriously, sleeping in his bed in the apartment the whole time.

After that one message, she heard nothing at all until Monday morning, when he texted, *Should be there by six tonight. Lots to talk about. See you soon.*

It was a slow day, hot and lazy, which Evvie spent at the grocery store and the bakery and a little shop where she bought herself a necklace with a white and red enamel baseball charm hanging from it. She kept looking at her phone to see what time it was, to see if he'd texted. He'd been gone three days, but she'd quickly gotten spoiled on the utterly entitled feeling it gave her to know she could reach out whenever she wanted and put her hand on his back, or her arms around his waist, or she could kiss him and pull him into the apartment and get him half naked in seven seconds.

As six o'clock passed, she walked around the kitchen, sat down again, got up, sat down in the living room, got up, went back to the kitchen, poured a glass of water, went into the bathroom and brushed her hair, and wound up back at the kitchen table. And at about twenty minutes past six, she heard the truck pull in and stop. She wondered whether to run out the door, or open the door, or stand up, but she sat where she was until the side door opened and he stood there with his bag over his shoulder and his keys in his hand. "Hey," he said. He dropped the keys on the table.

"Hey." Now she stood, went over to him, and slid her arms around him. "I'm happy to see you." She reached up and kissed him.

"I'm happy to see you, too." He kissed her again, this time on the forehead. "What did I miss?"

"Nothing big, I don't think. I mostly hung out here. It's been hot. I had lunch with Kell one day." *Why,* she wondered, *are we talking about this? Why isn't he saying anything?* "How did it go?"

They stepped back from each other, and he slid off his jacket and put it on a hook by the door. He turned back to her and crossed his arms. He shook his head. "I threw it into the stands, Ev."

She felt it in her chest. "What do you mean?" She held up one hand. "Sit down and tell me. I'll get you a drink." She went to the refrigerator and got him a bottle of beer.

"I threw it into the stands. I threw it two feet wide, I threw it a foot high, I threw it all over the fuckin' place. That was Friday, so we tried it again on Saturday, and I hit the poor kid they had standing in the batter's box. Clocked him right on the fuckin' elbow. They'd brought a specialist—or *another* specialist, a new specialist—and I talked to him for quite a while yesterday. And by the afternoon, we'd all agreed that it was a nice chance to catch up, but that was about it." He drank from the bottle and shrugged. "I'm sorry."

"Why are you apologizing?" she said.

He sighed like he was trying to blow out a candle with it. "I don't know. I don't know why I thought this was going to be different. It was like the shittiest practice any of us ever went to. I threw a couple that were not quite where I wanted them, and he was like, 'Form looks good, looks good, stay loose.' But I knew. I can tell."

"What do you think happened?"

He looked down at the table. "The same thing that happened for two years before I came up here, which is I don't have a fucking clue what happened." He didn't even say this unkindly. He said it as if he were telling her what happened, as if he were saying, *Well, the flange needed tightening, and they were using the wrong washer.* "The specialist asked me a lot of questions, had me do a bunch of exercises. I passed everything. They did a couple of MRIs, and other than the fact that my shoulder and my elbow both basically look like they got weedwacked from the inside out, there's nothing wrong."

"You don't have the thing where your arm falls off?"

He smiled. "Not falls off. Comes apart in the middle."

"That's not a *lot* better."

"Well, I don't have that, no. But I don't have anything. I'm still a fucking head case, so nothing's changed. Apparently, a year is about how long it takes me to forget that I already tried everything, most things five or six times, and it's time to stop fucking embarrassing myself."

"Wait, you're quitting?"

He looked up at her slowly. "Yes. It's fully, totally over."

"But I saw you pitch a month ago."

"And a bunch of people watched me throw into the stands yesterday."

The thump of the ball into the mitt. "You can't quit."

"Yes. I can quit. I am quitting. I am not pitching anymore."

She shook her head. "I'm so sorry. I feel like I should have gone with you."

He shook his head, his shoulders, all in a gesture of loose bafflement. "To do what?"

"I don't know. To be there with you, I guess."

"You didn't miss a good time."

"Not to have a good time. Just, do you remember when you asked me to be behind the plate at the Spring Dance? Do you remember that you said it helped that I was back there, even if you couldn't see me? I feel like this is what happened, we didn't follow the rules of what made it work, we didn't do it the same way. It can still work, but we have to do it the same way—"

"Please stop," he said, shaking his head. "Please stop, okay, Ev?"

"I'm trying to help."

"I know you are, but you have to listen. You have to listen to me. I'm fucking tired, and I had a long weekend, and even though I know you're trying to help, I'm telling you this is how it is." He was a little sunburned, she noticed. He looked older.

"I just . . . I'm just surprised."

"Evvie, I worked on this back in New York until I drove myself crazier than I already was. I did every goddamn thing they told me to do, *everything*. I don't understand what you expected to happen. I don't understand what I expected to happen." He leaned against the counter. "I mean, did you think I was going to be able to pitch now because we're sleeping together?"

Hearing this question was like biting down on a bad tooth, right to the nerve. "I didn't think that." *Oh, but you did, you did, you did.*

"It's over," he said. "I'm telling you it's over. All this is over." He took a drink, and then he shook his head. "I really fucking wish you hadn't forced it."

Evvie flinched. "I was trying to help," she said. "I thought you wanted to work."

"Well, I didn't," he said. "And I can't anyway. We should have left it alone. It's time for me to get on with my real goddamn life already."

She looked around the kitchen. "I'm sorry if I misunderstood."

"It's fine," he said. "I should have known better." He ran one hand through his hair. "I'm starving," he said. He opened the refrigerator and swore under his breath, and just as Evvie realized what was about to happen, he set down the bottle of champagne she had chilled, right in front of her, hard enough that it rattled the table. "Please stop it with this."

When he had disappeared into the apartment, she picked at the champagne label until it peeled away in sections, then she left the bottle on the table and went upstairs to lie down. *All this,* he had said, *is over.*

That night, once it was dark, Evvie wriggled into soft cotton jersey shorts and a gray T-shirt, and she shut off the lights in her bedroom. She went downstairs, stopping to stash the champagne in the back of a high cabinet, and she went to the apartment, where the door was standing half-open. She peeked in, and she saw Dean in bed, earbuds in, eyes on his iPad. All the lights were off but one, right next to him on the nightstand. She stood still until he looked up, smiled, took one little white earbud out, and extended it toward her. She crossed the room, feeling the quiet and the carpet under her bare feet. Dean lifted the sheets and the cotton blanket on her side of the bed, and she scooted in beside him.

He was watching *Raiders of the Lost Ark*, and she slid in her earbud at the moment Indy got to Marion's bar. Dean resettled the pillows behind his head so she could curl around his shoulder. "I'm sorry, Ev," he said into her ear. "I'm sorry, I'm sorry."

She turned a little to look at the curve of his jaw and the scar above his eye, and she said, "I'm sorry, too."

"It was a hard trip. I didn't mean to take it out on you."

She shook her head. "No, I pushed, you're right. I'm not at my best right now, either."

"Probably no chance you called Andy while I was gone."

She played with the charm around her neck. "No. I can't say I did."

"Or that he called you?"

She pulled on the chain. "I'm trying to give it some time to blow over."

"Can I ask you something?"

"Sure," she said, resting her hand on his side.

"The night you guys had that fight, you said, 'I should never have tried to be happy.' What does that mean?"

What Eveleth hated the most about being drunk, and what she already hated the most about having been drunk that night, was all the things she barely remembered but knew were true. She had said this; she was sure of it. She had no idea why. And so she ran her hands over her hair and said, "I don't—just a drunk thing, I guess?"

"You know, it's been a week. More than a week. It's not going to get any easier."

She nodded. "I'm going to miss this kind of really depressing advice."

He turned to her with his brow furrowed. "Am I leaving?"

"Aren't you? It's been almost a year. You said it yourself. It's time to get on with everything. Your regular life. It is for me, too."

"Are you sure?"

"Sure about what? That fall is going to follow summer and that will be a year? Yes. Yes, I'm sure." She put her hand flat against his chest, gave him a pat, and leaned back against his shoulder. She wasn't magic, she couldn't help, and he'd said it himself when he moved in: New York was where his life was. Might as well get on with it and not make it harder. It was going to be bad enough already.

Thirty-Two

A BOUT A WEEK after Dean got back from Connecticut, Evvie
saw a cardboard box on the table in the apartment with a stack
of books in it. This was the first sign that it was real. As July wore on,
everything continued largely as it had been: they slept in his bed or
hers, they pushed the windows wide open when it was cool enough,
they read the news on their phones and binge-watched seasons of *30
Rock* and *Archer*, eating takeout or spaghetti or burgers or something
she improvised from leftovers. He slept soundly at night, not getting
out of bed to pitch and not icing his shoulder in secret when it began
to bother him. Gradually, it stopped bothering him at all.

She read and she worked, and she started to plan for the clients she
would need to pay the bills after he was gone. She didn't ask him any
questions when he'd come home from hanging out with Andy, and he
didn't tell her anything. The longer it went on that way, the less she
could imagine how anything with Andy might be fixed. Or even
part-fixed.

But the boxes kept appearing on the table, and when he handed
her a check on the first of August, she looked down at it. "End of the
month, I guess?" he said. She looked up and nodded.

As the end of August approached, Dean began to leave in earnest. He sent someone to open up his apartment in New York and have it cleaned. He started selling the things he'd bought that he wouldn't need: the toaster oven and the smoothie blender, then the dresser, once he put his clothes into bins. He told Evvie he was leaving the big TV on the wall, in case she ever wanted a properly enormous screen on which to watch *Halls of Power*.

She wanted to have a party for him before he left—or, really, she wanted to be the kind of person who would throw a party for him before he left—but he didn't want one. He went and watched a ball game with her father one afternoon, and the kids he'd coached had a cookout for him and gave him a sweatshirt that said, COACH TENNEY. The Claws took him out drinking, and Andy's girls got out their paints and made cards for him, and Andy and Monica took him to The Pearl while Evvie stayed home on a deadline she claimed was slightly more urgent than it was. He spent a day at Kell's, helping her with her garden.

He packed his powders and potions from the counter. He packed his Xbox games. He packed the crooked little trophy and the plastic water bottles from the drying rack. With a week to go, he sold his bed and his table, and the last few nights, they slept in her bed, sometimes waking up in the middle of the night to have sex or eat cereal or watch *Match Game '76*, which ran all night on cable. On the last night, he took the pinball machine apart and wrapped the pieces in a couple of old blankets Kell gave him, and he put them into the back of the truck.

She woke up on the last day, went into the bathroom, and saw that he'd taken his toothbrush from the plastic cup on the vanity. The day before, she'd teased him about how their toothbrushes were bumping against each other, sharing all their germs, and he had said, "I think you already have all my diseases." When she saw her blue brush leaning against the side of the cup by itself, she felt the breath go out of her lungs. She leaned down and turned the tap, and she splashed cold water into her eyes and on her cheeks.

Evvie padded down the stairs in her socks, and Dean was there, making breakfast at the stove. "Hey," she said, coming over and leaning up to kiss him on the cheek.

"Hey. I made eggs, and coffee's on. And don't forget, there are still mini-donuts in the bag over there." They'd hit the bakery a couple of days before so that the next morning, they could stay in bed until noon eating pastries and arguing about which version of *Law & Order* was the best one.

"Are you all packed?" She poured herself a cup of coffee.

"I think so. I got everything out of the apartment, bathroom—I got my stuff out of the dryer, I got my charger from upstairs. I got your car charger out of my glove compartment and it's on the counter over there. I think it's everything."

He slid her breakfast in front of her and sat down. "I figure if I get on the road pretty soon, I'll be there sometime before the evening rush, which would be good."

She took a bite. "You know, your eggs have come a long way since I met you."

He laughed. "Well, it hasn't been a total loss, then." He leaned on his elbow. "So I guess it would be dumb to ask if you're ever down in New York at all."

"Not very often," Evvie said as she nibbled on a piece of toast. "But I'll call you if I am. And I'll call you anyway. I mean, I'm not dying. You're not dying."

"I hope I'm not dying," he said.

After breakfast, they cleaned up the dishes, they cleaned off the counters, they divided up an electric bill, and they checked the traffic on the route he was driving. They wound up leaning on opposite sides of the doorway between the kitchen and the living room. "I think I'm out of stalls," she finally said. "You should get on the road if you want to be ahead of the rush."

"Okay," he said. He stepped toward her and opened his arms wide, like she was a classmate at a high school reunion. She stepped close to him and let him hold her, and they stood that way for a long minute. "Thank you so much, Ev," he said. "I don't know what I would have done."

"Me, neither," she muttered into his shoulder. "I mean . . . you know what I mean."

He stepped back. "I'm going to miss you a lot."

"I'm going to miss you a lot, too. I'm sorry things didn't work out how you hoped."

Dean looked all around the kitchen, then back at her. "I don't know that they didn't." He reached out and squeezed her shoulder. "Walk me out?"

She nodded. Out by his truck, he turned back and kissed her, and her knees tried to buckle again, and her breath tried to leave her again, but when she stepped away from him, she steadied herself on her own feet. "Drive safe. Let me know when you get there?"

He nodded and slid into the driver's seat. He started the truck, and it pulled out of the driveway, and he was gone. She stood in the yard for a minute, looking at the fence, at the house, at the way that her own car needed to be washed, and then she pulled herself up the steps, hanging on to the banister, and went back into her kitchen.

Just as she started to ease herself down onto the living room couch, her phone buzzed. It was a text from Dean, who would be sitting at the light right about now.

Look under sink in apt bathroom. Take care. Call Andy.

She went into the apartment, now totally empty again, and ducked into the little bathroom. She opened the cabinet, and she took out a black baseball glove with pink laces. A sticky note was in the palm.

Go be great, champ.

Thirty-Three

I T WAS SEPTEMBER. The leaves would start to turn in the next couple of weeks. It would start cooling off at night, but for now, Evvie would still get sweaty, throwing off the covers most of the time and waking up tangled in her top sheet.

Dean had texted when he got to New York, and again two days later to tell her he was looking for coaching jobs in the city. She said she was glad both times, and she sent him a blue heart both times. The blue heart was *I have a hundred things to say*. But, of course, only to her. He lived there, and she lived here. That was all. It was fine. It would be fine, and saying all the other things would only make it harder.

Instead, she told herself to do one thing at a time. In fact, she stuck a note to the mirror that said, *DO ONE THING*. So on the hot Wednesday night after he left, she decided to replace the burned-out light bulb in the fixture over the kitchen table. She dragged the stepstool up from the basement, but when she climbed up and poked away the cobwebs, she realized she had to take the cover off of the fixture with a screwdriver to get to the bulbs. "That's stupid," she muttered.

Evvie glanced around her kitchen and remembered that her screwdriver was sticking up out of a coffee can filled with screws and nails. The can sat on the end of a high shelf over the stove that she could reach if she went up on her toes. She went over to the shelf, but as she reached for the can, she accidentally tipped it off the shelf. It hit the edge of the stove on the way down, and screws and nails skittered across the slippery kitchen floor. At the same time, a heavy cookbook she didn't realize had been leaning on the can fell over, and as it fell off the shelf, it took out both a plastic jar of applesauce and a big canister of rice. The applesauce hit the floor and split down the side, splattering across the bottom of the stove, the floor, and the legs of the kitchen chairs and table. And the top came off the canister of rice, which formed a pile in front of the stove—mixed with applesauce, of course—but as it fell, it tumbled and spun, spraying dry rice across the kitchen floor and into the hallway.

Once all the noise stopped, once everything stopped moving, Evvie stood and looked around. There was rice under the stove and inside the burners. There was applesauce on the undersides of the kitchen chairs. There were nails and screws covered with applesauce spilled all over her floor. She walked, dazed, toward her bathroom to see how far the rice went, and there were grains of it even in there. She looked around her kitchen, and she dropped her chin to her chest.

She started to cry, but she could barely breathe. She tried to ignore it and grabbed the roll of paper towels and walked toward the stove, slipping on rice under her feet. She kneeled on her kitchen floor and started to mop up piles of rice and muck, but she had to go get the trash can first, and she wasn't sure if she should try to pick out the screws and the nails or throw them away, and oh God, there was rice that had fallen into the drawer at the bottom of the stove that was open an inch, and she'd have to take out all the pots and lids, which would all have rice in them, and the stove was too heavy to move.

On her knees, on her floor, in the house she'd never wanted, she couldn't catch her breath. She felt like she was floating above herself, observing this woman on the floor who was sobbing, and then wailing, and then this woman on her knees on the floor was screaming. Part of Evvie was watching and thinking, *What is happening, am I having a panic attack, am I crazy, am I dying?* And part of her gulped air into her lungs and made it into this sound over and over again, a sound she'd never heard herself make before. Whatever was angrier than crying and much bigger than yelling and felt more like a seizure than a shout, that's what this sound was, and even as she was still making it, it registered: *Thank God I am the only person who will ever see myself like this. Thank God, thank God.*

She had no idea how long it went on. She knew enough to be terrified a neighbor would hear; she was steeled for a knock on the door from someone who thought she was being murdered. If she'd heard herself from inside someone else's house, she would have called the police. She heard her own words in what barely seemed to be her voice: *I can't do this* and *What did I do?* and *I break everything.* Several times, the last one. *Everything. Everything, I break everything.* She was making this sound, nearly howling these words, and she could hear it, but she couldn't stop it. She passed through long minutes when she couldn't imagine how it would ever end except with her emptied out or inside out or reduced to a stick figure that stood for a person who had once existed.

But it ended, for the same reason arm-wrestling matches and overtime games come to an end: there is only so much. Finally, finally, she felt the process reverse. That terrifying sound turned back into raw sobbing, and then to ordinary crying, and then she took a breath, and another, and another. Slowly, she stood, brushing the rice off her bare knees, which were now covered in painful, pebbly red marks. She went into the bathroom and flipped on the light. Her eyes were swollen in a way she'd never seen before. Her throat felt raw and her ears were ringing. She ran cold water on a cloth and held it over her face, breathing in, feeling the cool water on her lips and smelling her laundry detergent.

She felt strangely loosened, like she'd run a mile or gotten a massage. It was like she'd drained herself so utterly that nothing in her could stick together. What was left was floating like the fuzz you blow off a dandelion.

Cleaning up took about an hour. She scooped up what she could with paper towels and dumped it into the trash; she swept and swept and swept; she moved the stove after all. Drawers came out. She cleaned cabinet doors and chair legs with a wet sponge.

At the end of it, she sat on the floor of her kitchen and took out her phone. *Can you come over?*

Are you OK?

OK/safe, but need help.

Give me 15.

Side door's open.

It was closer to ten minutes later that the door of her kitchen opened and Andy, sweaty in basketball shorts and a Red Sox T-shirt, stepped into her house for the first time in about two months. He saw her sitting on the floor, leaning back against the cabinets under the sink. "Jesus, Ev, are you all right? What's going on?"

"Just sit with me," she said.

He dropped down to sit next to her, stretching his legs out in front of him. He waited, then leaned toward her. "Why are we on the floor?"

He had grown his hair out a little, and realizing she hadn't seen him in such a long time that his hair was different made her chest tighten. "I was changing the light bulb," she said, looking up above the kitchen table. It was a start.

He followed her eyes up there. "From down here? That seems like the hard way."

She smiled. "I went to get the screwdriver."

He turned and looked up at the shelf. "Did you have it in the Giant Screw Can? Evvie, I *told* you that was asking for trouble."

"It was in the Giant Screw Can. Knocked over the can, knocked over the applesauce, knocked over the rice."

He cringed. "The giant rice thing, the enough-for-*Survivor* thing?"

She nodded. "That's the one."

"And it fell?"

"It fell. It all fell."

He crossed his arms and looked around, then took a quick breath and said, "I have to admit that sounds amazing."

"Oh, it was amazing all right. There was rice in the bathroom."

He gave a low whistle. "Wait, you cleaned it all up already?"

"I did."

He laughed. "Ev, you're supposed to call *before* you do the whole thing yourself."

"I didn't feel like calling you to come clean up my kitchen would be the thing to do. You know, considering." She turned toward him and sighed. "I said a lot of things that I should not have said."

"We both did, Ev."

"It shouldn't have taken me this long to call. It was stupid, and I'm so sad, and something is wrong. Everything is wrong." She rubbed the spot between her eyes. "My mother called. Not today. I mean, she had called while I was working on dinner, the day you guys came over."

"Oh shit," Andy said. "What happened?"

"She wants to see me, and she's been leaving messages. I can't put her off anymore. It's been weighing on me so much, but I didn't want to bother you about it—"

"Oh, Evvie, God, you wouldn't be—"

"I know. I just . . . I want to be the kind of person who . . . I don't know, who—"

"Does exactly the right thing all the time? Yeah, I do, too." He wiped his damp forehead with the bottom of his shirt. "Every day, I worry that I'm screwing up my kids, screwing up with Monica. Hell, I worry I screwed everything up already." He scooted closer to her and picked off a piece of rice stuck to her bare knee. "You're not going to make everybody happy all the time."

"I want to, though."

He put his arm around her shoulders. "I know you do."

"Baggage," she said. "So goddamn much. I should have my own cargo plane."

"Well, you're not alone. You remember I told you that night that Lori had the girls for a weekend?" Evvie nodded. "She told me that day that she wanted to have them with her for six weeks every summer."

"Oh, no."

"I've never been away from them for six weeks. Ever. I don't think I've been away from them for six days since Lilly was born. But Monica and I didn't want to wreck the night, so we decided to keep it to ourselves." He nodded. "Which wasn't a very successful plan."

Evvie smiled thinly. "What happened?"

"What usually happens when Lori makes noises about wanting to see them more. She sees them, and she remembers that she loves them, and they love her, but she'd rather take them out to Chuck E. Cheese's and on cruises than be the one who makes them eat plants and go to school. And she backs off. She backed off again. Door's open to longer visits in the future, but . . . not for now."

"Well, I'm glad it passed, at least."

"Can I ask about Dean leaving? I wanted to call you, but . . . I didn't."

"I already miss him a lot." She nodded. "A lot. That's the truth. I don't know how much else there is to say, but I'm at least trying to stop lying."

"Lying about what?"

"I lie a lot," she said simply. "I lied about the dishes."

"Goddammit, I knew there was something weird about that."

She laughed. "Yeah. Well, I broke the yellow dishes. Or, Dean and I broke them. Really, I broke them. It felt better than anything I had done in months, which I can't explain. I didn't know how to tell you about it. Just like I didn't know how to tell you I wanted to get a divorce."

"Can you tell me about it now?"

She told him that Tim was mean. She told him about the worst things he'd ever said that she could remember. She talked about his temper, how he hollered at her when he couldn't find things, the bruise on her back from the dresser. And then she caught sight of her own toes, and it reminded her of something. She took the deepest breath, maybe of her whole life. "Do you remember the cut on my foot? When I got stitches?"

He turned and looked at her. "You said you dropped a glass."

"I did say that. But Tim dropped a glass." She paused. "No, that's not even true. Tim *threw* a glass. He threw a glass at the living room floor, because he was mad at me. He threw the glass, and I stepped on it."

Andy shook his head. "Goddamn."

Evvie nodded very slowly. "You know, he told me once a week since I was in high school that I overreacted to everything. That everything with me was drama. After a while, I knew what he would say. He didn't even have to say it. So I think I just stopped telling anybody anything."

"I should have figured it out, though."

She shrugged. "I'm a better liar than you think." She picked at a spot on her knee. "Speaking of which, I should tell you there actually was insurance money, but I felt too guilty to spend it, so I haven't touched it. And you shouldn't bother arguing with me, because I'm not going to."

His eyes widened. "Holy shit."

She smiled. "Yeah. That's why I'm broke. That's why there's no way I can stay in this house. I'm going to look for something, maybe something smaller but closer to the water." She looked over at him. "I know I'm laying a lot on you. But I think that's about it for now. That, and I'm sorry."

"Well," he said, picking up a grain of rice from under the edge of the cabinet and tossing it over his shoulder into the sink, "I'm sorry, too."

"It's okay. I'm glad you showed up now."

"And I'm glad you called."

Evvie pulled her knees up and hung on to her shins with both hands. "I scared the shit out of myself tonight. I don't even know what to do next."

He put his arm around her shoulder, and she leaned on him. "It's okay. I've got you. You're going to figure it out."

Thirty-Four

A FEW DAYS LATER, Monica texted. *Long time no see. I'm baking bread. Can I bring you some this afternoon?*

Sure! Thank you. Come in the kitchen door and yell—might be working upstairs and not hear the knock.

But instead of working, Evvie, distracted and exhausted, eventually wandered into Dean's apartment—no, *the* apartment. She rested her hand on the counter of the kitchenette, and she looked around at the emptiness of the big rectangular room where she once drank bourbon and told stories and where she sometimes slept with the most famous disaster in Calcasset besides herself. In the middle of the floor, right under the ceiling fan, she stretched out on her back and closed her eyes.

She heard a knock on the door, but she stayed where she was, and before long, she heard it open. "Evvie?" came Monica's voice.

"I'm in here," she called out. She heard Monica drop her keys on the kitchen table.

"Oh, hi," Monica said.

"Hey."

"Can I join you?"

"Sure."

Monica came over and sat down on the floor, then lay back until they were right next to each other. "It's good to see you."

Evvie smiled at the ceiling. "Yeah, you, too."

Right there, stretched out on the floor, looking at the popcorn ceiling Evvie had always meant to replace, Monica updated Evvie on Rose's upcoming dance recital, Lilly's current obsession with collectible toys called Monsteroos ("like Beanie Babies if Tim Burton made them"), and everything she was trying to get done now that school had started. "How are things with you?" Monica finally asked.

"Okay. About to be busy. I'm going to sell the house, I think. It's too big for me. And I'm trying to get back to work. And right now, I'm putting off calling my mother."

Monica laughed. "Oof."

She hadn't planned to, but Evvie told Monica about Eileen: how she left when Evvie was little, how her visits and calls diminished gradually, how she would pop in at inconvenient times of her own choosing but miss all the weddings and the funerals. "But," Evvie said, "she's my mother. I don't want to have regrets. I know I have to see her and suck it up, but it always stresses me out."

"Well, you don't *have* to."

"No, I know. But I'm trying to . . . I don't know. I can't cut her off, so I might as well have peace with her."

"Hmm."

"What?"

"Well," Monica said, "I don't know why you're the only one who has to show up every time. If she can wait when she's deciding to wait, why can't she wait when *you* decide to wait? It doesn't have to be forever."

It was quiet, except for the jangle of Monica's bracelets as she shifted on the floor. "What's your mom like?" Evvie asked.

"Overprotective. Fun. Smart. She works for a law firm. Big Cuban family, a bunch of brothers and sisters, just like I have."

"Your mom's Cuban?"

"Yep. If you're thinking you wouldn't know it from looking at me, you're thinking the same thing a guy said to me when I was applying for a summer fellowship once. Right before he asked me if I'd ever seen the TV show *Jane the Virgin.*"

Evvie turned her head. "Seriously?"

"Seriously."

"But they're not Cuban."

"No, they're not."

"What did you do?"

"Nothing. But my brother called the guy two days later. He claimed to be from the law firm of Rodriguez, Rodriguez & Rodriguez, and he told the guy if he ever asked another question like that, he'd be sued for a million dollars."

"Is your brother a lawyer?"

"Not only is he not a lawyer, but he's my littlest brother. He was fifteen." Monica shrugged. "He has a low voice."

Evvie laughed.

"I want you to know I never spilled the beans about the lingerie thing, by the way. Andy came right out and asked me whether I thought you were sleeping with Dean."

Evvie turned to her. "What did you say?"

"I said, 'I hope so. I would be.'"

Laughing made Evvie's shoulders shake on the carpet. "Bet he loved that."

"I mean, it's the truth. I told him, the closest I ever came to sleeping with a professional athlete was the guy who wore the mascot costume at my college."

"You slept with the mascot?"

"Swear to God."

"And how was that?"

Monica hesitated, and then she turned to Evvie. "One time he told me he wanted to wear the tiger head to bed. He expected me to think it was, like, a very exciting idea."

"What did you say?"

"I said, 'As far as my own experience, I'd rather you wore the body.'"

They cackled, and it echoed in the empty apartment. Monica shifted her position on the floor. "Hey, is it okay if I call you up sometime and we can see a movie or something? I meet a lot of guys around here, and I need women friends or I lose my bearings."

"That would be fun. I used to have women friends," Evvie said. "I'm not sure what happened. When I was married, Tim wanted us to only have, you know, *couple* friends. He thought I'd complain about him to people. Eventually, it was easier not to start anything, and I stopped going out very much."

"Wait . . . what?"

"Yeah, I know. He was weird."

"That's not weird, Evvie," Monica said. "That's sort of . . . emotionally abusive."

Evvie had told stories about cutting her foot open on the debris of her husband's anger, and about his temper. She had dreamed over and over about his red face and his hot breath. She had told Dean, right from the beginning, that he wasn't good to her. That she didn't love him. She had whispered that she didn't miss him. *He was mean,* she had told Andy. But there it was, a diagnosis like you'd give someone with a fever and a red throat, where you'd peek with a flashlight and say, *hmm,* and then say that you'd be spitballing, that you're no expert, but it sure looked like strep to you.

That's sort of emotionally abusive.

"Yeah," Evvie finally said. "I keep saying I'm going to get into therapy one of these days."

"I'm in favor of all that stuff," Monica said. "One of my doctors said, 'Your head is the house you live in, so you have to do the maintenance.'"

"That's . . . weird."

"Yes. Mental health metaphors are sort of hit or miss in my experience. But I've been on antidepressants since I was seventeen, so I can give you a name if you need somebody."

I need somebody all right, Evvie thought to herself.

Two days later, Evvie lay on the floor of the apartment again with her phone in her hand and her heart pounding. *It won't get easier. You might as well just do it. Then you'll be done.* She couldn't say quite why she'd taken out her black and pink baseball glove and had it resting against her hip.

She went into her history and found the call she was looking for. She highlighted it and hit the button.

"Hello?" Her mom's voice was always eager and never completely believable. She was probably sitting on her patio, her cat on her lap, her sunglasses pushed up on top of her head.

Evvie could feel her hand shaking. "Hi, Mom."

"Evvie! I'm so glad you called! I was starting to be afraid you hadn't gotten my messages. How are you, sweetie?"

"I'm fine." She scratched the carpet with the fingers of her free hand. "How are you?"

"Busy. All over the place. I had a craft fair, and that went very well. And I saw a very good play, you know, it was on Broadway last year, it's touring now. It's about an affair, do you know the one I mean?"

"I'm not sure."

"It's wonderful. You should see it. It's so moving."

Evvie closed her eyes. "Listen, Mom, I don't have a lot of time, but I wanted to get back to you about what you said about being in town."

"Yes! Yes, I'm going to be around at the end of September. What would be a good day for you to come down to Portland for lunch? It's been ages. I know we've both dropped the ball a little on staying in touch."

Evvie clenched and unclenched her fist and played with the pink laces on the glove. "I don't think we're going to be able to get together this time."

There was a pause. "Oh? You're not in town then?"

For a second, she thought that maybe for once, her mom had thrown her a rope. She opened her mouth with such gratitude, she was about to say yes, yes, she was traveling, that was it exactly. But she remembered being in Dean's truck with him on the way back from Thanksgiving, and she remembered him saying she had to start telling somebody the truth.

"No, I'm not traveling. I just don't want to, Mom. I'm not saying forever, but not right now."

"I'm not sure what you mean."

"I don't want to get together right now."

"Don't be silly. I haven't seen you in ages. We'll check in."

"No. No, not right now."

Now Eileen's voice got tighter. "Well, now I really don't understand. What's all the drama about?"

She kept her eyes closed. "It's not drama. I don't have the energy to bring you up to speed on everything that's happened to me in the last two years in two hours just because you think it sounds interesting. I just broke up with somebody, I might be selling the house—I have a lot going on, and I'm not going to add to it."

"I'll make time whenever it's convenient for you," Eileen said, as if Evvie had said none of it.

"Mom, you're not listening. I don't want to. I'm—" *Take a class in not apologizing all the time,* she heard Andy's voice say. "I don't want to."

"Honey, I know it's been hard for you. But I'm not asking for much; it's lunch. If there's something we need to talk out, we'll talk it out. I want to help. And I want to hear all about your boyfriend."

"I understand that, but I don't want to talk about it with you."

"Eveleth," Eileen said. "You only have one mom, and I only have one daughter. And I don't want either of us to have any regrets." There it was. The crescendo of Eileen Ashton's symphony for telephone and preprinted greeting card always ended here, with the same cymbal crash: *But how will you feel if I die?*

"Mom, I'll talk to you later."

"Evvie, it's not like you to be like this."

"No," Evvie said. "I know it's not."

Thirty-Five

"EVELETH," SAID DR. Jane Talco with a smile as she swung open the door of her office. "Come on in. It's good to see you again. Pardon my stacks of paperwork."

Evvie stepped into the room, beige and blue and calming, feeling her heart pound so fast she thought she might pass out. She lowered herself onto the couch and tried to smile a mentally healthy smile, whatever that was. "It's good to see you, too," she finally said, as evenly as she could, which was ridiculous, because it wasn't good at all.

"So," Dr. Talco said, settling into her wing chair. "It's been a while. Tell me what's going on."

The surprising thing to Evvie was not that she cried, since she'd been doing that on and off for the last four days, but that she cried so *soon*. "Shit," she whispered to herself.

"There are tissues on the table. Take a breath."

Evvie dabbed at her eyes, managed a long exhale, and then focused her eyes on a painting of gulls on the wall behind the doctor's chair. "I feel like I'm already bad at this."

"You're doing fine," Dr. Talco told her.

"What, crying as soon as I sit down?"

"I've had people cry for six months," the doctor said. Evvie felt her eyes widen a little. "I'm not saying you will."

"I don't know what to say," Evvie told her. "I guess 'help.' But I don't know what else."

"Well, what made you pick up the phone and call me?" Dr. Talco was holding a silver pen, rolling it a little between her fingers.

"I dropped something. In my kitchen. And I don't know what happened, I just . . . flipped out. I guess I thought I might be going crazy. Or whatever is less offensive than that." She explained about the rice and the can and hearing herself wail. It sounded as strange when she described it as it had felt when it happened. If her head really was the house she lived in, Evvie was increasingly afraid that walking through it and stomping on the floorboards, rattling the beams, might make it all collapse right down to the concrete slab. "I ended up screaming on the floor of my kitchen over having to clean up some stuff I spilled. And like I said, it made me think I might be crazy. It just didn't seem normal."

"I don't know about that," Dr. Talco told her. "When we talked last time, I told you that I thought in your situation, most people would need some help. Remind me how long ago your husband died?"

"Almost two years." She shook her head. "Yeah, wow, in a couple of weeks, it'll be two years," Evvie said. She instantly felt fraudulent, letting this doctor treat her like she might be grieving. "I also just ended a relationship I was maybe getting into. And I might have broken up with my mother, too. I'm not sure my husband's accident is what's wrong."

"You know, nothing's necessarily *wrong*."

"You didn't see me on the floor of my kitchen."

Dr. Talco smiled. "You would be shocked how many people tell me that they got through cancer or divorce or having their house burn down, but then they lost their keys or they ran out of coffee or the dog chewed on a slipper, and they fell to pieces. It's just that last insult."

"I feel . . ." This was all Evvie said for a while. She said, *I feel*, and she stopped. She looked out the window and at the floor, and she kept expecting Dr. Talco to take over. She expected her to lead. It went beyond an awkward silence until it was a cooperative silence. One with intent. Evvie finally cleared her throat into her fist. "I feel like I should be able to figure this out. I keep telling myself, you know? Pull it together. You're not starving, and you have friends, and just . . . get a grip."

Dr. Talco tapped her index fingers together. "Did you know it's possible to remove your own teeth with pliers?"

Evvie looked at her blankly. "That's not what I thought you were going to say."

"No, no, probably not. But it's true. If you have a bad tooth, you can take a pair of pliers, stick them in there, and pull as hard as you can. Is that something you would do?"

"This feels like a trick question."

"Stay with it."

"No, I don't think I would pull out my own tooth with pliers."

"That's what I always tell people about therapy. It's not a question of whether you could try to do it by yourself. You can always try it. But it can be dangerous, and it's harder. Trying to buck yourself up is the tooth pliers of mental health."

She remembered Monica saying *Mental health metaphors are a mixed bag*, and it made her smile. She sort of bought this one.

"Evvie, if it helps you to hear it, given everything you've said in the last five minutes, this is a whole lot to tackle alone."

"So you think I'm a candidate for therapy."

"Oh, practically everyone's a candidate for therapy. Myself included. The question is, do you want to give it a try? Do you want to talk about you?"

Evvie nodded. "Yeah."

Evvie put the Bancroft house on the market. It sold fast once she let her realtor sweep in and remove half of what was in it, making it look even bigger, even emptier. They replaced the living room rug, meaning whatever remained of the spots of her blood from the glass that Tim broke went out the front door. One last time, she lay on the floor in the apartment, pushing her palms into the floor, missing Dean so much that she felt dizzy. And then she packed, and she left, and she lived with her dad for a couple of months and looked for a new place.

She picked it out on a chilly fall day when she'd just taken her heavier jacket out of storage. Betsey, her real estate agent, brought Evvie in her boxy little red car across the short bridge from Calcasset to Kettle Bay Island, sometimes shorthanded as KBI. The island was mostly little cottages with one or two bedrooms, some of them were rented out in the summer. "I think you might like this one," Betsey said. "I thought of you as soon as I saw it. It's not big, but it looks right out at the water."

It was a house with a name—Kettlewood, they called it. When Evvie opened the door, she saw a woodstove in the corner and the kind of cheap and durable carpeting that was common in rental houses, with a worn path from the kitchen to the living room and then out to the sitting room facing the harbor. Most of the water side of the house was picture windows, and then there was a small deck, big enough for a couple of lounge chairs and maybe a charcoal grill. The kitchen was small, and she'd have to replace the appliances. But it turned out the furnace was sound, the roof passed muster, and when her father came and walked around, he said, "Yuh. Looks like a good one, Eveleth."

Before she finished emptying the Bancroft house, Evvie had invited Tim's mom, Lila, to have a look around and see if there was anything that she'd like to take as a keepsake. Lila wandered around the house, and Evvie knew she was staring at all the places Tim had stood, sat, or held court about medicine. Whatever else he had been, Tim had been hers. "Sometimes I still can't believe it," Lila said. "It's so sad."

Evvie didn't even know which sad thing she meant. So much was sad. *Everything* was sad here. Sadness lived in the walls like a poltergeist, and it was time to run. When Lila left an hour later, after a cup of coffee and a chat about the scholarship at the school in Tim's honor and the work Evvie had to do at Kettlewood, she said, "I hope you're as happy in the new place as you were here." It didn't even feel like lying when Evvie hugged Lila again and pretended to want the same. It felt like dropping a gift into her pocket, passing a talisman to someone for whom it could do some good. It was just giving Lila back Tim's death to grieve as she would, like she'd given his shirts to Goodwill. And like she'd finally made a fire in the fireplace and burned her box of receipts and ticket stubs and his flash cards from college.

While she waited to move, she called Nona and managed to catch her between classes.

"Nona, it's Evvie Drake. I'm so sorry it's been such a long time. I've had a lot going on. I should have called."

"Well, I'm glad to hear from you," Nona told her. "I was about to give up and call somebody who's not nearly as good as you are." They did not talk about condolences or regrets. They didn't talk about Tim, because Nona didn't know him, and she didn't care. They didn't talk about Dean, because she didn't follow baseball. She knew only Evvie. She knew only Evvie's work. Not family, not good deeds, not the broken-legged birds she might have saved. Just her work.

They agreed to collaborate on a book examining the effects of industrial fishing operations and climate change on the lobstermen of Maine. The work would start in April. Nona sent her a new voice recorder and a bottle of champagne with a note that said, "We're going to do great work together. Thank you." Andy took her to dinner to celebrate.

At Thanksgiving, her father carved the turkey, and when he told everyone what he was thankful for, he said that he was thankful for his daughter, "and everything she does every day to make me so proud, even though she lost so much." It was a start. Maybe someday, she'd tell him more, about the blue suitcase and the bruise on her back. But Dr. Talco had assured her that she shouldn't unless she wanted to. "You have nothing to confess," she'd said.

For Christmas, Andy and Monica gave her a gift certificate for a spa day at a resort in Bar Harbor. When she opened it at their house on Christmas morning, Monica leaned toward her and said, "We're going together, if that's okay." Evvie nodded. When they got their massages in January, Evvie breathed deeply and blissfully while a woman spread a hot clay mask across her back and shoulders. But when the woman moved a bit of her hair out of the way to keep it clean, Evvie gasped, struck by a sense memory of Dean nudging her hair off the back of her neck with his fingers. Her eyes stung.

In February, Evvie moved into Kettlewood, and a week later, she went to Thunderous A-Paws, a dog rescue in Thomaston that Diane Marsten had recommended to her. Evvie stepped up to the desk and said, "Hi. I think my new house needs a dog." The woman at the desk grinned at her.

Back in what they called their "dormitory," she went into a small room where a brown puppy with big feet was dragging around a plush baseball as big as his head. She laughed out loud and bent down close to him. "Oh, hi, buddy." The pup kept the ball in his mouth as he made his way over to her. Without letting go, he looked directly into her eyes and said, *Rrr?*

Evvie sat on the floor. The puppy dropped the baseball and devoted himself fully to what seemed to be an effort to touch every part of her with his nose before leaping into her chest through her rib cage. She kept talking to him, feeling his soft coat under her fingers, laughing when he tried to crawl up onto her bent knees and landed in a heap on his side, still wagging his entire back end.

Four days and a home visit later, she was lying on the floor of her new house with a puppy stretched out on her chest while she skritched his ears and watched his sleepy, moony eyes droop shut.

Evvie had been in her house for a few weeks when she decided it was as good a night as any to hook up the speakers she'd bought used from a friend of Andy's. The system was all wireless, with a long sound bar in the living room and smaller ones for the kitchen and the bedroom. She connected it all to her phone, and as soon as she pressed play, she jumped. The dog jumped, and his ears stood up like a kangaroo's. It was *so loud*. She started to reach for the volume, but she stopped, amused by the feeling of her feet, in socks, buzzing with vibrations in the floor.

The nearest neighbor wasn't close. There was no one trying to sleep upstairs, or trying to make a phone call, or trying to get work done. So she stood for a minute, and she let the soles of her feet thrum. She walked over to the wall and laid her hand against it, and she felt it there, too, and she laughed. "Holy shit." There were sounds that felt thick and round under her palm and ones that felt sharp and thin. She walked over to the window and leaned close to it, and where the lights were reflected, she could see the glass shaking just a little. She laid her flat hand against the cool pane and when the bass pounded, it tickled her skin. When she moved away, she could see her greasy handprint, like a high five from a ghost. It was, she suddenly knew, her window to smudge.

She started to bounce on the balls of her feet with what now seemed to be the pulse of the whole house. Webster was beginning to gather that this was playtime, so he came over next to her and crouched down with his butt in the air. "Puppy dance!" Evvie said to him, and she did the twist for her little brown dog as he beat his tail against the ground and then offered a yip. She shimmied and ponied over to the kitchen, where she soloed on an imaginary piano, skimming her fingers across her beat-up laminate countertop.

She spun down the hallway from the kitchen to the bedroom, and she dropped onto her back on the bed, feet wiggling, hands waving, screaming out the last chorus. As she finished holding the final note with her eyes shut, she felt a damp nose nuzzle her forehead. She emerged from her reverie to find Webster trying to climb onto her chest.

Evvie sat up and scratched the dog's ears. Her face was hot and sticky, she was entirely out of breath, and she owed nothing to anyone.

Thirty-Six

D EAN STOOD IN his parents' study and stared at his Little League trophies, some framed articles about his career—the good parts—and a variety of Marlins and Yankees swag. It was March, and he wasn't getting ready for a season, and it still made his shoulder itch. He'd figured the visit would do him good.

"I'm about to put dinner on the table," his mom said, putting her arm around his waist.

He draped his around her shoulders. "You guys don't have to keep all this stuff, you know."

"You don't think we should at least hang on to your bobblehead?" She reached out and touched it, and it nodded enthusiastically.

"Man, I thought that was cool when they made that," he said, smiling. "My own bobblehead. Might have been the pinnacle of my career."

"Not the *SVU* cameo?" she asked. "You did meet Ice-T."

"I did," he said, and then he put his fingers on his own little image to still it. "Okay, you can keep that. But you could probably lose a lot of the rest of this stuff."

"Are you kidding? I still come in here to try on the big foam hand with the 'we're number one' finger. I wear it during fights with your dad."

"You do not."

"I could."

"You know, there's not a lot to be proud of anymore, Mom."

She knocked his hip with hers. "Of course we're proud. You were always going to stop playing at some point. You were always going to get old, if nothing else. You've got some gray in your hair, you know."

"Yeah, yeah, I know."

"Your dad put on your jersey every time you pitched. We were in the car one time when you struck out the side and he honked the horn until I thought he was going to get a ticket."

Dean looked at the *Daily News* headline that called him a hero. "I was a pretty good pitcher," he said to his mother.

"You were a great pitcher. You remember that?" She pointed to a picture cut out of *The New York Times* where they'd caught him in midair after a World Series win. He had leapt a couple of feet with his legs splayed like a hurdler's, his mouth open in a holler, his fists over his head. The photo had been on T-shirts and magazine covers, and he'd seen two different pictures of people who'd had it tattooed on their arms. "You still did that," she said.

"Yeah," he said. "I did. It's just . . . I'm the only one, you know? I'm the only one who knows I did every . . . everything I could think of, everything they told me to do. I'm going to spend the rest of my life hearing from people who think I didn't care enough."

Angie slowly rubbed his back. "Dean, people don't like . . . fragility. It makes them nervous. They're scared thinking things just happen. They think there's always something you can do to keep monsters from getting under the bed. Do you know what I mean?"

"You're saying judgmental bastards feel invincible."

She shrugged. "I didn't say it was going to make you feel better. But what should make you feel better is that you get to keep every good day you had playing." She put her hand on his elbow. "And whether you ever pick up another baseball as long as you live, we're not going

to be any less proud of you than we were when they took that picture." She looked at her watch. "Now, I'm going to serve dinner in
about five minutes. Don't make me come back and drag you out."

"I'll be there," he said, leaning down to kiss her on the cheek.
"Thank you, Mom."

At the table, Stuart got right to the point. "You hear anything from
Evvie these days?"

Angie shook her head. "Stuart, I thought we were going to work up
to that. Is this working up to it?"

Stuart shrugged. "I'm up to it."

Dean spooned potatoes onto his plate. "I get a text from her here
and there. But not really. That . . . ended."

"Well, that's dumb."

"Stuart," Angie said again. "Maybe take it easy?"

"You don't think it's dumb?"

"I didn't say that."

Dean buttered a piece of bread. "Well, Dad, the head case stuff, she
couldn't get used to. She pushed and pushed and pushed for me to try
to get back into pitching, and when it didn't work out, she pretty
much invited me to leave."

"I didn't realize she cared that much about baseball," Angie said.

"Yeah, I gotta say that doesn't sound right," Stuart agreed.

"Believe me, she was pretty relentless," Dean told them. "It was like
you guys with All-Star Camp all over again."

Angie and Stuart looked at each other. "Now, wait a minute," Angie
said. "Tell me how you think you got to All-Star Camp."

"You guys badgered me until I agreed to go."

Dean's mother gave this contemptuous "Ha!" and his father, simul-
taneously, said, "You've got to be kidding me."

"What?"

Stuart speared a piece of chicken. "You're remembering that
wrong, pal."

"How? What's your version?"

"You brought home that brochure, said you'd been invited, but it was pretty clear it was going to be hard work with a lot of guys you didn't know. It seemed like it spooked you. You told me and Mom you didn't want to do it. We said, 'Are you sure?' You said yes. Next day, that brochure's on the table again. We ask you again, 'Well, now, do you want to do this, Dean-o?' 'No, no, I don't want to.'"

"You were adamant," Angie added.

"But the thing keeps showing up. Every time you walk off with it saying you don't want to go, it shows up again. I told your mother, 'Angie, either Dean wants to go to this or we've got a ghost that wants him to.'"

Angie laughed. "You did, I forgot that."

"So the next day, you come home and you say, 'You know what I found out today, Dad? I found out Teddy's going to that All-Star Camp.' And that's when I said, you know, 'Go. You're going.' 'Badgered' you, for goodness' sake."

Dean frowned. "That's bizarre. I don't remember doing that at all."

"You know I'd tell you if your dad was fantasizing," Angie said. "But that's the way I remember it, too. You dropped hints. And more hints. And even more hints. I think we were invited to badger you."

"What," Stuart said, "did you leave a bunch of brochures lying around for Evvie, too?"

Dean was quiet for a minute. "Dammit."

Thirty-Seven

O N THE LAST Friday in March, just before eleven in the morning, Evvie took the quick drive into Calcasset with a white box next to her on the passenger seat, addressed to Dean in New York. She pulled up to the curb near the post office and climbed out with the box in her arms. The sun was not fully out, but it was trying, and a gull soared over her, cawing. Just as she neared the doors, they swung open, and Dr. Paul Schramm came through them, with a huge pile of mail rubber-banded together. He'd finally retired, and now and then, Evvie's dad would tell her something he'd heard about where the Schramms were, where their postcards back to friends were coming from. "Eveleth, hello!" he said.

"Hi, Dr. Schramm." She shifted the package under her arm. "That's a lot of letters you've got there."

"Hey, I keep telling you to call me Paul," he said. He looked down at the stack. "Helen and I were in Nova Scotia for a couple of weeks, so they held it for us. I'm sure it's mostly junk. How are you? I heard you sold the house."

"I did, I did." She nodded. "A very nice guy who has a printing business in Augusta bought it. I'm sure you'll meet him in the next few weeks."

"Must have been hard to part with."

"It was. It was a beautiful house, but much too big now that it's only me." And just like that, Tim floated briefly between them like a stream of blown bubbles.

Dr. Schramm nodded gently. "I can imagine. And you're living out on KBI now, right? Nice as your old house was, I've always loved those cottages. My aunt lived out there for years. I used to sit on her deck and look at the boats."

"I do a lot of that myself. I still have work to do on it," she said. "I'll tell you what: once I get it in shape, I'll have you and Helen out for dinner, okay? We'll eat on the deck."

"I'm going to take you up on that," he said with a nod. "You take care, honey."

"You, too, Paul." She pulled the heavy door open and went up to the counter. She set the box down.

"First class mail?" said the clerk, without looking at her.

Evvie smoothed her hand over the address label, and closed her eyes for a second. *Please, please, please.* Then she opened them and said, "Yes. Please."

A few days after she mailed the package, Evvie woke up when the light started to brighten the bedroom, and the minute she opened her eyes, she was confronted by a plaintive, damp-eyed stare.

"Oh, hello there, pup," she said to Webster, reaching down to scratch him behind the ear. He closed his eyes blissfully but briefly, then resumed staring sadness daggers from his position sitting on the floor next to the bed. "Are you hungry?" she asked. His ears twitched. "Should we get food?" He hopped up and stood, and she threw back the covers. "Let's go get breakfast!" She heard Webster gallop around the corner, through the living room, and into the kitchen, where she heard his claws skid across the floor as he tried in vain to stop.

In the kitchen, she emptied a cup of food into Webster's dish, then put the coffee on. It was nine in the morning. Maybe Dean would be having breakfast. Maybe he was with someone. She should have asked Andy if he was seeing anyone before she sent that package. She should have asked *him* if he was. She put on sweatpants and her fleece jacket to take Webster for a walk along the lane that led from her house out to the main road.

She and Webster walked out the lane every day, through a thick swath of evergreens, and every day, she thought consciously about smiling and trying to meet the neighbors. This house was about twenty minutes from her old one, still near her dad, still near Andy and his kids. But it was a new neighborhood, to the degree it was any neighborhood at all, and one where the houses were so far apart that it was too easy to feel like she lived all alone.

Back at the house, she took Webster off his leash and then she made herself something to eat, checking her phone entirely too often, wondering if she'd hear anything today. After a while, she went into her living room, where she could see the fog was fading and she was beginning to be able to make out the boats through the window.

As she went to settle herself on the couch with a book, she froze in the living room and put a hand to her heart. If she'd been asked if she could still pick out Dean's truck's engine in a list of ten similar rumbles, she'd have denied that she could, but now she knew differently, because the minute she heard it, she was sure. She had only the dog to look at, so she said to him, "Hey, pup, who's that?" Still inexperienced and unsure what absolute loyalty required in the face of an obvious intruder, Webster yipped at the sound of the truck with as much menacing excitement as a twelve-pound puppy can muster.

Evvie went to the front door and opened it in time to see Dean pull up next to her car and step out. After six months of intermittent texting and the occasional wistfully sexy dream—okay, also the occasional wistfully sexy *daydream*—her mind had smoothed the edges of his looks. It remembered that he was tall and dark-haired with mossy green eyes, and it remembered the shape of his shoulders and the tilt of his hips. But as he approached with a sloping smile, she realized it had discarded the mole on his cheek and the fact that he walked with a slight hitch in his step.

They stood on opposite sides of the door, both smiling. And then he held up a black baseball glove with pink laces. Taped to the palm was her note. In big black letters, she had written: *I MISS YOU*.

"You lose your glove?" he asked.

She bit her lip. "I thought you'd text me. Or call. I didn't expect you to come all the way up here. I'd have come to you."

He didn't often smolder at her willfully, but he did in this moment. He met her eyes, and he said, "This was faster."

Her face got hot, her knees got wobbly. "You should come in," she said, opening the door.

Thirty-Eight

I T FELT SO familiar having him pass her in her new doorway, as she again encountered that shoulder, as she showed him into her house. As soon as he was inside, he turned around and pulled her in, his hands linked across her back. "I hope it's okay I showed up. I got home last night from a tournament where I was coaching, and it was too late to call. I was going to call you today, but I woke up at four in the morning, and once I figured out I could be here by lunch, I just . . . left."

She nodded, smiling. "It's okay you showed up." He leaned over and kissed her, and at first, she floated in it, putting her hands on his arms, remembering what it felt like, hearing her own heart. When she felt him pull her in tighter, she dug her fingers into his back. In the months without him, she'd forgotten and somehow not forgotten at the same time; it was like hearing the first lyrics of a song and realizing you can sing all the rest.

Suddenly, Webster yipped and jumped up on Dean's legs, inspecting him for signs of danger, hot dogs, or past encounters with cats. "Webster, Webster," she said as Dean pulled back from her, crouched down, and scratched Webster's ears, rendering any security function instantly moot.

"So this is the dog," he said.

"Yes. This is Webster."

"Because?"

Evvie laughed. "When I showed him to Andy and Monica, she asked me what kind of a dog he was, and I said a shepherd mix, because that's what they told me at the rescue. But Andy said, 'He looks like the dog who's in the dictionary under "dog."' So I named him Webster."

"You also got a house."

"I did! You want to see? I mean, can you stay a while?"

He pushed a bit of her hair behind her ear. "Yes."

"Okay. C'mon." She led him through the kitchen and showed him the new table in her combined living and dining room. "Big enough for my dad and Kell and Andy and all his people to come over for family stuff. Over there, I have a woodstove." They walked into the room with the huge picture windows, which were now offering a limited view of a few of the nearest boats. "And this is my view."

"Holy shit," he said softly. "This is great."

"Yeah. I love it. My realtor heard me say that I had always wanted a house on the water, so she brought me out here. The carpeting's all old, and the appliances in the kitchen are, you know. More 'charming' than 'modern'? But I love it. I'm willing to work on it." She hugged herself at the elbows. "How's New York? Should we sit down?" He nodded, and they sat in the two club chairs that were very much like the ones he'd had in his apartment.

"New York is good. I'm back in my old place in my old neighborhood, and a lot of my friends are around. I've gone back to being able to see guys I knew before without feeling fucking terrible, so that's a good thing. I do some coaching sometimes, I do clinics."

"How's . . . everything else? Are you happy?"

He was quiet, and then he said, "Are you? You want to tell me why you sent me your glove?" His words hung there and hung there. "You're up, Minnesota."

Finally, Evvie took a breath. "I have wanted to call you. But there was a lot I had to do that just couldn't wait," she said. "The house, my mom, work. A ton of therapy."

"Learn anything interesting?"

She fidgeted, picking at one of her fingernails. "Believe me, we'll get there eventually. There's plenty. Mostly, I just wanted to tell you that I wish I'd done a bunch of things differently. I should've listened better. Fixers want to fix, and I wanted to fix something. I wanted to help. And I shouldn't have pushed." She took a breath. "But I also think that in fairness to me, you—"

He held up one hand. "Evvie, I wanted to fix it, too, and I should have just said that, and it wasn't fair that I didn't. I said yes to the game. I said yes to everything. You were right. The pinecones, the park in the middle of the night. I really wanted it all back." He reached down to pet the dog. "But, Ev, when it didn't work, when it looked like I was maybe going to be a high school gym teacher, it seemed like you thought that wasn't enough."

This cut deep, right between her ribs. "Dean, I didn't want you to be able to pitch because it would mean you were enough." They looked at each other. "I wanted you to be able to pitch because it would mean that *I* was enough."

He wrinkled his brow. It wasn't even disbelief, just curiosity. And then it dissolved. "You're enough."

She nodded. "So are you." She smiled and took a deep breath. "Therapy, right? You know, the dog was her idea."

"You got a prescription for a dog?"

"Not exactly, she can't prescribe anything. If that happens, that will be the psychiatrist that I also have. No, my therapist thought that since I'm still trying to figure out my life and give it some structure, having somebody like Webster, who demands that I get out of the house, would be a positive thing."

He nodded slowly. "This is a lot."

"Yeah, well, I'm really broken," Evvie told him brightly.

"Oh, sure, me, too."

~~~~~

They sat and talked in the living room into the afternoon, and when it started to rain, they watched the drops speckle the water and wet down the lobster boats, and Evvie took her wool plaid blanket out of the trunk in the sitting room and draped it over her legs. She made tea and showed Dean how to put up a fire in the woodstove, and she shared her informal research about what kinds of wood burned best.

Dean picked up Webster's favorite toy, made from old T-shirts Evvie had braided together, and engaged in a lengthy battle of tugging and wrestling that also included significant growling by both parties. Evvie smacked Dean on the elbow and said not to torture her dog, and Dean said to take it up with the dog, and Webster wore himself out and walked over to lie by the woodstove.

When it got to the late afternoon, Evvie poured bourbon and made snacks, and they sat on the love seat with their feet on the coffee table and listened to the new episode of the true-crime podcast they'd both been following. Dean rolled his eyes and complained that the people were clearly never going to solve the case, and Evvie passed him a peanut butter cracker and said it was about the journey. He reached over and hooked his index finger through hers.

The show ended, and Evvie suggested they take Webster for a walk. They took the long way, up the lane and out to the road, then down around the curve of the inlet to a short little bridge that connected Calcasset to the island where Evvie lived now. There was so little water that cars rambled over the bridge in only a few seconds, but if you asked everyone along Evvie's curved road, they'd say they lived on Kettle Bay Island, as if it were an isolated hamlet. Evvie explained that there were, in fact, also islands in the bay that you couldn't drive to, that you had to take a ferry to. She particularly liked one where there was a lobster fishery and a tiny town that swirled with tourists in the summer. She'd take him out there sometime, she said, when the weather was warmer. As they walked, she held the leash in one hand and he put his arm around her shoulders.

When they got back, they curled up on the couch and turned on the TV. Immediately, they both cracked up. "It had to be baseball," Evvie said.

"Oh, it's not just baseball," Dean told her. "It's *opening day*."

She gestured toward the game with the remote control. "You want to watch this?"

"Are you kidding? I want to know how much you've picked up."

So they watched for a while. Dean told her which guys he knew, which pitcher he could tell could have used one or two more spring training starts, and which hitters had changed their stances. And sometimes, they stopped to make out or have a snack. That was the perfect way to watch a game, he told her.

They ate at the table as it got dark outside. Evvie explained that she was only a couple of weeks away from starting work with Nona. She'd added some transcription clients and was doing a few hours of paperwork a week for Betsey, with whom she'd become friendly while she was buying her place. It wasn't quite what she wanted yet, but it was work, and she was paying her mortgage with her own money.

They did the dishes, standing next to each other by the sink, and then they went back into the big room by the big windows and sank into the big chairs, and they could hear the water slapping the boats. She let Webster out one more time, into the little fenced-in yard her dad had built for him, and as she stood in the open door to call him inside, she felt Dean slide his arms around her waist. He whispered in her ear that he wanted to see her room, and she laughed, and the dog came inside and settled himself. She took Dean down the hall, where he noticed right off that she had a new bed. It was not the one she'd slept in with her husband; it was not the one she'd slept in with him. It was one she'd only slept in alone—and, of course, with Webster, when he jumped up, which he was emphatically not supposed to do. But tell that to a puppy.

They kissed, and when he let her go, he saw that her eyes were a little watery, that there were tears gathering on her lower lids. At first, he held her shoulders, asking what it was, asking if she wasn't sure.

But she chuckled and said it was not that with a dry certainty that made it clear it was not, at all, that.

He tugged off his shirt, and she pulled the white sweater over her head. She had skipped her rituals. She knew she was a little bit sweaty and flawed, but he seemed unconcerned. He was sweaty and flawed, after all, and it didn't stop her from feeling like her joints were dissolving when he kissed her, like every part of her that he touched was pulling her toward him.

He muttered—he growled—that he had missed her, and when she said she had missed him, too, it felt like she said it in a voice that no one else would have been able to hear from even six inches away, like she'd whispered it into herself and he'd felt it come out through her fingers on his back. She kept breathing; she kept listening to him breathing.

Later, so close to each other that they were sharing a pillow, Evvie and Dean lay face-to-face in her bed. "What do we do now?" she said. "Not *right* now. You know what I mean."

"Evvie, I'm doing pretty well in New York."

Her stomach dropped.

"I like my place. I like coaching. I like the clinics, and I like living around the guys that I've known my whole life. I love the city, I love being able to do a ton of things that aren't playing, and even though I've missed you—and I missed you a lot—I've been pretty happy."

All she said was "Ah," and she was so glad to be in the mostly dark room, where the way she was sure she looked could remain a secret.

"And I think you're doing well, too. This house is fucking great. You're on the water. You're where you love to be. And that's a great dog."

She smiled a little. This, she could not deny.

"It seems like you made up with Andy."

"Well," she said, "it's not like it was. We don't see each other every week. We don't talk every day. He has the kids, he's with Monica, he's busy with everything. But I'm getting used to it. My therapist calls it grieving the first call."

"What does that mean?"

"She says when something happens, good or bad, you can only call one person first. And if you've been somebody's first call, it's hard not to be their first call anymore. She says it's one of the reasons why parents sometimes feel sad when their kids are getting married. It's not just the empty nest. They're not the first call anymore. I'm not Andy's first call anymore. It doesn't mean I want to *be* his girlfriend, and it doesn't mean I don't like her. But it was sad. It's different. The doctor says it's important to be sad."

He reached over to kiss her forehead. "I'm sorry."

Under the covers, she shrugged. "It's okay."

"So you're good. And I'm good. And I feel like I could stay in New York and you could stay up here, and we'd be okay." He pushed a bit of her hair behind her ear. "But I don't think that's what we should do."

Evvie couldn't keep from smiling. "No?"

"I don't know a lot about . . . a lot. Where to live, what kind of job I want, what kind of family situation. But I am really in love with you. And, you know, unless I'm still throwing into the stands, I think that's how you feel, too. So I think we should be in the same place and then work on all the other stuff. Because when we're in the same place, I'm happier, and I think you're happier, too."

In the dark, Evvie closed her eyes and smiled.

"You should say something," Dean prodded, nudging at her with his knee. "I'm kind of flapping in the wind here."

"Sorry. It just . . . kind of freaks me out," she whispered.

He frowned. "Why?"

"The last time I tried to go off and be happy, somebody died. I feel like if it's too good, something terrible will happen."

There was a pause. "That's what you meant, that night when you were stinking drunk. *I should never have tried to be happy.*"

"Yes," she whispered.

He grabbed her hand under the covers and pulled it up so their clasped hands were under their chins. "I mean, Ev, if you wait long enough, something terrible is always going to happen. But I don't think that's because you try to be happy, you know? I think it just is. You . . . you wake up one day and you need a whole new plan. Not to brag, but that's my area of expertise." He squeezed her hand tighter.

"There are just a lot of things that get taken away," she said.

"I know. I know. But that happens even if you try to throw everything back first. You just have to hope in the end you'll have enough left."

She smiled. "I love you," she said.

He seemed to stop breathing for a second. And then he let go of her hand and rested his palm on her jaw. "Good."

She wriggled closer to him. "You want to live here for a while?"

He wasn't even surprised. "Yeah."

"I mean, you'd have to move all over again. What about your apartment?"

"Well," he said, adjusting his head on the pillow, "I would keep it. We could have both for now. You never know what you're going to want to do. You like history, New York has a lot of great museums. We can be down there part of the time if you want. It's not terrible having a place to go in New York."

"So you want to stay flexible."

"I know I'm making it sound half-assed. I don't mean to. Don't get me wrong, Ev. I want to marry you, probably."

She laughed. "Oh, *probably*."

"But right now, I want to live with you, in your house, with your dog, and listen to boats and walk in the woods and maybe get my job back at school. And when something terrible happens, we'll just figure it out." He draped his arm around her waist. "I guess that's my offer."

"Yes." She scooted over and kissed him. "I accept."

And Then

ANDY'S WEDDING WAS in the middle of October, when the leaves had started to turn. They were having the ceremony at First Presbyterian and the reception at Kettle Bay Hall, a converted fire station that was used for the Lobster Festival in the summer. Evvie came with Kell the day before to put up the tables and cover them with silver linens that Kell had ironed herself. The girls ran around between the tables while Evvie put the favors at each place: a little net bag of candy and a pack of playing cards with the wedding date on them. Andy had said he knew he and Monica were going to survive planning a wedding when they agreed, early in the process, on one ironclad rule: no Mason jars.

Andy and some of his buddies, including Dean, went out that night for what Andy called Boring Dad Bachelor Party, which meant two beers at the bar at The Pearl, then a viewing of *Caddyshack* and a *Madden* tournament that went on until about one in the morning and ended when Rose had a bad dream and woke up in tears. Evvie had been to Monica's shower a couple of weeks earlier and had learned that Monica's mother had gorgeous silver hair and called Andy her daughter's "intended."

On the morning of the wedding, Evvie walked Webster while Dean picked up his tux. She and the dog got back in time to see Dean come out of the bedroom ready to go, and Evvie raised an eyebrow. "Hubba hubba."

"I gotta tell you, this is not the most comfortable thing I've ever worn."

"Welcome to Formal Occasions for Women: An Introductory Course in Empathy."

"I feel dumb in this."

"Yes, but you look *so hot* in it. Honestly, if I'm not allowed to wear a white dress, I don't know why you're allowed to wear a tuxedo."

"All right, pipe down, horndog. Kell is bringing my parents to the church. I'm going to meet up with Andy, and I'll see you there?"

"Yes."

He came over and gave her a kiss, then ruffled the dog's ears. "Love you," he called over his shoulder on his way out.

"Love you," she sort of sing-songed back as she unclipped Webster's leash and hung it on the post. She showered and dried her hair, and in the bedroom, she changed into her dress, which was emerald green with elbow-length sleeves. She put a gold pin in the shape of a maple leaf near her collar and filled her little bronze bag with tissues and lipstick and a vintage Volupté compact that Dean's mom had given her to celebrate the summer day when she'd legally changed her name back to Eveleth Ashton.

Evvie gave Webster one last skritch on the ears ("I love you, too, puppy," she said in her only-for-talking-to-the-dog voice) and got into her car. As she rumbled over the bridge into Calcasset, she beeped and waved at Morris, who lived two properties down and walked his dog, whose name was *actually* Fido, at around the same time she usually walked Webster in the evening. She passed the medical building, passed Tim's little memorial trees that she could see from the road, and adjusted her hands on the steering wheel.

The Tim money, the death money, was gone now. Dean had taken her to see his lawyer in New York, and she'd fixed it so that Evvie could give the money to Dean, and Dean could give the money away, so nobody would ask why Evvie Drake—Evvie Ashton—was throwing money around like a . . . well, like a professional athlete. They sat on her deck on a late summer afternoon drinking beers with their feet up, and they drew up a list of the places to send it: a big women's shelter in Portland, a tiny domestic violence prevention nonprofit in Calcasset, youth baseball, the food bank, the library, the ACLU, and the Ida B. Wells Society, which was helping train Nona's niece to be a journalist. Public radio, public television, the zoo, the chamber orchestra. Shelter bought with death, symphonies bought with broken glass, jars of peanut butter and cans of soup bought with the catered wedding she never should have had.

There were plenty of cars at the church, including Dean's truck, and when she got out, she felt surrounded. They all knew now, about her and Dean, about her selling the house. Tim's parents had been very unhappy that she didn't return to mark any more anniversaries of his death after that first tree was planted. Her father, unfortunately, had overheard them at the bank saying that it hurt to know she'd forgotten their son so quickly.

When she got inside the church, she ran into Kell, whose smart raspberry dress was overlaid with lace. "Oh hello, honey, welcome, welcome."

Evvie kissed Kell on the cheek and looked around at the church as it filled up. "Good turnout."

"And beautiful weather outside, too. Perfect fall day. I know he'll want to see you, so why don't you go on back?"

Andy was getting ready in a small room in the back of the church, and when she knocked on the heavy wooden door, the person who opened it was Dean. He leaned over and kissed her. "Hey."

"Hey," she said. "I thought I'd say hi."

"Absolutely," Dean said. "I have to step out anyway and talk to my parents, so you guys should talk. I'll be back in a couple minutes."

"Thank you. You still look hot," she said as he squeezed past her. He turned and winked. Evvie stepped into the room and saw Andy straightening his tie. He spotted her in the mirror and turned around.

"Evvie," he said. "I'm nervous."

"Well, of course you are," she said, walking over. "All these people are out there and they're going to stare at you. Who wouldn't be nervous?" She ran her palm down the front of his shirt. "You look great, though. And she's great. And you're going to be great."

He turned around. "I love you."

She took both his hands. "I'm not going to hug you, because I don't want to squish your handsomeness, but I love you, too. And I'm very happy for you." She squeezed to make sure he knew. "I am very, very happy for you."

"I'm happy for you, too," he said, flitting his eyes toward the door.

She shrugged. "Who knows? Fingers crossed."

He smiled. "Fingers crossed."

"Are the girls all ready?"

"The girls are dressed, they had their hair done, they've had about a pound of candy each from what we bought to make the favors, and they're in with Monica giving her the whole 'old, new, borrowed, blue' thing. Everything seems to be taken care of."

Evvie remembered when she'd gotten Rose ready for Halloween, helping her wriggle into a fairy princess costume and pinning on her wings. "Yeah, it sounds like . . . you guys have everything covered."

"Can you do me a favor?" he asked. "My mom's going to sit with the girls during the ceremony, but can you be nearby? Just . . . I'd feel better if you weren't far."

"I won't be far."

"Evvie! Don't cry."

She squeezed his hands. "It's a wedding. Crying is allowed. Go get married."

"Okay, I don't care if we get squished, come over here." Evvie went over and put her arms around him, avoiding the flower in his lapel, keeping her makeup off his tux. She had held on to him like this on the day his wife moved out, on the night her husband died, on the day he told her he was engaged, and on the morning she showed him her new house. They had, for years, marked their new chapters with her chin on his shoulder and his arms around her waist.

Dean came back in and said it was time. Evvie kissed Andy's cheek and paused to swipe her pale lip-print off with her fingers. She made her way back out to the church, where she slid into a pew right behind Kell, next to Dean's mom and dad on one side and her father on the other. "Well, you look pretty," he told her.

"Thank you." Evvie briefly laid her head on his shoulder. "Love you, Pop."

"Love you, too, Eveleth."

So Andy got married, and Dean stood next to him, and Evvie cried. After the ceremony, she waited by her car for Dean with her jacket wrapped around her. There would come a time, she knew— she supposed, she even hoped—when it would have lasted long enough with him that it would be relaxed and familiar. It would feel so beautifully ordinary that seeing him emerge from anywhere and move toward her wouldn't turn her cheeks pink. But that time would not be today, as he walked out of the back of the church in a tux with his bow tie undone and his top button open. He came over and put his hands on either side of her, leaning on the roof of the car. He said nothing. He just smiled that third of a smile.

She busted out laughing.

Acknowledgments

I AM BLESSED WITH more people to thank than I can possibly mention, but I am determined to do my best.

My literary agent, Sarah Burnes, has understood me and this book perfectly from the minute we got on the phone. Her advocacy meant everything to getting the book into your hands, and her support meant just as much to my ability to both survive the process and enjoy it. My editor at Ballantine, Sara Weiss, was a joy to work with, as well as the ideal diagnostician who told me what the book needed but knew when to let me find my own solutions. She also helped me cut a lot of things that you will never have to know you didn't need to read. (She could have improved this paragraph.) Thanks also to Elana Seplow-Jolley for her thoughts, and to everyone at Ballantine in copy-editing and production.

I am so indebted to Stephen Thompson, my great friend whose adventures in single parenting informed my interest in it and my high regard for it. I regret any time he may have to spend explaining that this book is not about our friendship (it isn't). To the Thompsley family, including my dearest Katie Presley: I love you all.

My thanks to Margaret "Hulahoop" Willison, who read the first pages of this book years ago and never lost her ability to throw hand-fuls of figurative confetti every time I picked it up again. Other early readers who helped me see things more clearly included Alan Sepin-wall, Marc Hirsh, and Sarah Wendell.

My friend Julia Whelan stepped in to help the first draft see the light of day, as did the generosity of Breck and Mary Montague and Carter Williams.

I was fortunate to have the wise counsel of people in and around publishing and writing who answered tricky beginner's questions like, "I don't know anything that happens after I write THE END." They included but were not limited to Pam Ribon, Jennifer Weiner, Rainbow Rowell, Heather Cocks and Jessica Morgan, Rachel Fershlei-ser, Maris Kreizman, and Danielle Henderson. Thanks to Michelle Dean for the DMs and for being just far enough ahead of me in the publishing process.

I greatly appreciate the baseball and baseball-adjacent writing I read while I worked on this story. It includes all or parts of: Jason Turbow's *The Baseball Codes*, Rick Ankiel's *The Phenomenon*, John Feinstein's *Living on the Black*, and Jeff Passan's *The Arm*, along with David Owens's 2014 article about the yips in *The New Yorker*. I also greatly appreciate the openness that guys like Mackey Sasser and Steve Blass have shown in talking about the yips. Thanks to Will Leitch and Joe Posnanski for writing about sports, always, in a deeply human and deeply entertaining way that has helped me stay con-nected.

A special thanks to Hilary Redmon. (Hilary, *look what happened.*)

Thanks to Sarah Bunting, Tara Ariano, and Dave Cole for their role in everything that has happened to me since 2001.

Thanks to all the friends: my high school friends, my college friends, my recapping friends, my law school friends, and the Minnesota friends I miss terribly, including my treasured Alexanders. Thanks to my NPR family, including Jessica Reedy, Gene Demby, Barrie Hardymon, Mike Katzif, Audie Cornish, and many others. Thanks, too, to my boss, Ellen Silva.

Thanks to the people who were once strangers who became readers and listeners as well as pals. Thanks to the sprawling collection of audio people who have taught me entirely new things about good stories. (And I hope PJ will forgive me for appropriating his dog's likeness.)

Thanks to Glen Weldon, whose enthusiasm for the book meant so very much to me that it got me through several awful convulsions of doubt. (I promise, Glen: I am only hugging you in my mind. *And I always will.*)

Thank you to Alex Kapelman, whose unwavering belief that I could do anything I wanted to do was—and is—like plugging myself into a supplemental power supply. You are the absolute greatest, my SVP of Hustle, and I wouldn't trade you for anything.

This book was written to the sounds of the Avett Brothers. High-fives to the FedEx office outside Colonial Williamsburg. Thanks to Spruce Head Island, Rockland, Camden, Spruce Spray, Pooh, Captain Gargan, and the St. Paul Saints. Thanks to the Phillies, Twins, and Nats. Thanks to my distressingly tall nephews and my brother-in-law, all of whom love baseball so much.

I decline to thank my dog, only because he can't read. Besides, he knows how I feel, because sometimes I feed him peanut butter off my fingers.

Thank you to people who do beautiful things with words that make me want to assemble mine half as well.

Thanks to all my teachers, including but not limited to Nona Smolko, Christine (Powell) Tate, and Kerry Brown.

Thank you to my family—my clever grandmothers, the kind-hearted grandfather I knew and the kind-hearted one I never did, my aunts and uncles and cousins, and especially my fabulous parents and spectacular sister.

ABOUT THE AUTHOR

LINDA HOLMES is a pop culture correspondent for National Public Radio and the host of the podcast *Pop Culture Happy Hour,* which has held sold-out live shows in New York, Los Angeles, Washington, and elsewhere. She appears regularly on NPR's radio shows including *Morning Edition, All Things Considered,* and *Weekend Edition.* Before NPR, she wrote for *New York* magazine online and for *TV Guide,* as well as for the influential website Television Without Pity. She shares her Washington, D.C., apartment with a dog who patiently indulges her desire to take his picture a lot. In her free time, she watches far too many romantic comedies, bakes bread, reads in bed, and recently knitted her first hat.

thisislindaholmes.com
Twitter: @lindaholmes
Instagram: @lindaholmes97

ABOUT THE TYPE

This book was set in Minion, a 1990 Adobe Originals typeface by Robert Slimbach. Minion is inspired by classical, old-style typefaces of the late Renaissance, a period of elegant and beautiful type designs. Created primarily for text setting, Minion combines the aesthetic and functional qualities that make text type highly readable with the versatility of digital technology.